STORY
THIEVES

STORY
THIEVES

JAMES RILEY

ALADDIN

NEW YORK LONDON TORONTO SYDNEY NEW DELHI

ALADDIN

An imprint of Simon & Schuster Children's Publishing Division

1230 Avenue of the Americas, New York, NY 10020

First Aladdin hardcover edition January 2015

Text copyright © 2015 by James Riley

Jacket illustration copyright © 2015 by Vivienne To

All rights reserved, including the right of reproduction in whole or in part in any form.

ALADDIN is a trademark of Simon & Schuster, Inc., and related logo is a registered trademark of Simon & Schuster, Inc.

For information about special discounts for bulk purchases, please contact Simon & Schuster Special Sales at 1-866-506-1949 or business@simonandschuster.com.

The Simon & Schuster Speakers Bureau can bring authors to your live event. For more information or to book an event contact the Simon & Schuster Speakers Bureau at 1-866-248-3049 or visit our website at www.simonspeakers.com.

Jacket designed by Laura Lyn DiSiena

Interior designed by Gabe Levine and Laura Lyn DiSiena

The text of this book was set in Adobe Garamond.

Manufactured in the United States of America 0618 FFG

10 9

Library of Congress Cataloging-in-Publication Data

Riley, James, 1977–

Story thieves / James Riley. — First Aladdin hardcover edition.

p. cm.

Summary: Except for reading the Kiel Gnomenfoot magic adventure series, Owen's life is boring until he sees his classmate Bethany climb out of a book in the library and he learns that Bethany is half-fictional and has been searching every book she can find for her missing father, a fictional character.

[1. Books and reading—Fiction. 2. Characters in literature—Fiction. 3. Adventure and adventurers—Fiction. 4. Magic—Fiction.] I. Title.

PZ7.1.R55St 2015   [Fic]—dc23   2014028133

ISBN 978-1-4814-0919-3 (hc)

ISBN 978-1-4814-0921-6 (eBook)

Dedicated to my fictional characters:

I'm so, so sorry.

STORY
THIEVES

CHAPTER 1

Owen wanted to scream at the horror before him. But the sound wouldn't come and the nightmare only continued, forcing Owen to ask himself, deep down, one question:

"Can anyone tell me what three-fourths times two-thirds is?"

Mr. Barberry stood at the board at the front of Owen's classroom, his arms folded, waiting for a hand to raise.

No, not *that* question. The real question was this: Was there anything in the world that could possibly be more boring than fractions? Owen frowned as Mr. Barberry gave up on volunteers and just picked someone. "Mari? Three-fourths times two-thirds?"

Being locked in a room with no windows or doors, without anything to do, while wearing a blindfold and being forced to name various types of trees? That'd be pretty boring, but not fractions boring.

"One-half," Mari answered, and Mr. Barberry nodded.

Maybe if someone gave you enough soda to keep you awake for hours, then read furniture building instructions to you? In another language?

Except what if you accidentally started to learn that foreign language without realizing it? That'd almost be considered worth it to some people. So that was instantly out.

"Owen?" Mr. Barberry said. "How about you? One-third times two-thirds."

"Two-ninths?" Owen said, faking enthusiasm.

"That's right," Mr. Barberry said, and turned back to the board while Owen let his mind wander again.

Maybe being stuck home sick and too feverish to think or do anything except watch TV, and the only channel that came in was an infomercial for other infomercials. *That* would be pretty boring.

"One-third times one-third?" Mr. Barberry asked. "Gabriel?"

"One-ninth?" Gabriel answered, his eyes glazed over.

Nope, fractions still won. And by a lot.

If only the bell would ring early from some freak electrical surge. Sure, it had never happened before, but Owen was nothing if not optimistic. And that was something he was pretty proud of, since it wasn't easy to be optimistic in the face of all these math problems.

"How about four-fifths times one-eighth?" Mr. Barberry asked. "Bethany, want to take this one?"

There was no answer, so Mr. Barberry turned around. "Bethany?"

Owen threw a look over his shoulder and saw Bethany hunched down behind her math book, her head not even visible. She wasn't actually sleeping, was she? That'd be brave. Dumb, but brave.

Either way, at least something was happening, and that meant class got just a *fraction* less boring. Owen covered his smile with his hand. Fraction. Ha!

"Bethany!" Mr. Barberry shouted.

Bethany jerked back in her chair, and her math book tumbled forward, revealing something else behind it: *Charlie and the Chocolate Factory*.

Uh-oh.

Mr. Barberry just glared at Bethany for a second as she looked around, a mix of confusion and fear on her face. Owen winced, waiting for Mr. Barberry to start yelling, but fortunately the bell rang right at that moment, releasing them for lunch.

"Okay, go," Mr. Barberry said. "Everyone but you, Bethany."

The girl nodded, her long bronze-colored hair falling forward over her face. Owen threw a sympathetic look back at her, then noticed something weird.

Was that chocolate on her chin?

But then the other students blocked his view, and he shrugged, not willing to chance getting yelled at too. Besides, lunch meant at least he had a half hour of no fractions.

After waiting in a lunch line that he'd have to remember to add to his list of the most boring things ever, Owen carried his tray of pizza and milk around the cafeteria, looking for a seat. He considered one table with some boys from his class, but they ignored him as he walked over, so he kept going, pretending he'd always meant to sit by himself.

That's why he brought a book, anyway. Sitting by himself wasn't exactly new.

Owen had read *Kiel Gnomenfoot and the End of Everything* twice now, but the seventh book in the series was coming out next week, so it couldn't hurt to catch up. It'd been hard enough getting a copy out of the library anyway, despite the fact that his mother worked there. This was the book that ended with Dr. Verity surprise attacking the Magister, Kiel's teacher, after all. Owen personally knew at least five people who had cried at the idea that the Magister might die. And ten people who called the series a Harry Potter rip-off, which it sort of was, but everyone still loved it.

As Owen started to read the last chapter, where Dr. Verity broke into the Magister's upside-down tower, he saw Bethany stomp into the cafeteria out of the corner of his eye. She plopped down at a table on the other side of the room, then pulled out her book and looked around suspiciously. Then she dropped her head, ate something, and sat back up, glancing around again.

What was she was doing? Eating behind the book? Did she even have food? Was she—

Whoops. What she was now, was staring at *him*.

Owen immediately looked everywhere but at Bethany, but it was too late. She slammed her book closed, threw him a dirty look, then exited the cafeteria with an annoyed huff.

Owen sighed and dropped his own book onto the table. She was probably feeling embarrassed after getting yelled at and didn't want anyone staring at her, which meant he'd just made things worse. Awesome.

His guilt pushed Owen up out of his seat and after Bethany to apologize or make a joke. Only, by the time he got to the hallway, there was no Bethany. In fact, the entire hallway was completely empty, except for the copy of *Charlie and the Chocolate Factory* Bethany had just been reading, which now lay on the floor just beneath a locker.

Huh? Not only had she just left her book on the floor, but worse, Owen could tell even from a distance that it came from his mom's library. That wasn't even her book!

And were those chocolate stains on it?

That was *not* cool. What was Bethany thinking? Who checked out a book and got chocolate all over it, even if it, you know, fit the story? Other people wanted to read these books too, and didn't want to have food stains on their copy.

Shaking his head, Owen grabbed the book and dropped it into his bag, then walked back into the cafeteria to get back to important things, like Dr. Verity's attack on the Magister. Unfortunately, the bell decided to ring then—cruel, but expected. Owen sighed, threw away his garbage, and tromped back to another few hours of mind-numbing semi-learning.

Eventually, mercifully, the day ended, and Owen exploded out the front door like he was launched from a cannon. It felt so good to be out that he walked that much quicker to his mother's library, where she worked almost every night. As usual, Owen would go by and help out where he could, mostly because she made him, but partly because it was just fun being around all the books.

He said hi to his mom, who was running around with too much to do, then took his usual spot at the front desk, where he checked people's books out for a few hours. This job could be either interesting (seeing what people were reading), embarrassing (seeing what people were reading), or boring (seeing what people were reading). Usually it managed to cover at least two of the three every few minutes, and tonight was no different.

When things finally cooled down, Owen sighed and pulled out his homework, knowing that his mother, no matter how busy she was, would notice *he* wasn't busy and make him do it anyway. Only, when he went to pull out his math book, there was Bethany's copy of *Charlie and the Chocolate Factory* in his bag.

Um, whoops. He'd sort of forgotten all about that. He'd picked it up meaning to give it back to Bethany and glare at her judgmentally for the chocolate stains. But now that he thought about it, had she even been in science after lunch? He couldn't remember her being there, or in any other class that afternoon. Maybe she'd gone home sick after eating too much chocolate and using a library book as a napkin.

Owen shrugged and checked the book back in to the library. She knew where to find it if she wanted it again.

His mother caught him putting the book on a pile that was supposed to go back out onto shelves, and gave him a look. He sighed and stood up, knowing where this was going. "Those all go in the children's section," she said. "I'm locking up, but I have a few things to take care of in the office after that, so finish your homework when you're done."

Ugh. Of course. Owen picked up a pile of books about half as tall as he was, then walked them slowly back to the children's section.

As usual, it was a mess, like a hurricane had plowed into a nuclear bomb right around the Rick Riordan books. Owen sighed and dug in, pulling a few interesting books aside as he noticed them. That was the only good part about cleanup—he'd sometimes find things that looked like a good read.

Ten minutes later the children's section was at least cleaner, with random piles stacked on top of over-full shelves. Owen looked sadly at the stack of books he'd carried here to put back, then sighed again and picked up *Charlie and the Chocolate Factory*, knowing there'd be no room for it.

But then, as he found the *D* section for Roald Dahl, something weird happened. His hand . . . jumped.

He looked down at his hand and the book in it, thinking he'd just imagined the jolt.

The book in his hand jumped again.

"Gah!" he said, dropping the book. It smacked the floor hard and just sat there for a moment.

Then it jumped a third time.

What was happening? Owen backed away as the cover and a bunch of pages flipped open all by themselves. Was the book haunted? Was the entire library haunted? Was it okay to find that awesome even while being scared?

And then, the last thing in the world that Owen ever expected happened.

Five chocolate-covered fingers pushed right out of the center of the book, grabbed the edge, and began to pull themselves out.

CHAPTER 2

As Bethany slowly pulled herself out of *Charlie and the Chocolate Factory* by her chocolate-covered hands, she sighed. Why had she stayed so long? She was beyond late now. It'd just been incredibly relaxing to sit hidden behind the chocolate river, watching the Oompa-Loompas work and not being yelled at by Mr. Barberry or her mom.

Her head popped out of the book, and suddenly she worried a lot less about being late and a lot more about Owen, a brown-haired, ordinary-looking boy from her class, staring at her like his eyes were going to explode.

"Bethany?" Owen croaked, his voice almost too quiet to hear.

"Owen!" she said, cringing, and quickly pulled herself the rest of the way out of the book and kicked it closed.

"You . . . were in the book?" he said, glancing between her and the still-chocolatey book.

"Don't be stupid," Bethany told him, forcing a fake laugh. "You just didn't see me. I was back here the whole time reading."

Owen shook his head. "I had the book in my hand," he said, pointing at it on the floor. "It started jumping around, and you came right out of it. I *saw* you!"

"That's crazy," Bethany said, picking the book up and showing it to him. "How could I have been inside a book? They're made of paper!" She dropped the book to her side and snorted. "You've been reading too many books yourself."

Owen started to say something, and then his gaze dropped to her side, and he began to make odd squeaking noises. Bethany glanced in the same direction and groaned as she saw her thumb sticking right into the book.

Okay, *that* really didn't help her case. Ugh.

Owen's squeaking noises got louder, and he began to back away from her in a hurry.

Bethany cringed at how loud he was getting and started to shush him, when she remembered something. Owen had seen her in the cafeteria, when she'd been pulling chocolate out of the book to eat at lunch, because some days were so bad that you just wanted candy. He was the one who'd sent her over the edge.

After her mother being upset that morning; after the long, horrible day of Mr. Barberry going on and on about fractions, then yelling at her; after being forced to sit in class when she could have been searching in Prydain or Oz or Wonderland instead, Owen almost catching her at lunch had been the last straw. That had just been it: She was done with school, her teachers, her mother, *everything*. She walked out of the cafeteria, resolving to spend the rest of the day in the fictional world, so over things that she couldn't even wait to get somewhere safe before jumping right into the book. She might get detention, yes, but she'd gotten it before and her mother never found out, since she got home from work so late. As long as Bethany was home before her mom, she'd be fine.

Except she *wasn't* home, and now Owen had seen her jumping out of a book. This had gone *way* too far.

"Owen," Bethany said, grabbing him by the shirt and pushing him back into the children's section. "You're going to listen to what I say, quietly, or I'm going to throw *you* into the Chocolate Factory. Do you understand me?"

Owen nodded quickly, and she let go of him. Instantly, he made a jump toward the library's exit.

Bethany gritted her teeth, grabbed his hand, and pulled him

down into the pages of a book from a nearby pile on the floor without even looking at the title. First Bethany, then Owen passed right into the pages so fast that he probably didn't even see how it happened.

And that's how they found themselves in the middle of a burning London as huge green rays exploded into buildings all around them.

"GAH!" Owen shouted, then quickly shut up as a death ray sizzled through the air above his head.

Bethany shoved him into the burned shell of a building, then followed right behind. "Those are Martians," she shouted over the roar of the invasion, pointing at the huge round space-ships crawling around the city on robotic tentacle legs, firing green rays at anything and everything. "We're in *The War of the Worlds*. Now calm down and be quiet, or they'll shoot you full of Martian lasers." Something exploded right outside and Owen jumped, but Bethany just grabbed him by his shirt again. "If you stay quiet and don't get seen, then we'll be fine. They're all going to get sick and die from getting colds or germs or something."

"Martians?" Owen said, his voice almost too quiet to hear over the craziness outside. He glanced out, then jumped back in as another ray exploded a car right outside. "For real? Martians?"

Bethany paused, not exactly sure how to answer that. "It's real *here*, in the book. It's not like Martians really destroyed London. That probably would have made the news."

Owen gave her a confused look, then stuck his head outside again. "But . . . where's the army? Who's fighting them?"

Bethany scrunched up her nose. "It's been a while since I read it, but I think the army gets beaten pretty bad. They can't really fight the Martians with just guns. But that's not why we're here!" She pulled Owen back inside again and stared him straight in the eye. "You can't tell anyone about this, Owen. In fact, you can't even tell *me* about it, because we're never going to speak again after this. Mostly because you'll be so good at keeping this a secret. Do you understand me?"

He just stared at her for a second, then shook his head and pushed her out of the way. "Shouldn't we help them?" he shouted, pointing outside. "We can tell them how the Martians get sick, so they can protect themselves. Sneeze on the aliens or something!"

The boy really wasn't getting the point. *"No,"* she told him. "The book's already written. We can't change it. You don't seem to be grasping what's happening."

"But how is it written if it's going on right now?" Owen shouted. "Look at it!"

She sighed, grabbed his hand, and jumped them both up and out of the book, this time not bothering to exit slowly, since she didn't have time to be careful. They shot right out of *The War of the Worlds*, slamming into the nearby bookcase a bit harder than Bethany had meant. Before Owen could even say one word, Bethany grabbed another book and jerked him straight into its pages. He shouted in surprise, but then went quiet as they landed on a checkerboard field, mostly because he couldn't stop looking all around.

"See?" she said. "We're inside the books. This is the fictional world, Owen. You can't change things here, because they're already written. If we'd jumped into the last page of *The War of the Worlds*, the Martians would have all been defeated. I just didn't really look before leaping." Which, admittedly, was horrible, and something she never, ever did. But this was a special circumstance.

Owen didn't seem to hear her. Instead, he reached out a hand and let a small rocking horse with wings land on his fingers.

"Where are we now?" he whispered, and the horse neighed at him.

"Wonderland," she told him. "Well, *Through the Looking Glass*. I think that's still Wonderland, but I was never really sure how that worked."

"Wonderland? As in Alice?" he asked her as a bread-and-butter-fly landed in his hair.

"She's probably on her way to the nameless woods around this page," Bethany told him. "I make sure to avoid the main characters, since that's the easiest way to not mess up the story. Plus, then I don't have to get involved with all the plot stuff, and I can just enjoy myself."

He turned back to her, various impossible insects hovering all around him. "Please tell me this isn't a dream. I know it has to be, I must be asleep at the front desk, but *please* let it not be a dream—"

She reached out and pinched him as hard as she could, letting out some of her annoyance. He gasped and yanked his arm away, then gave her a dirty look. "You could have just said no!"

She shrugged. "So remember what we were talking about? How we're never going to speak of this again?"

"How can you *do* this?" he asked her. "How . . . how can you just jump into books? They're words on paper."

She sighed. "They are, but right now, so are you. If you can be quiet, I'll show you what I do. But no shouting or anything this time, okay?"

He nodded, and she grabbed his arm, and again, jumped

them both right out of the book into the library, just a bit more gently this time. She let go of his arm, held up her hand for him to see, then slowly pushed it into *Through the Looking Glass*.

As her fingers touched the page, they melted and re-formed, becoming various words like "knuckles" and "fingernail" and "thumb," all describing whatever part they'd been. Those words then spread over the page like brownie batter, absorbing right into the book. Finally, she just shoved her arm in up to the shoulder.

"I'm wriggling my fingers at you right now in Wonderland," she told him.

Owen laughed oddly, then made a weird face and fell backward to the floor, unconscious.

Bethany sighed, shaking her head. "Alien invasions and rocking-horse-flies are fine, but *this*, you faint at?"

CHAPTER 3

Owen woke up to his mother calling him and immediately pushed himself upright, looking around quickly for ray guns or white rabbits or something.

Unfortunately, there was nothing but a cleaned-up children's section.

No. No no no! Had he dreamed all of that? Did that mean that he really was still stuck in real life? AGH!

"Owen?" his mother shouted again. "What's taking you so long?"

"Sorry, I was just reading!" he shouted back to her, then grabbed his Kiel Gnomenfoot book and ran to the front of the library, getting more and more depressed with every step. No! It *had* to be real! If it was real, then that meant there was more to life than boring classes and boring chores after school and boring everything else. Bethany jumping into books was the opposite of boring, and therefore it had to be real, if life was going to be fair at all!

Owen spent that night staring at the ceiling, waiting to sleep and not even feeling a sliver tired. Would Bethany be in school tomorrow? Would she deny it all? Had he just made it all up? And if not, how did she do it? What did she do in books . . . just explore, or did she mostly go for eating fictional candy? Who had she met? Did she have autographs?

Sometime during the night he must have fallen asleep, because his alarm pulled him out of dreams of Bethany introducing him to Aslan the lion as the people of Narnia cheered. Owen slapped the alarm off, then leaped out of bed, wide awake despite getting almost no sleep.

His mother asked him if everything was okay as he almost choked on his breakfast, and then he raced out the door, easily twenty minutes early for the bus. When it finally came, Owen sat alone in the very first seat, his legs shaking from nervousness and excitement the entire way.

He pushed his way off the bus as fast as he could and speed-walked to class, so he wouldn't get in trouble for running. Once there, he took his seat and waited, the first one to show up.

Other kids filed in, none looking that happy to be there,

and more than a few gave him an odd look as he sat at his desk, grinning in anticipation. He couldn't help it, though. Bethany would be there soon, and then he'd get his answers. It *had* to be real. It just made so much more sense than math and school and chores!

Mr. Barberry stepped in, and the bell rang a second later with no sign of Bethany. Owen almost slapped his desk in frustration. Where *was*—

And then Bethany slid in the door, right behind Mr. Barberry. She edged along the side of the room and quickly took her seat, sitting down just as Mr. Barberry turned around to start class, completely missing the fact that she was late.

Owen glanced over his shoulder at her as subtly as he could, but Bethany had her eyes locked on the front of the room, where Mr. Barberry had started talking about geography.

Owen groaned. So, what, he'd have to wait till lunch now to talk to her? Life was both boring and very, very cruel.

What followed were the worst three hours that Owen had ever experienced, like Christmas Eve, the night before vacation, and waiting for the new Kiel Gnomenfoot to come out all rolled into one. Minute by minute rolled by, and Owen was so frustrated, he didn't even bother daydreaming. Instead, he threw looks back at Bethany, who seemed to be paying more attention to Mr. Barberry than anyone had ever before, in all of history.

Finally the lunch bell rang, and Owen had to hold himself down, letting the rest of the class leave before him. Bethany seemed to be waiting too, but seeing that he wasn't going anywhere, she quickly got up and left, ignoring him when he called out her name as she passed.

Owen paused, psyched himself up, then walked out directly behind her, following her to the cafeteria. She sat down alone at a table with her paper bag lunch, and he sat down right across from her, completely lunchless.

"Hi!" he said, grinning widely.

She sighed loud enough to be sure he heard and gave him a dirty look. "What?"

"What are you reading?" he asked, pointing at the book next to her lunch tray.

She flipped the book over even as he asked about it. "None of your business."

"Is it any good?"

She made an annoyed growling noise. "Owen. *Tell me what you want.*" Her voice lowered to a whisper. "Are you going to blackmail me or something? Turn me in to the library police? All unless I jump you into a book and steal you a time machine or something?"

That threw him. "Blackmail? . . . A time machine? Where would you get that?"

She glared at him. "From *The Time Machine*. It's a book, and the title kinda gives it away."

"Oh right!" he said. "But no, I just came over here because, honestly, I thought I might have imagined the whole thing. But you saying it happened makes me feel so much better." He grinned again.

She stared at him, openmouthed, then rolled her eyes. "This is what I get for not letting you talk first."

"So how does it work?" Owen whispered, looking around to make sure no one else was watching or listening.

"How does *what* work?" she asked, looking tired of this whole conversation.

"You doing . . . whatever it is that you do? With the finger waving in Wonderland? And bringing us into *War of the Worlds*?"

She glanced around. "Can we *not* talk about this here, in the middle of the cafeteria? Everyone's staring at us."

Owen glanced in the direction she nodded in, but saw no

one looking at them. He turned back and realized she'd been about to make a run for it. "Nice try!" he said, standing up too. "We can go somewhere else, but you're not running away into a book or something. Not without me!"

"Is that a threat?" she demanded, giving him a cold glare.

"No?" he said, his confusion making his smile fade. "I just . . . You can't know how amazing this is, how it makes up for everything. I knew that there was something like this out there, because if there wasn't, then life is just dental floss and vegetables and word problems. That can't be everything. Deep down, I think we all know there has to be more. So for books to be real? To know they're out there, all my favorite characters? That would make it all worth it!"

She stared at him for a moment, then shook her head. "I'm an idiot for even talking to you. But if I tell you about it, will you *promise* to never tell anyone else?"

Owen crossed his heart, and she rolled her eyes again. "Not good enough?" he asked. "How about, I solemnly swear that I am up to no good—"

"Don't Marauder's Map me," she told him. "I'll talk to you at the library tonight. Until then, you don't speak to me, look at me, or even know I exist. Now leave me alone."

Owen beamed and stood up to go get food, too excited to eat but knowing he'd better, since he might need his strength. There'd *have* to be dragons, whatever story they'd visit tonight. And magic. And spaceships, and aliens who weren't allergic to human colds, and flying squirrels, and volcanoes, and superspies, probably, and everything else he couldn't even imagine right now.

All this time, his favorite books hadn't been lying. All you had to do was wait long enough, last through enough boring lessons on fractions, live through enough chores and homework and evil stepmothers, and eventually you found something . . . *better*. A fairy godmother, a dying alien with a power ring, or a doorway to a magical world.

And Owen's doorway just happened to be a girl named Bethany.

The rest of the day went by in a blur, mostly because Owen didn't even bother trying to pay attention. Instead, he went through all his favorite books in his head, trying to pinpoint which one they should go into first.

Obviously, Harry Potter would be near the top of the list. Not even to Hogwarts, just to Ollivanders for a wand. That'd be perfect. Next, *The Lightning Thief.* And *The Graveyard Book*, and a trip to *Fablehaven*, and—

And then Owen stopped short, right in the middle of the sidewalk as he walked home from the bus. What was he thinking? What was everyone at school talking about? The seventh Kiel Gnomenfoot book, out next week. And why? Because they all wanted to find out if the Magister had lived, and if not, to see Kiel get revenge on Dr. Verity.

But what if . . . what if someone *saved* the Magister from Dr. Verity? What if Bethany brought Owen into the book right at the moment when Dr. Verity attacked, and Owen stopped him?

He would be a hero. A hero in a book. *A hero in a book that everyone read.*

Owen's mouth dropped open, and pure joy exploded in his chest. This would be *huge*. Bigger than saving Dumbledore, since Dumbledore came back anyway as a ghost or whatever. The Magister was like everyone's favorite character after Kiel. It might even change how the books ended!

That was it. None of the tourist, autograph type stuff. Clearly, Owen had been pulled out of his boring world for exactly this reason. It was meant to be. Fate or something. He'd been chosen, and it was time to save the greatest wizard ever, the Magister.

And all Owen had to do to make it happen was convince Bethany to take him.

CHAPTER 4

Bethany stood outside the library's sliding doors, watching Owen at the front desk. He wasn't actually doing anything, just staring off into space like he always did in class. Daydreaming.

When was the last time she'd daydreamed? Bethany couldn't actually remember. Why imagine a world in your head when you could just go visit another one in a book?

Of course, to do that, you had to sneak the book into your house to make sure you didn't get caught by your mother, who absolutely forbade you from ever jumping into another book. And then you'd have to hide it from her at all times, waiting to actually jump into it until there was no chance she'd catch you missing.

Bethany sighed, smushing her face against the library's window. Maybe daydreaming *was* better.

This was going to be bad, talking to Owen about . . . everything. The how and, even worse, the why. But there was no way to avoid him, not with him working in the library. Without money, the library had always been the only way to get more books. And without new books, she'd never find what she'd been looking for.

She sighed again. Either she stopped sneaking books and gave up her search, or she disobeyed her mother and felt horrible. At least feeling horrible would eventually go away.

It had to, didn't it?

This was dumb. She'd just tell Owen enough to satisfy his curiosity, then bribe him so he'd leave her alone. She dropped a hand into her pocket to make sure the Everlasting Gobstopper she'd taken from Willy Wonka's factory was still there. Candy that'd never lose its flavor or get smaller, no matter how long you sucked on it? That seemed like a good trade-off for keeping your mouth shut.

For just a moment she watched Owen smile at someone as he checked out their books, and she felt a little sick. There hadn't been many people lined up to be her friend, not since her birthday party all those years ago. After the party her mother hadn't let her out of the house without watching her closely, and she'd even pulled Bethany out of school for the next few years. And here was Owen, someone who might be fun to talk to, or even come with her when she searched through books. But instead, she was bribing him to stay away. Great.

Ugh. Why couldn't she just be back in a book right now, avoiding all of this?

Taking a deep breath, Bethany stepped through the sliding glass doors, gave Owen a look, then nodded toward the computerless tables in the back, the ones no one ever sat at. He smiled at her, then winked way too obviously, which almost made her turn right around, no matter what he knew. She pushed on anyway and kept walking toward the tables, where she threw her bag onto a chair and sat down to wait.

Less than a minute later, Owen slid into the seat across from her. "My mom's watching the desk. I told her we were meeting to go over some homework." He grinned. "A book report. You know, because—"

"I get it," Bethany said. "So, what, you just lie to your mother? No big deal?" Guilt swirled in her stomach, but she decided Owen deserved it more.

Owen sat back in his chair, his face turning red. "Well, not usually, but I promised not to tell anyone, so I had to think of an excuse—"

"Right, whatever," Bethany said, waving a hand as she inwardly tried to ignore how he'd done it for *her*, which made this lie her fault too. "Listen. I brought you something." She reached into her pocket and pulled out the gobstopper.

His eyes widened, and he took the candy in his hands almost reverently. "Is . . . is this a Wonka original?" he whispered.

Wow. "Yup. And it's all yours. You just have to agree to leave me alone and never tell anyone about what you saw last night."

His eyes widened even more, and he held the candy up so he could look at it more closely. Then he sighed and passed it back to her. "You keep it," he said, shaking his head. "There are too many books I'd rather visit!"

Bethany narrowed her eyes and pushed the candy back toward him. "It's not a choice. You either get the candy and leave me alone, or you *don't* get the candy and leave me alone."

He took the candy back, but set it to one side. "We can talk about that in a minute. I want to know how you do all of this in the first place."

Bethany glanced around to make sure no one could hear. "My . . . my father. He's, um, fictional. You know, from a book." She swallowed hard, knowing what was coming.

Owen gave her a confused look. "I'm sorry, he's . . . what?"

"My father is a *fictional character*," she said, her anger grow-ing, which wasn't really fair. It's not like she had just told Owen her father was from Sweden or something. This wasn't some-thing that most people dealt with on a daily basis, so she should maybe cut him some slack.

But why did she have to be fair to Owen about this? How was it any of his business anyway?

". . . What?" Owen repeated, still confused.

"My *mother* read books about my *father*, and somehow my father found his way out of those books, and they fell in love," Bethany hissed, her anger growing with each word Owen said. "You know, I'd really like to not talk about this—"

"How does a fictional person just . . . get out?" Owen asked.

"I don't know!" Bethany said, annoyed at herself for letting Owen bother her so much. "Maybe I could ask him if he was around. Only he's not, okay? Are we *done* here?"

"Where did he go? Back into his book?"

"Where did he *go*?" Bethany said, her voice getting louder. "For my fourth birthday party, my mom told everyone I wasn't allowed to get books for presents. All my friends' parents thought that was weird, but they listened. All except one. While my mom was in the other room, I opened a present and found a copy of *Fairy Tales for Kids*. And since I didn't know what I was doing, I pulled myself, all the other kids, and my *father* right into the book."

She paused, swallowing hard. "Somehow, I got me and the other kids back out," Bethany said, her voice now quieter. "They all thought it was some kind of cool magic trick for the party. But my dad . . . I don't know what happened, but he got left behind. Except he's not in that book now, not anymore. And I don't know *where* he is."

"Couldn't he just leave that book too?" Owen asked. "The same way he did the first time?"

Why was she telling Owen this much? "Maybe? I don't know. Maybe he tried, and left that book looking for another way out. Maybe . . . maybe he couldn't leave, because something hurt him in the story. Or maybe he just figured, why come back to the real world when the fictional world is so much *better*?"

She turned away, ran the backs of her hands over her eyes, then sighed. "I look for him everywhere I can," she said, staring at the table. "After my dad got lost, my mom wouldn't let me jump into books anymore, no exceptions. For years after, she

31

wouldn't even let me read a book the normal way without watching me do it, not even schoolbooks. And what am I going to do with those, jump into a word problem? As soon as she started to trust me, I hit the library and checked out that fairytale book first thing. I tore that thing apart, inside and out, but he wasn't there. Not anywhere in it! I keep trying, bringing home new books every night, hiding them from my mom, but there are so many other books out there. How could anyone possibly look through them all?"

Owen put up his hands, and she realized he was trying to quiet her down. She looked over his shoulder to where several people had turned to look at whatever the crazy girl in the corner was yelling about. Her eyes widened, and she gritted her teeth in an effort to not punch something. "I don't know why I'm even talking about this," she hissed. "You're just some jerk who won't leave me alone. *Now, do you want the gobstopper or not?*"

He glanced at the candy again, staring at it like it was made of gold. Then he pushed it back to her side. "No. But if you really don't want to ever hear from me again, then I've got a different deal for you."

That's what this was all about. She should have known. "So you *do* want a time machine."

He shook his head. "I don't want anything from a book. Just for you to take me into one. Five minutes, in and out, that's all I ask."

Bethany sighed. Of course that's what he wanted. Meet Percy Jackson, or Ron Weasley, or that knockoff Harry Potter kid, Kiel Giant-toes. And if she didn't do what he asked, he'd tell her mother, and that'd be it. So much for making a friend. "And which book is that?"

He pulled a book out from his backpack. *Kiel Gnomenfoot and the End of Everything.* Kiel Giant-toes it was.

"So, what, you want his autograph?" she asked, keeping her voice as level as she could. "Want to go gush over him like he's a celebrity? That'll be *perfect*, Owen. He has no idea anyone even knows who he is, but yes, go tell him how much you love his gnome feet or whatever, and how *The End of Everything* is the greatest title you've ever heard. Do you know how dumb that idea is? You'd change the entire story! Do you have any idea what would happen if you did that?"

Owen's eyes lit up like Christmas lights. "No?" he said.

"Neither do I!" she whispered. "Maybe it's not possible, I don't even know, because I'm too smart to have ever tried. The last thing I need is for my name to show up in a book like

I'm a character, where *everyone* can see it. You think no one would notice that, if suddenly there's a Bethany Sanderson in *Frankenstein* where there'd never been one before? And what if I change a book's story, especially one that's as popular as Kiel Nope-Fingers? People are gonna notice something like that in seconds! I have nightmares about what could happen."

He started to say something, then stopped and opened the book. "I don't want to meet Kiel," he said finally. "He's not even in this chapter. I just . . . His teacher, the Magister, has this spell book, and—"

"Magic?" Bethany almost shouted, then quickly quieted down when everyone turned to look at them again. "Are you kidding me? You want to learn *magic?* Did you hear what I just said about nightmares? That'd be like ten times worse!"

"There's a spell," Owen told her. "Kiel's used it before. It helps you find things." He paused, as if he were considering something. "I didn't know about your father, not before. But now that I do, there's a spell in this book that could find him for you. You learn the spell, and cast it here, or there, however it works. And it'd locate him." He shrugged. "I just thought that might help you. And if after that you want me to forget all this, that I ever saw you, that's up to you."

Bethany stared at him, her mouth hanging open. He wanted to help her? "No. *No.* It's way too risky. I'm sorry, that was actually . . . nice of you. But no." She stood up and turned to leave, then paused and pushed the gobstopper over to him before walking straight out of the library.

As soon as she passed through the sliding doors, she stopped and turned around. Owen had picked up the candy and was staring at it sadly, like it was all that was left of his Christmas after the Grinch came through.

Ugh. UGH! He'd been trying to do something nice. Obviously, he wanted to visit the book too, just for fun, but besides that, he'd been thinking about *her.* And this is how she treated him for it?

But there was no way she could do that. It was just asking for trouble. She couldn't!

Bethany fell back against the library wall. She hadn't even checked out a new book to search for her father. But there was no going back in now, not with Owen still there. Great. Was she going to have to avoid the library all the time now?

At least she still had some books back home. Okay, she'd already looked for her dad in them, but sometimes you just needed a *Little Prince* night, sitting alone on his planet while he was down on Earth, talking to the pilot.

She gave Owen one last look through the library doors, then tried to forget this whole night ever happened as she set off home.

Ten minutes later, turning the key in her front door, she heard the TV and knew her mother was home. It sounded like the news was on, but not about anything important, just something about how some first issue of a comic book had sold for hundreds of thousands of dollars since no one could find any other issues in the series anymore. Hugely important news, obviously.

But her mom being home early meant something was wrong. Something wrong like maybe Owen had said something he shouldn't have?

"Mom?" Bethany said in a voice even quieter than she meant to use.

She heard her mother sniff loudly, and the TV sound disappeared. "Bethany?" her mom said, and sniffed again. "Is everything okay? Why are you late?"

"Just, uh, stayed after school to do some homework with someone from my class," Bethany said. "Why are *you* home?"

Her mother appeared in the hallway, a smile on her face despite her red eyes. "Oh, I just felt a little sick. It's going away, though."

Relief flooded through Bethany, and she gave her mother a

hug. "Want me to make you some soup or something?"

"Oh, that's ridiculous. I'm fine," her mother said, sniffing again. "See? Probably just a cold."

Bethany nodded. It wasn't a cold. Her mother only got this way when something reminded her of Bethany's father.

It could have been the color of Bethany's hair, the same bronze color that her father had—at least that was the color her father had in Bethany's memory of him. Sometimes it was just a word or a random memory. Bethany never knew exactly what set her mother off, but it always came down to her mother sitting in front of a fire, even in the middle of summer, and staring into an old hand mirror that had been a gift from her father. Then her mom would go to bed, and the mirror would disappear, never to be seen again until the next time this happened.

"Are you hungry, Beth?" her mother asked.

"No, I had a snack at school. I'm good for now," Bethany told her. "You go sit down. You still sound sick. I'll make you something."

Her mother gave her a sad smile, then nodded. "You're far too sweet, you know. I'm so proud of you, of the person you're growing up to be, you know that?"

Bethany returned the smile, but inwardly wanted to groan. What would her mother say if she knew Bethany was reading every single night? Breaking the one rule her mother ever really cared about? And would probably be in a book right now if it meant not having to watch her mother cry?

An hour later her mother had a fire going and was sitting with her hand mirror on her lap, staring at the flames. Bethany kissed her forehead, then quietly went upstairs to her room and closed the door behind her.

She pulled a copy of *Goodnight Moon* out from underneath her bed and ran her fingers over the cover. Years and years ago her father had walked with her through the book's rooms, narrating the story by heart to her as they went. It was her first memory of him, and her favorite one.

All this time, she'd wondered where her father had gone, and now she had a way to find him.

But what if he hadn't come back because . . . because he didn't want to?

She stuffed the book back beneath her bed, pulled *The Little Prince* out from a different spot, then jumped in to spend the rest of the night alone with the stars.

CHAPTER 5

*O*wen stared at Bethany across the cafeteria, an empty feeling in his stomach. It wasn't entirely a trick, honestly. There *was* a spell in the Magister's spell book that might help her find her father. And after learning that Bethany's father was missing, Owen really did want to help.

It just felt wrong, though, to use that as an excuse to get him into the book. Even if all he wanted to do was perform an amazing, heroic, lifesaving, awesome act of goodness. Even if this was clearly the thing he'd been meant to do with his life, saving the Magister.

Maybe he should just tell her the truth? He knew that Bethany would never go for it, since he'd be changing the story, and that seemed to freak her out more than almost anything—anything other than learning magic, at least. But then he wouldn't feel so guilty, and besides, what did he have to lose, since she wasn't taking him anyway?

Owen glanced over at her, at her long reddish-brown hair, and wondered who her father might actually be. Was it someone famous, like Sherlock Holmes? James Bond? He came from books too, didn't he? Or maybe someone like Gandalf? The wizard seemed kind of old to be someone's father, though. Grandfather, sure, but father, maybe not.

Or maybe it was some character from one of those romantic books that people were always checking out, but trying to hide the covers from Owen at the counter like they were embarrassed. That seemed like a possibility, considering her mother had fallen in love with her father by reading about him. Who did that? Who fell in love with a character in a book?

Whoever Bethany's father was, maybe Owen could still help. Not by jumping into the books with her, but by reading and keeping an eye out. *That* was what he should do. Tell her the truth, that he really wanted to go into *Kiel Gnomenfoot and the End of Everything* to save the Magister, then say how sorry he was and offer to help her find her father to make up for it.

He stood up to do just that, only to notice that Bethany had disappeared from the cafeteria. But she had left something at her table. The book she'd been reading.

He walked over, making sure no one was watching him too suspiciously, then grabbed the book.

Kiel Gnomenfoot: Magic Thief. The first book in the series.

And stuck inside like a bookmark was a note:

I'm in.

—Bethany

What? She was in? Owen's eyes widened and he began to shake. He quickly sat down so no one would see his trembling, but he couldn't stop the grinning. It felt like the smile was bigger than his face, but he didn't even care.

THEY WERE GOING TO SAVE THE MAGISTER! Everyone in this cafeteria, everyone in cafeterias all over the world would read the book, see Owen's name, and watch him save Kiel's magic teacher.

Would they throw him parties? Come up to him all shyly to ask for his autograph? Start a national holiday for his birthday, and no mail would be delivered because too many postal workers had to celebrate everything about Owen Conners?

Or would something *really* amazing happen, like he and Kiel would become best friends, and Kiel would ask him for his help now that Dr. Verity was taken care of? "Help with what?" Owen would ask. "Something mind-blowing," Kiel would say, and wink.

Kiel always winked. That was so Kiel. Especially with his best friends.

A small, tiny, miniscule part of Owen decided to be a downer and reminded the rest of him that Bethany knew none of this and was going to be extremely not happy when she found out. That same part suggested that he still apologize and tell her the truth.

And the rest of Owen knew that the small part was right. He should. *He should.*

On the other hand, was an apology worth letting a great man like the Magister die? Of course not.

Owen crumpled Bethany's note up, tossed it into the trash, then left the cafeteria to make some plans. Plans to take down a mad scientist, save a master magician, and become a hero to the entire world.

CHAPTER 6

Owen's bedroom was where books went to die, Bethany realized. Every shelf in the room overflowed with books without covers or with splitting spines, and even, every so often, just collections of pages held together with rubber bands.

She gestured toward the books, raising an eyebrow, and Owen turned red. "Uh, my mom brings them home," he said, sitting down on the floor with *Kiel Gnomenfoot and the End of Everything* in front of him. "Whenever a library book gets too beat-up to lend out anymore, she gives it to me."

"So you live in a book graveyard," Bethany said, sitting down across from him.

Owen's eyes widened. "Ooooh, that'd make a fun story! Have you ever been to a graveyard in a book? Like *Pet Sematary* or something?"

"No horror books," Bethany said quickly. "That's rule number

one! Horror is a good way to get yourself killed. And speaking of rules, let's go over them while we can still back out of this."

"Bring 'em on!" Owen said a bit too loudly.

Bethany shushed him, despite the fact that no one was home. Owen's mother was still at the library, so they weren't exactly going to be caught doing anything they shouldn't be. Still, Bethany half believed her own mother would pop in and yell "AHA!" at any moment, so the more quiet they could be, the better she'd feel.

"There are five rules total," she whispered, giving Owen an annoyed look. "Rule number one: MAKE NO NOISE. Either here or in the book. Quiet is key."

"Got it," Owen mouthed silently.

She rolled her eyes. "Rule number two: NO TALKING TO CHARACTERS. No matter what. Talk to a main character, you might show up in the book, and that's the absolute last thing we want to happen. Even if it doesn't change the story, everyone who ever read the book would see our names. *That cannot happen.*"

Owen nodded, but his eyes lit up with excitement in a way that fundamentally disturbed Bethany, so she quickly continued. "That brings us to rule number three: WE DO NOT CHANGE THE STORY. No way, no how. If we touch something, it goes back exactly the way we left it. This is maybe the most important rule, except that *all* the rules are the most important. Do you understand?"

"Sure, but you've eaten chocolate and taken gobstoppers. How did that not change the story?"

"Because they'd never notice a little chocolate missing from a chocolate river, or a gobstopper that I took from the gobstopper machine while the Oompa-Loompas were teaching the kids a lesson," Bethany said, feeling a little guilty since she really shouldn't have done either thing. But that had been a really bad day. "Anyway, these are *my* rules for *you*. If you want to come, you follow them. Got it?"

"Got it," Owen said, nodding again.

She gave him a suspicious glance, then grabbed the book. "Okay. Are we ready?"

"What about the last two rules?"

Bethany wrinkled her nose. "I really only had three. So the last two are LISTEN TO ME AT ALL TIMES and DON'T DO ANYTHING STUPID. That work?"

"I'll do my best on the last one," he said, and laughed.

Bethany stared at him without cracking a smile, and he slowly stopped laughing.

"Now, you've got a chapter where Kiel and his teacher aren't around?" Bethany asked him.

Owen reached over and opened *Kiel Gnomenfoot and the End of Everything* to a marked page. "Yup, the spell book is just sitting out. Kiel's off beyond the edge of the universe, where he just found the Sixth Key, but he hasn't gotten back to existence yet. The Magister is distracted, casting a spell to locate the Seventh Key. It's the perfect time to sneak in and learn the location spell. No one will ever know."

Bethany glanced at the page.

It wasn't easy sifting through the past, especially for things deliberately mislaid. The Magister carefully wove one thousand and eleven spells together into an elaborate tapestry, threading them in and out of one another. Some showed his life, or his children's, his children's children's, or the school he once ran, or even old enemies.

Other spells went back further, to the very beginning. The Seventh Key hadn't been seen since the locking of the Source inside the Vault of Containment. To find the key meant finding the location of those who had been present, which meant only two: the original president of Quanterium, Favora Bunsen, and a figure lost to history: the very first magic-user.

The spells pushed hard against the curtains of time, straining to part them. But something kept him out. Something from the very beginning.

He banged his fist down. There was no time left! Dr. Verity had an infinite army from a multitude of alternate dimensions ready to attack Magisteria, and citizens were being rounded up and jailed for even owning spell books, let alone using the now-illegal magic. And if the hints Kiel had heard were true, the entire planet might be in even more danger than they'd thought.

And all the Magister could do was search desperately for the seventh and last key and do what he could to help the boy who was never meant to be.

Suddenly, the nine hundred and tenth spell opened a blazing portal, revealing President Bunsen, only much more elderly, recording her memories into a computer of some sort.

The Magister gasped. This was it, the first clue to the location of the Seventh Key, the one most hidden, the one designed to keep any and all from ever opening the Vault of Containment hidden beneath Quanterium and unleashing the greatest power known to all of mankind: the Source of Magic.

Kiel would have to know!

Over the hills of Magisteria, through the Forbidden Space separating Quanterium from the magic planet, and into the Cities of Science traveled a new spell, searching for Kiel. The spell passed beyond Quanterium's atmosphere, back into the nothingness of space, then beyond even that, to true nothingness, to the end of space itself, to Charm's ship, the *Scientific Method*, and then past, to whatever lay beyond everything, and into Kiel's mind.

"I hope I'm not disturbing you," the Magister said through the magic, directly into Kiel's thoughts, "but I found a clue to the Seventh Key's location. You must locate the Original Computer on Quanterium."

"The original what?" Kiel thought back. "Sorry, I'm having a bit of trouble thinking, since I'm beyond the edge of existence. I'm not even really sure that I'm existing myself right now."

The Magister smiled to himself. "You are thinking, therefore you are existing," he said. "Do what you need to, but you must find the very first computer ever created. Listen closely, as this information is of the utmost importance!"

Owen reached over and grabbed the book from her hand before she could turn the page. "See?" he said. "It's the perfect time to sneak in. He'll never even know, because he's doing all kinds of magic and talking to Kiel. In and out, five minutes. Ready?"

"Ready," Bethany said, inwardly terrified. This was *such* a bad idea.

But maybe . . . maybe things would go better than she expected. Maybe it'd even be fun to do a little magic, and they'd laugh and have a good time, and maybe—probably not, but maybe—she'd find that Owen really could be trusted, might even be a friend. That'd be nice, wouldn't it? To have someone to hang out with in books? To talk about things? Maybe even help her look for her father?

She smiled, strangely optimistic. Could this be the first time in her life where things actually went well?

CHAPTER 7

Bethany took the book from Owen at the marked page, then began to push in with one hand, holding the other out to him.

Owen took her hand, and then as soon as her head went inside, grabbed the baseball bat he'd left on his bedroom floor. There was no way he was going to face down Dr. Verity without *some* kind of weapon. The guy had beaten Kiel Gnomenfoot like five times already, and had all the powers of science on his side. The *least* Owen needed was a bat. A metal bat. It was perfect.

Now armed, Owen took a deep breath and followed Bethany in. This time they went slower into the book, and he could feel his fingers, then his arm, melting into words, then those words pouring out over the page like brownie batter. When his head went through, though, it was more like stepping through a bubble. First he was in his bedroom, then a tingling, and there he was, standing in the upside-down tower of the Magister.

The Magister's study could have stepped right out of Owen's imagination, if rooms could step. Every wall had bookcases, and every bookcase overflowed with books, almost all of which held spells or potion recipes or a million other things that Owen would have given almost anything to read. Potions bubbled over small flames in various places, and dark shadows snapped and bit at the metal bars of their cages. Kiel's winged cat, Alphonse, sat cleaning himself on a table, ignoring them. And the Magister himself stood staring into nothing, his mind communicating by magic with his apprentice beyond the end of the universe.

Owen knew that above them, where the upside-down tower met the underside of a cliff, thousands of magical traps awaited any unauthorized visitor. He also knew that at this moment, Dr. Verity was working his way through them without a sweat. They only had a few minutes before the mad scientist showed up, which meant Owen needed to be in place. And *that* meant giving Bethany something to do.

"Spell book," Owen whispered, nodding toward the center of the room, where a monstrously huge book lay open on a pedestal. "In the Kiel Gnomenfoot books, you learn a spell by reading it, but can only cast it once without the spell book. Then you have to relearn it. So don't cast the search spell by accident. . . . You'll only get one shot."

"Does it have a table of contents or something?" Bethany whispered, her eyes widening at the size of the book. "How am I supposed to find the right spell?"

Owen shrugged. "In the books, the spell book always opens up to whatever spell Kiel most needs. Maybe just try thinking hard?"

Bethany nodded and slowly approached the book, trying not to make any noise. Not that the Magister would hear her, as intent on his magic as he was. That was the only way Dr. Verity had been able to surprise him.

But not anymore! Owen shuddered at how amazing this was going to be. "I'm going to keep watch," he told Bethany, then backed away into the shadows next to the door, giving himself a clear view of anyone who came in, as well as of Bethany and the Magister. He pulled the bat from behind his back and held it ready. Too bad he couldn't use some kind of magic on Dr. Verity, but the doctor would expect that. Baseball bats, though, not so much.

Bethany reached a hand out to the spell book, but before she could touch it, the book leaped to life, pages turning on their own, making Bethany gasp and step back in surprise. The book came to an abrupt stop, and she glanced down at the page. Immediately a warm glow spread from the book to Bethany's hands, and she leaped backward.

"What was that?" she whispered to Owen, her eyes still on the spell book.

"That's how it works," Owen whispered back. "It's teaching you the spell. That's what the glow was. Was it the location spell?"

She shook her head. "'Amnesty of Amnesia,'" she read. "'For removing memory.'" The glow began to light her up, and she quickly stepped backward again.

"Why would it give you that?" Owen said, starting to worry. Bethany needed to be done before Dr. Verity got here, or the doctor would see her. The last thing they needed was a spell book that couldn't do its job.

Bethany glanced at him, and he quickly shoved the bat behind his back. "Uh, who knows," she said, sounding almost guilty. "But I don't remember the words to the spell, so I guess I didn't give it enough time. Doesn't matter. Let me try one more time to find the location spell."

She put her hands on her forehead and stared at the spell book, apparently trying to make it turn to the spell she wanted. The book complied, flipping its pages to a new spell near the beginning, and Bethany glanced down at it, then gave Owen a thumbs-up.

She must have found it, because this time as the book began to glow, Bethany laid her hands on the page and allowed the light to slowly sweep up her arms and into her body.

"It's like hot chocolate on a cold day," she said, a tiny smile on her face. The light quickly faded, and she turned back toward him. "That was almost . . . nice!"

"Great," Owen told her, nervously looking at the door, where he could swear he heard explosions getting closer. "You sure you have it? Like I said, all spells are one-time things if you don't have the spell book, so let's make sure before we go."

Bethany closed her eyes. "I think so. I can remember the words. They're all here in my head." Her eyes opened, and she held out a hand toward Owen. "Come on, let's get out of here. This was much easier than I thought it'd be!"

Owen bit his lip, then shook his head. "Hold on, just let me take this in for one more minute, okay? Since it's my only chance to ever see it."

Bethany looked like she wanted to protest, but instead nodded. "Just don't take too long," she said, then went to hide from view behind the Magister's desk, waiting for Owen.

Perfect, because Dr. Verity ought to be coming through the door any—

The door exploded out into the study, knocking Owen against the wall hard.

"Hello?" Dr. Verity shouted, glowing with the light of his force fields and from the large green ray gun in his hand. "Sebastian? I rang the bell upstairs, but you must not have heard me, so I destroyed most of your tower instead."

From across the room and just out of Dr. Verity's sight, Bethany's eyes went wide with terror, and she frantically motioned for Owen to stay still. She had no idea what was happening, that the Magister sensed Dr. Verity was there, that Kiel was telling the Magister to save himself, but the Magister refused to stop his spell so the information about the Seventh Key would not be lost.

"If you're busy, I can come back later," Dr. Verity said, then shot his green gun directly at the Magister's giant spell book, which first exploded, then imploded immediately after. He stepped forward, aiming the gun at the Magister's back. "Or, we could just take care of things right now, once and for all, my old friend."

Dr. Verity's force field protected him from magic, fire, lasers, and a million other things. But one thing it *didn't* protect him from was solid objects, especially metallic ones. For some reason the force field energy got disrupted by metal, which wasn't a big problem when your enemies all used ray guns or magic.

Of course, the doctor always had other protection as well, but here, after making his way through the entire tower, all he had left was his force field and Owen knew it, since the book had been pretty explicit about that fact.

Owen hefted his metal bat and took his baseball stance. Just like Little League.

Bethany's mouth dropped open, and she shook her head over and over.

Owen just smiled.

"Good-bye, Sebastian," Dr. Verity said, and his gun began powering up to fire.

"Hello, Dr. Verity," Owen said, then swung his bat right at the doctor.

The bat hit the mad scientist with a hollow metallic thunk, and the evil doctor actually spun around once before collapsing to the floor, hitting his head hard. The force field powered down with a whine, leaving just an old man in a lab coat lying on the floor of a magician's study.

For a moment there was silence, as Bethany was too shocked to even move. That moment quickly passed, though, and she stood up. "What did you do?" she asked in a tiny voice. "Owen . . . what did you just *do*?"

"I saved the Magister," he told her, raising the bat in the air like a sword. "Bethany . . . I just saved the Magister! Do you know what this means?" He shouted in triumph, then turned his gaze toward the ceiling and addressed his audience. "Hey, everybody reading the book! Don't worry, the Magister doesn't have to die now! I saved him! He's going to be okay! You're *welcome*!"

CHAPTER 8

Bethany stared at Owen, her mouth hanging open. How could he have done this? He changed the story! He *changed* the *story*! In all her years of visiting books, she'd never interfered with the story, not *once*. She'd avoided the main characters, no matter how much she wanted to see them, just so there wasn't even a chance of this happening.

Owen must have come in specifically to do this, to save the Magister. He'd tricked her. He'd *tricked* her! Had he said all that stuff about the location spell as a way to fool her into bringing him into the book?

"I know what you're going to say," Owen told her, backing away from what must have been a pretty upsetting look on her face.

"Oh, I don't think you have *any* idea what I want to say,"

she told him, her voice dangerously low. How could this have happened? Would the readers see them, after he'd just yelled out to them? Would it change the next book that hadn't come out yet?

Owen held up both his hands in surrender. "I'm sorry, I really am, but it had to be done! He was going to kill the Magister! How could I let that happen? Besides, as of right now, I don't think anyone's even noticed that you're here, so your secret should still be safe—"

"And who might you two be?" said an old, half-amused voice. Owen flinched, while Bethany spun around, hoping that whoever it was intended to shoot fireballs or something at Owen.

A man wearing robes down past his feet and a beard past his robes stepped over to them, his eyes twinkling, his hat twitching like a living thing. "Visitors!" the Magister said with a wide smile. "And I hope with no intention of killing me? That's my favorite kind of visitor. And what brings you to my tower?"

"Don't. Say. Anything," Bethany whispered, trying to step back into the shadows. "We're going. *Now.*"

She grabbed for Owen's hand, but he pulled it just out of reach. "I came to save you, Your Magister-ness," Owen said.

"It was all me. My plan, no one else's. I heard about Dr. Verity trying to kill you, so I figured I should stop that." He shrugged. "You know, no big deal. Something anyone would have done, if they'd thought of it. And been brave enough. Like I pretty much was."

"Saved me?" the Magister said, then gave him a curious look. "Then you have my everlasting thanks. But you *also* have my curiosity." He sniffed the air. "You don't smell as if you're from Magisteria. Or Quanterium, for that matter. You smell . . . *distant.*"

Despite his friendliness, the Magister's tone gave Bethany a chill. She grabbed for Owen's hand again, but this time he smacked her hand away, and she almost punched him.

"Distant is a good word," Owen told him. "Where I'm from, we're all big fans of yours. *And* Kiel's."

"I have fans, do I?" the Magister said, his eyes twinkling. "What a curious thing. And how did you learn of me? I don't recall visiting a land with people like you in my travels. Perhaps Kiel has?" He gestured for them to sit down. "He should be back in a moment, if you'd like to wait."

Dr. Verity moaned, and the Magister's gaze fell on the scientist. "Ah, my good doctor," the Magister said. "This boy seems to have done me a great favor. Not only did he protect me, but he left you vulnerable to my tender mercies." The Magister gestured, and the mad doctor's body sprang into the air. Snake-like chains slithered up from hidden parts of the study to wrap themselves around the scientist until no part of him except his head was uncovered.

Dr. Verity screamed in rage, jerking his head around to no avail. "You couldn't have seen me coming!" he shouted. "It's impossible! I had this planned out, and you were meant to die, *tonight*!"

The Magister looked him right in the face. "Oh, but I didn't, Doctor. See you coming *or* die, for that matter. In fact, I still don't know how these children knew of your attack." One finger flicked on his right hand, and invisible hands yanked Bethany out into the light. "The boy has spoken, but you have not, my dear," the Magister said, turning to face her. "What can you tell me about all of this?"

Bethany went absolutely silent, her face bright red. Anything she said now would be seen by *every single reader* of the book, from now until forever. This was her worst nightmare, worse than forgetting to wear clothes to school or the one where she dreamed that her father was actually Mr. Barberry.

"I . . . ," she started to say, then froze, her mind blank.

The Magister smiled gently. "Don't be afraid. I mean you no harm." He sniffed the air loudly again. "You smell distant too, though not from as far as your friend. In some ways, you *could* be from Magisteria. But in other ways, not." He raised an eyebrow. "You glow with power as well, my dear. Now which would that be? Magic or science?"

The invisible hands held her tighter, and something electric and cold shot through her spine, giving her the chills.

"No time for explaining, sorry," Bethany said quickly, shaking off the odd feeling as she frantically reached for Owen.

Owen, though, just shook his head, an excited look on his face. "Are you kidding?" he whispered. "We're not going yet. *Kiel* is coming. We have to meet him!"

"You'll pay for this, Sebastian," Dr. Verity said, almost spitting with hate. "My infinite armies will attack Magisteria with or without me! I don't care where you imprison me. I'll find a way out and will destroy all who profane reality with that blasphemy you call magic. You, that boy of yours, this whole science-forsaken planet of Magisteria—"

The Magister sighed. "I take no pleasure in doing this, Verity. But you leave me no choice in the matter. You're far too dangerous." The Magister gestured, and the destroyed spell book on the podium popped back into existence, then flipped pages faster than Bethany could see, finally landing on a page called "Exile from All Reality."

Dr. Verity's eyes widened. "You wouldn't! Kill me instead!"

"So your death can trigger further clones of yourself, as it has for centuries?" the Magister asked with his gentle smile. "I think not. In exile, you'll never age, or hunger, or thirst. Time will stand still, and you'll find yourself with far more freedom than those you would make war against. Freedom to reflect on the choices that have brought you here." He patted Dr. Verity on his cheek. "After all, freedom is the right of all beings, is it not?"

"I think Optimus Prime said that," Owen whispered to Bethany. Bethany elbowed him in the gut, hard.

The Magister began his spell. Dr. Verity tried to scream, but the sound was lost as the scientist slowly faded away. The chains, having nothing to hold on to, fell to the floor with an enormous clatter.

"Um . . . I thought there was supposed to be a seventh book," Owen whispered to Bethany. "It's coming out in a week, and Kiel was supposed to have a big final battle with Dr. Verity. How's that going to happen now?"

She shot him a look of pure hatred, but it didn't even register with Owen. The Magister, however, registered just fine. "A book, you say?" the old man asked. "With Kiel and Dr. Verity? What book would that be, then?"

This was all *far* too far. Whatever spell had been holding her had disappeared when the Magister had exiled Dr. Verity, so Bethany leaped right at Owen, her hands spread wide. The boy jumped backward in surprise, but she tackled him around his waist and kicked them both right up out of the book.

They crashed out of the book's pages and onto the carpet of Owen's bedroom, landing hard enough to knock the air out of Owen. Bethany quickly sat up, grabbed Owen's shirt, and shook him back and forth. "WHAT DID YOU DO?" she screamed.

"Boof!" Owen said, not able to form words yet.

"YOU JUST TOLD A CHARACTER IN A BOOK THAT HE WAS *IN* A BOOK!" Bethany couldn't even think, she was so angry. "Do you have any idea what that means?"

"No?" Owen squeaked.

"ME NEITHER!" she shouted. "And that's what scares me!"

She leaped off of him and grabbed the book, frantically turning back to the last page.

"Good-bye, Sebastian," Dr. Verity said, and his gun began powering up to fire.

. . . To be continued in *Kiel Gnomenfoot and the Source of Magic.*

Bethany let out an explosive breath. They weren't there! The book ended too soon!

"What does it say?" Owen asked her, looking nervous.

"It says you are *so* lucky!" she shouted, then threw the book at him. He flinched, and the book fell back to the floor, falling open. Bethany yanked him up by his arm and stared him right in the face, so close she could feel his breath. "You don't *ever* speak to me again, do you understand? And if you ever tell anyone about me, I'll find the deepest, darkest math book I can find, and drop you into the most boring part!"

Owen shuddered and slowly nodded. "I . . . I'm sorry," he started to say, but she just glared at him, and he immediately shut up.

"We don't talk, remember? EVER AGAIN!"

And with that, Bethany slammed his bedroom door and stomped down the stairs to go home. For a moment, she was so angry she couldn't even get his front door open. In frustration she smacked the door so hard that her hand stung, and she groaned in pain.

A friend would have come out to see if she was okay. Or just come out to apologize again for ruining her life in the first place.

Bethany gave Owen five seconds. He didn't show.

Maybe even angrier now, she yanked the front door open, then slammed it shut, too furious to notice the bright light exploding from Owen's window.

CHAPTER 9

Bethany looked in her living room window before going in, just to see. Her mother seemed to be reading something, maybe a magazine.

And her eyes were red.

Not again. Not tonight. Bethany just didn't have the strength to deal with *this*, too.

Instead, a few minutes later Bethany found herself in the library, walking through the stacks, checking to make sure no one else was around. Forget her mother, forget that jerk Owen, forget everything else. It didn't matter. None of it did.

Not if the location spell worked and found her father.

She took a deep breath, running through the spell in her head. This was *so* wrong. Magic, in the real world? What if other people saw? What if it created a gigantic flaming arrow that pointed out the book her father was in? What if it started screaming the name of the book, and she couldn't turn it off quickly enough, like she'd forgotten to turn her cell phone off in a movie?

Didn't matter. Not anymore. This was it. All she had to do was say the words, and she'd know exactly where her father was.

So why couldn't she? And why couldn't her legs stop shaking?

But she knew why. Because as bad as today had been, it could get much, much worse.

What if she found her father and he didn't want to come home?

The words to the spell were ready, right on the tip of her tongue. Her father had gotten himself out of a book to begin with, hadn't he? Why couldn't he now? Wasn't that the real question? What if her father just didn't care? What if he didn't remember her, somehow?

Or worse, what if he didn't . . . if he didn't . . . ?

A one-time-only spell. She could find her father. She could *find* her *father*!

No. She couldn't.

Someone turned the corner and gave her a concerned look, and she realized she was sweating, that her legs were still shaking. She forced a smile, then walked too quickly to the children's section and fell into a seat.

The books helped. Being around all the stories somehow let her breathe again. They didn't want anything from her, or think badly of her. They were there just to tell their stories.

When her legs stopped shaking, she wiped her forehead with her sleeve, then stood up to walk along the shelves, touching random books here and there. Something would be here to distract her, some strange world that didn't care about fathers or mothers or Owens. *Island of the Blue Dolphins?* Beautiful, but way too dangerous with the dogs and devilfish and everything. *A Wrinkle in Time?* A little too much quantum theory for a night like this.

"Can I help you find anything?" asked a woman behind her, and Bethany glanced over her shoulder to find Owen's mother giving her a pleasant look.

Bethany quickly turned away, shaking her head. "Oh, no thanks. I'm fine."

"I can make some suggestions, if you want," the librarian said, standing next to Bethany. "What kinds of books do you like?"

"I'm not really a big reader," Bethany said quietly, turning her body away as much as she could.

"Oh, I always see you in here," Owen's mom said, running her hands over the books like she was looking for something.

"Don't worry. Maybe you just haven't found your favorite book yet. I honestly don't think anyone has. Just when you think you might have a favorite, something even better comes along. It's the one rule they taught me in librarian school."

"You went to librarian school?" Bethany asked in spite of herself.

"You can quiz me on the Dewey decimal system if you want. Ask me about what number Victorian biographies go under. I dare you."

Bethany smiled, then remembered what was happening. "I'm okay. I just wanted . . . this one." She grabbed something random off the shelf and tried to make an escape, but Owen's mother stepped in front of her.

"*Half Upon a Time*? I met that author once. He misspelled his own name in my book when he signed it. Weird. If I were you, I'd try . . . Here, what about this? It's one of my favorites."

"I thought you couldn't have favorites," Bethany said.

"Nah, the second rule they taught us in librarian school is that you can have as many favorite books as there are books," she said, not cracking a smile. "Do you want to know what the third rule is?"

"That there *are* no rules?"

The librarian laughed. "That's the fourth rule, actually. The third is that if you want to find a new favorite book, ask a librarian. They always know." She handed Bethany a copy of something called *The Great Brain*. "Give it a try and let me know what you think."

Bethany nodded, giving up, then followed Owen's mother back to the checkout desk and signed the book out. She turned to leave, then paused. "Um, thanks. For the book. That was nice of you."

"Let me know if you like it," the woman said. "And next time, maybe you can recommend something for me."

Bethany smiled and waved good-bye, then left the library holding her new book close, her mind not at all on what she was doing. Weirdly, it took her longer to get home from the library than usual. Even weirder, she found herself at Owen's house again without even realizing it.

Ugh. What was she doing? It's not like she owed him anything. He should really be the one apologizing to her.

But what had he really done wrong?

He'd told a character in a book that—

Okay, there was that. And that was *huge*, yes. But it hadn't shown up in the book, and for all she knew, maybe it never would. After all, that wizard guy had been supposed to die, right? So maybe he wouldn't even have a chance to tell anyone what had happened. She could go back and check in a few days, before the last Kiel Gnomenfoot book came out, just to make sure that nothing had changed.

Too bad she hadn't actually let the forget spell infect her or whatever. That would have made things a lot easier.

In the meantime, she *could* go in and at least listen to Owen apologize again. That wouldn't be the worst thing in the world to sit through, at least for a few minutes. Better wrap it all up now than have to deal with him throwing her guilty looks in school or whatever, assuming he'd even care.

Besides, Owen's mother wasn't the worst or anything, so somewhere in there Owen had to be not so bad too.

She knocked on his front door and waited for a few seconds, then knocked again. No answer. Maybe he couldn't hear her, up in his room? He was probably listening to depressing music, thinking how sad it was that he'd betrayed her like he had. That just made sense.

She tried the door, and it was still unlocked, so she pushed it open and walked in. It wasn't breaking and entering if you'd just been in a place and had stomped off, she was pretty sure.

The lights hadn't been turned on since she left, so it looked like Owen hadn't even come out of his room. That made Bethany feel even more sure about letting him apologize again. Obviously, he was upset. So upset he couldn't even bear to go downstairs.

Unless he was playing video games in his room or something.

No, he had to be upset. You couldn't just do something like he'd done and not feel horrible. No one was that heartless.

She took a deep breath, practiced a stern but forgiving face, then knocked on his door at the top of the stairs. "Owen? It's Bethany. I, um, forgot my book." Yeah, that sounded like a good reason to come back. "I'm still mad, obviously. Because you were a huge jerk, and you never should have done what you did. It was like you betrayed me, Owen, you know? You promised one thing and lied. You know how messed up that is?"

She paused, waiting for a response, but didn't hear one. He probably felt too guilty.

"It's very, *very* messed up," she said, answering her own question. "So let me have my book, and we can go back to never speaking to each other again." There. Now that she'd made her point, she could take the high road and let him apologize his way back into being friends with her. After a while, at least.

Feeling good about things, she opened the door to an empty room.

Empty except for the Kiel Gnomenfoot book, which was still lying open right in the middle of the floor.

He couldn't have. *No way.* He *couldn't* have gone back. It wasn't possible. Only she could jump into books, right?

Right?

She slowly picked up the Kiel Gnomenfoot book and opened it to the last page.

"Good-bye, Sebastian," Dr. Verity said, and his gun began powering up to fire.

So it still read the same as before. But maybe it wouldn't hurt to check?

She pushed her head in, just to make sure, since it was impossible, but—

Something slammed into her head, and the last thing she could see before everything went black was Owen's surprised face as someone yanked her all the way into the book.

CHAPTER 10

As Bethany slammed his bedroom door, Owen sighed, then started to go after her. This wasn't how things were supposed to go. How was he going to be best friends with Kiel Gnomenfoot now? Would anyone even know that he was the one who'd saved the Magister if his whole saving scene hadn't made it into the book?

Plus, what about Narnia?

And there was that other small issue of, well, Bethany being hurt. Not just annoyed or irritated, but actually hurt by what he'd done. And that gave Owen a heavy feeling in the back of his shoulders, like when his mother wasn't mad, just "disappointed."

Stupid guilt.

"Bethany," he tried to shout after her, but for some odd reason his lips didn't move, and all that came out was a weird sort of "hunnnnh." Why couldn't he move his lips? He tried to bring his hands up to touch his mouth, but now his hands decided to play the same lip game and not move either.

Arms, legs, toes . . . nothing worked.

And that's when Owen noticed that his bedroom seemed quite a bit brighter than it had a minute ago.

"I'd just like a minute of your time, if it's all the same to you," said a voice from behind him. Owen's body froze from disbelief, along with whatever it was that had already frozen him a few seconds ago.

That was the *Magister's* voice.

The Magister shouldn't even have a voice, because books don't have voices, unless they're audiobooks, and really, that wasn't the character's voice so much as the person who read the audiobook. And yet, there it was in Owen's house, all polite and magical and Magistery!

"I apologize for such treatment," said the Magister, and Owen's legs turned the rest of him around like some kind of puppet. There, behind him, was a doorway made from brightness, lighting his entire room.

And inside the doorway stood a fictional character.

Um. This had to be a mistake, right? Sure, the Magister

existed in the book, but this was the real, actual, *nonfictional* world. Wasn't it?

The magician raised a hand, and Owen's body jerked forward, walking like some kind of zombie toward the doorway.

"It's just that you disappeared in such a hurry," the Magister said, beckoning Owen forward with one finger. "And after riling up my curiosity in such a way! We can't have that, now, can we? I promise this won't hurt a bit." He frowned. "Well, I shouldn't think, at least."

Well, *that* didn't bode well. Owen tried to shout again for Bethany, hoping she'd hear and rush back upstairs to shut down this doorway made of light and save him, but his lips still wouldn't move. His legs kept jerking him forward, though, and soon he was just inches from the doorway.

And that's when he saw the one thing in the world that would cheer him up.

"Are you taking on a new apprentice without asking me?" said a younger voice, and Kiel Gnomenfoot—KIEL GNOMENFOOT—stepped into view behind the Magister.

Just like in the books, Kiel was dressed in black pants, shirt, and cloak, the better for sneaking in and sabotaging Quanterium labs. A rope belt weighed down by pouches hung around his waist, and two different knife-wands were holstered at his side like pistols.

All in all, he looked like the coolest thing Owen had ever seen in his entire life.

"Ah, Kiel," the Magister said. He gestured toward Owen. "This is the boy who saved me from Dr. Verity. And somehow knew that I would *need* saving."

"You fought Dr. Verity?" Kiel Gnomenfoot, the actual *real*, *live* (sort of) Kiel Gnomenfoot, said to Owen. "With *what*?" He grinned. "I'm just kidding. Nice job, buddy! I owe you one. Doesn't matter when or where. You just tell me what you want done. The more dangerous, the better. In fact, if it's world-being-destroyed dangerous, that's the most fun, so really, you'd be doing *me* a favor." His grin widened, and he winked.

Owen fanboy-giggled in response, only since he couldn't move, it came out like a weird moaning ghost. Kiel *winked*! That was just so Kiel!

Kiel's grin faded and he gave Owen an odd look, then turned to the Magister. "So the Seventh Key's location is in the Original Computer? You *know* how much I hate going to Quanterium."

"That will have to wait for just a moment, apprentice. This might be of greater importance."

"But even if you captured Dr. Verity, there's an infinite army of Science Soldiers waiting in orbit around Magisteria, ready to attack! We still have to shut them down. And all the magic-users that were arrested, I need to free them—"

"If this child knows of Dr. Verity's plans, we might do well to find out how that is possible, before you run off again," the old man said, flashing a patient smile at Kiel. "Something already worries me. Do you see what I see, through the portal?"

Kiel squinted past Owen. "Someone doesn't know how to hang up his clothes?"

The Magister shook his head. "The world this boy comes from has no magic. None at all. We could be looking at another alternate reality, where magic was truly destroyed. It's even possible that this boy knows of Dr. Verity's plan because, in some manner, Dr. Verity exists there, as well."

Uh-oh. *That* didn't bode well *either*. "No Dr. Verity!" Owen tried to shout. "No Dr. Verity! And magic wasn't destroyed! It just never existed here!"

None of that got said, of course. Just a lot more moaning.

"He says that magic never existed there," Kiel translated, then paused. "You know, I've seen alternate worlds, desolate futures, and the nothingness beyond the end of the universe.

But I've never seen anything like that room." He shook his head. "It just screams boring. You have to feel bad for whoever grew up there."

"Ah, appearances might deceive," the Magister said. "Look closer. This boy and another, a girl, mentioned a book while they were here. Take a look at those books on his shelves." The Magister gestured, and several books popped off Owen's shelf and began flipping their pages. "There's magic in their histories, Kiel. Magic everywhere. Schools for magic. Wardrobes leading to magic lands. Gods and monsters, impossible things. And yet, that magic no longer exists in their world. How would that have happened?"

Kiel frowned. "Let him talk. Maybe he knows why. Maybe he even wants to help?" He turned to Owen. "You *do* want to help, don't you? You saved my master here. I bet you want to learn magic and become amazing and do impossible things, yeah? Of course you do. Everyone does. That's all science people are, just jealous of magic. Want me to teach you some right now?"

Owen's eyes widened, and he tried to nod vigorously. Tried and failed.

"Answers it shall be," the Magister said. "If you wouldn't mind, my boy, just a short trip back to my study?"

"Let's keep it as short as we can," Kiel said. "I still have to find the Seventh Key."

Owen's feet picked up off the floor and walked him into the shining doorway, then over to the wall in the now-familiar Magister's tower. There, his uncontrollable hands reached down and fastened chains to his ankles, then to each wrist. The chains magically tightened, making sure he wasn't going anywhere anytime soon.

"Just for your own safety," the Magister said, giving a friendly wink.

This *really, really* wasn't boding well.

The Magister murmured something, and suddenly Owen was free to speak, to move, and to escape.

Unfortunately, the chains kept him from doing two of those things, so he went with the third.

"You're making a big mistake!" he shouted. "There's no magic in my world. Those books are just made-up stories! You know, for entertainment! We love magic so much that we tell each other stories about it, like we wish we could do it! That's it! Trust me, if any of us could, we'd be magicians in a minute!"

The Magister watched Owen for a moment as Kiel made "see?" gestures with his hand, fidgeting from foot to foot, clearly anxious to get on with his quest/book series. But the Magister ignored his apprentice. Instead, he whispered something else, and a weird sort of fog slid into Owen's brain.

"Now," the magician said, his voice low and commanding, "tell me again how there is no magic in your world."

"There isn't," Owen said, meaning to repeat exactly what he'd just said. Only the strange fog didn't want him to. And for some reason, the fog seemed to be in control of his mouth now. "Just in fictional stories. Like you. You're made up. You don't really exist. None of this is real. It's all just the product of someone's imagination, a writer, an author, his name is Jonathan Porterhouse. He made you all up. You don't really exist. All this? Your whole war with Dr. Verity? Made-up. It's not real. There's no such thing as magic, never was. You are just a bunch of words on a page, and the only reason I'm here is because my friend Bethany—well, not really my friend, because I annoyed her—she brought me here, because she does that kind of thing."

Wait. *What?*

CHAPTER 11

hat had the fog just made him say? Owen tried desperately to lie, to take back everything he'd just spouted out, but the fog filled all of his thoughts, arranging them like soldiers in a line, ready to march out the door of his mouth and into battle. And no matter how much he ordered them to stop, they just kept marching.

Or something like that. It was honestly a little hard to think of analogies with his brain so magicked.

The Magister's eyes bore in on Owen. "I'm sorry, my boy. You didn't just suggest that we don't actually *exist*, did you?"

Kiel tapped his own arm. "I feel fairly solid to me. Could we get back to more important things now?"

The Magister closed his eyes for a moment, then reopened them. "The spell is working. Somehow he actually believes that we aren't real."

"You're *not* real," Owen's mouth said. "You're just characters in a book." He frantically tried to bite his lips closed to keep from saying anything else, but his lips just pushed out into a fish-face expression to escape his teeth. Ugh, those clever lips of his!

"He's probably been science brain-cleaned, washed, whatever they do," Kiel said. "Charm told me about it. They use their electric lights to flash your eyes until you believe whatever they say." He shrugged. "Science people do weird things for fun. Magi, I *need* to find the Seventh Key—"

"Why would you think us not real?" the Magister asked Owen, giving him a quizzical look. "You can see us standing in front of you, and you are responding to my magic. Could an unreal person have cast such a spell?"

"Apparently!" Owen said. "I know you're not real because I've read about you in books, especially Kiel. I'm a huge fan. Everyone is! We know all about your quest to find the Seven Keys to the Vault of Containment, then use the Source of Magic's power to defeat Dr. Verity once and for all. But there are things you don't know yet. Like the Magister was actually born on Quanterium, and Dr. Verity was born on Magisteria, and they were switched as some kind of peace offering, to let each side experience the other's culture. See? I couldn't have known that except that it's in the books."

The Magister took a step back, his eyes wide. Kiel turned to him, one eyebrow raised. "That isn't true, is it, Magi?" he asked quietly.

"*No one* knows that," the Magister said quietly. "It happened thousands of years ago! No one alive still knows apart from Dr. Verity. How could you—"

"It's all in the books," Owen's mouth continued. "Just like how Kiel found out he's a clone of Dr. Verity in the fourth book, and that the parents he'd always been searching for never actually existed. Which made him wonder that if he was actually from Quanterium, like Dr. Verity, how could he do magic, since no one from Quanterium's ever been able to do it." Owen paused for a breath, while inwardly he screamed at himself to just shut up already. "Obviously, you're from Quanterium, Mr. Magister, and you can do magic, but he didn't know that part yet. Not that it matters, since Dr. Verity was from Magisteria to begin with anyway. And remember how you originally told Kiel that his parents were killed by a time bomb that Dr. Verity sent, since you didn't think he was ready to know that he's a clone of Dr. Verity? You thought that'd turn his life upside down—"

"And it did, at the time," Kiel said quietly.

"Enough!" the Magister shouted, and Owen's mouth clamped shut. "There is no way you could know these things!"

"None of this changes anything, as . . . surprising as it might be," Kiel said. "If you really know what is happening here, why not tell us what Dr. Verity has planned?"

"Oh, he's going to blow up Magisteria using a huge science bomb," Owen's mouth said. "That's what I read on fan sites, at least. Someone went through and pieced it all together from various threats. And somehow, it's going to be your fault, Kiel. That's what I read, anyway."

"*My* fault?"

The Magister gave Kiel a quick glance, then turned back to Owen. "Tell me how you know these secrets. I must know!" He gestured, and the fog became even thicker in Owen's head.

"I *read* them!" Owen said. "I told you! There's a guy who writes all of your books, Jonathan Porterhouse. He made you up. I don't know how you're here now, trust me. That's all Bethany's thing. Somehow she has the power to jump into books like they're windows or something. Not that you'd jump into windows usually, but you know what I mean—"

Kiel tapped the Magister on the shoulder. "Did you hear

what he said? The part about Dr. Verity *blowing up the planet*—"

"This Bethany girl," the Magister interrupted. "She travels between your world and this one? My world? The one you claim doesn't exist?"

"Yeah, because she's half-fictional," Owen said. "I don't honestly get it at all, but she said that her father was fictional, so, you know, imaginary, and somehow he came out to the real world and married her mom or something, but then he disappeared, so she wants to find him. But she can travel between here and there, yeah. Between fiction and the real world. Nonfiction? Would that be it?"

"She brought you here the first time," the Magister said, turning away and rubbing his temples. "She could take me to your world myself, and I could see if these wild statements have any truth to them."

"Didn't you bring *me* here?" Owen asked. "Why don't you just go back the same way?"

"I borrowed a bit of her power," the Magister said absently. "When I first met the two of you. I meant no harm by it, and solely wished to learn about her abilities. However, I used up what little I could take, bringing you back. To do more, I would need her at hand, if not taking me herself."

88

"I don't know why you'd ever want to leave here," Owen said. "You've got magic and time machines and dragons and—"

"I would wish to meet this . . . *writer*," the Magister told him. "The man you mentioned, Jonathan Porterhouse. The one who knows my deepest secrets, who has recorded my entire life."

"He's not really recording," Owen said. "He's making it up in his head. There's kind of a difference." Okay, really? *That* was the point he had to keep driving home here?

"Magister, we're all in danger!" Kiel said, but the Magister just waved him off.

"That shall wait, Kiel!" he shouted. "I must learn the truth of this! If what this child says is true, none of this might be real! We would have been fighting a war that never should have happened." He sighed, leaning against his spell book. "All my thousands of years of life, learning everything I could, seeing the impossibilities of magic . . . all those years, dreamt up in someone's head?"

"It can't be true," Kiel said, shaking his head. "That's all there is to it."

"I put this boy under the Fog of Truth spell," the Magister said. "Everything he has said is objectively the truth as he knows it, or his brain would collapse like a dying star."

"Really?" Owen said. "Cool!" Stupid truth spell! Okay, it *was* cool, but it was also scary! Apparently, scary wasn't objectively true enough to be said by a truth spell, though.

"We need this Bethany girl, then," the Magister said, turning back to Owen. "When will she be returning here?"

"Oh, she won't be," Owen said, finally happy to be saying good news. "She hates me now, and wants nothing to do with me. You'll never see her again. She'd *never—*"

Bethany's face popped out of nowhere right in the middle of the air.

Kiel shouted in surprise, grabbed the Magister's spell book, and banged Bethany over the head with it. Her eyes rolled back into her head and she tipped forward, but Kiel grabbed her head before it could fall, then helped her the rest of the way into the room.

He laid her gently on the floor, only to back out of the way as the Magister gestured. Bethany's body glowed with magic, then stood up on its own like a puppet, her eyes still closed.

"Perfect," the Magister said. "And you," he said, pointing at Owen, "shall wait with Dr. Verity beyond time and space until I return. You won't need to eat or drink, as your body won't actually exist as anything beyond a possibility until you come back out."

"That's all well and good, but what about bathroom breaks?!" Owen shouted as the Magister mumbled a spell. "*Seriously*, that's an important question!"

But neither Kiel nor the Magister answered, and Owen began to disappear. The last thing Owen saw was the Magister reach out and take Bethany's hand as Kiel took the other.

"Take me to your world," the magician said to his puppet. "And then I shall take us to this Jonathan Porterhouse writer."

The unconscious Bethany body nodded, then jumped the three of them right out of the book, just as the entire room disappeared into nothingness.

Owen sighed. Bethany was totally going to blame *him* for this.

CHAPTER 12

The first thing Bethany noticed when she woke up was that she wasn't in Owen's bedroom. Instead of a bed, a desk, and a few bookshelves of dead books, there were . . . well, hundreds of bookshelves, maybe thousands. And all the books had their covers, too.

It looked like she was in some kind of massive library, with the shelves rising at least two, maybe three floors, with those rolling ladders you only see in movies with rich people's houses. That, combined with the marble floor and enormous oak desk, meant that whoever owned this house probably had a very large bank account.

That was the first thing she noticed. The second was that she was alone.

Where exactly was she, and how had she gotten here? She must have jumped out of a book, but since when did she not come out of the same book she went into? And if she *had* jumped out of a book, which one was it? There weren't any books on the floor around where she'd woken up, and the last thing she wanted to do was have to figure out which book to jump back into out of the hundreds of thousands on the shelves.

That, and even worse, she had no idea what time it was, or how far from home she might be.

Could she use the location spell to find out where she was? But then she'd have wasted it, and how would she find her father then?

"Owen!" she yelled, not even caring. "If you can hear me, I will make you pay for all of this!"

Two double doors swung open at one end of the room, and a man in robes with a long beard and a twitching hat strode in. The Magister.

Well, that explained things. She hadn't jumped *out* of a book because she was still *in* a book. That made a little sense, at least. She had stuck her head into that Kiel Gnomenfoot book.

"I'm glad to see you're awake," the Magister said. "We have quite a lot to talk about."

"No, actually, we don't," she said, and immediately jumped out of the book.

Except . . . she didn't. Instead, she just hopped a foot in the air, and landed right back where she'd started.

A little more panicked, she tried jumping out of the book a second time, then a third, her heart starting to race as nothing happened. "What did you do?" she shouted at the Magister. "Why can't I leave?"

The Magister gestured to a huge comfy leather chair nearby, and it waddled toward her on its little feet. "Please. Sit."

Bethany began to hyperventilate. She'd had panic attacks before, usually when her mother had almost found all her hidden books beneath her bed, but this was something else altogether. Where *was* she? How could she not jump out of the book? And if she wasn't in a book, *how was a fictional character here too*?!

Why had she ever, EVER trusted Owen?

"Sit," the Magister repeated, and this time, her legs sat her down without her doing anything.

"I don't know what you want," she said, words just tumbling out of her mouth. "Please just let me out. Let me go, *please*! I don't want this. I need to fix it, before it gets worse, whatever's happening. Please!"

The Magister just tented his fingers in front of his chest and waited for her to finish. She realized he wasn't going to answer her, so she took a deep breath, then another, and waited.

"You are no longer in my world," the Magister said finally. "I apologize, but I used your power to transport myself and my apprentice here. Your magic is . . . strange to me. And my spells weren't able to replicate it. In fact, if I hadn't siphoned a bit of your power from you when we first met, I wouldn't have been able to find your world at all."

Okay. Okay. This was about as bad as it could possibly be.

"You . . . you took some of my power. But how?" She paused, remembering the chill she felt when the Magister had first noticed her. "You mean, back in your tower?"

The Magister nodded. "More to learn about it than anything, at the time. I wasn't sure what you were capable of. As I said, the power seemed strange, foreign. Unreal, in a way."

She swallowed hard. "You've got no idea."

The Magister raised an eyebrow. "Actually, I do."

The implications of that statement made Bethany's heart skip. "You . . . do?"

"I do. But perhaps we should discuss where we are." He gestured around the library. "What you see before you is the home of a man named Jonathan Porterhouse." He stopped, apparently thinking Bethany should recognize that name. It did seem familiar, actually. Where had she heard it before?

And then it hit her. Not heard, but seen. An image of a book cover came to her, and her heart just completely gave up for a moment.

"Oh," she said, sinking back into the chair. "Oh, oh, *no*."

The Magister nodded silently.

"NO, NO, NO!" Bethany shouted, jumping to her feet. "You need to get back now! *Please!* Where's the book? I'll take you back myself. Give me your hand! You can't be here, this is so, *so* bad!"

"Sit down, if you would," the Magister told her, gesturing back to her chair.

"No, I can't!" she yelled. "You have no idea how awful this is! It's impossible, it *is*! NO. You're going back, right—" And then she stopped, something horrible occurring to her. "Where is he? Where's Jonathan Porterhouse?"

The Magister just stared at her until she sat back down. Finally, he spoke. "Owen told me that your father comes from my world. Is that true?"

Did Owen just give away *everything*? And speaking of, where was he? "What did you do with Owen?" Bethany asked, feeling sick to her stomach.

"He waits outside of time for my return just as Dr. Verity does," the Magister said. "He will be completely comfortable until I free him, and no harm shall befall him."

"I'd be more worried about the harm he'd cause, actually," Bethany said, but at least Owen was safe. Safe, in a nowhere prison beyond time and space, only able to be freed by a fictional character. So maybe "safe" wasn't the best word so much as "trapped."

"Be that as it may. Answer my question, please."

"We're not doing this," Bethany said, shaking her head. "Whatever you know, it's *way* too much. Just let me bring you back. You'll be so much better off. I found a forget spell in your spell book. I can use that on you, and none of this will ever matter again. You can free Owen, and we'll all go back to our lives!"

"Is that *true*? About your father?" the Magister repeated.

"It is and it isn't, okay? He's . . . he's from a world *like* yours, but not yours. And beyond that, I don't know much more than you."

The Magister nodded. "How is it done? How do these writers, in this world, chronicle the stories of worlds like mine?"

"They use these things called computers," Bethany said, just trying to hold herself together. "I know you don't know science, but—"

"THAT IS NOT WHAT I WANT TO *KNOW!*" the Magister roared, and the lights in the room dimmed as his entire presence grew. He seemed to gather ahold of himself, though, and everything lit back up to normal a moment later. His voice was once again measured as he continued. "I want to know *how* they know what they write. Can this man see into my world?"

Bethany stared at him. "I don't honestly know," she said in a quiet voice.

The Magister's eyes grew hard. "Because if he cannot see into my world, but instead my world sprang from his head in some way, that would mean my entire life, as well as the lives of everyone and everything I hold dear, have all been a lie. Made up. A *fiction.*"

Bethany swallowed hard again, but didn't say anything.

"I can remember back thousands of years, Bethany," the Magister said. "I remember my childhood, when the original magic-users first built the great cities of Magisteria. I remember the first time I met Sylvia, the love of my life. I remember centuries upon centuries of magical study. And my children. I watched them grow and age and have children of their own. I remember the school I once taught in, before the Quanterians destroyed it and put my planet under martial law, outlawing all magic. I remember those whom a mad doctor has imprisoned just for living their lives the way they wished, with magic." He leaned forward. "My power kept me alive for all this time while others, dear friends and loved ones, passed away. It did so because I knew I had purpose, a reason to keep living in spite of time. So you might imagine how it would feel if, in reality, my entire existence amounts to nothing more than *six adventure books for children*."

"Seven, in a week or so," Bethany said, her voice barely above a croak.

"If you won't answer my question, you give me little choice but to find out the truth another way," the Magister said, his voice dangerously low. "I used my Fog of Truth spell on your friend and did not yet have a chance to relearn it, but there are other methods."

"I . . . I really don't know!" Bethany said. "I swear, I don't! I know some authors say they hear their characters' voices in their heads, like they're talking to them—"

"Their characters?" the Magister said softly.

"The people they're writing about, that's all I meant! And if that's true, then they couldn't just make them up, you don't just hear voices. I mean, some people do, but they've got mental diseases, and authors probably don't have that kind of mental disease. I mean, they could, but—"

"I see that we'll have to do this another way," the Magister said. "Come."

He stood up and gestured. Invisible hands yanked Bethany out of her seat and carried her along behind the Magister as he strode back to the double doors.

Outside the library was some sort of large entryway, with marble floors and stark-white columns. Two people stood in the middle of the entryway, right in front of a large staircase: one younger, wearing some kind of black cloak, with twin wands in what looked like holsters at his waist, and the other middle-aged in jeans and a sweater, his eyes filled with terror as ropelike snakes wrapped and unwrapped themselves around his arms and legs, holding him in place.

"The girl has not been as much of a help as I'd hoped," the Magister said. "So we'll have to try a different way to find out the truth."

"Please, *no*," the middle-aged man said. "I told you, I don't—"

The Magister gave him a look, and the man's mouth disappeared right off his face.

"Magi, we don't need to do this," the boy in the black cloak said, not seeming too happy himself. "Honestly, I get it. I nearly gave up entirely when I found out I was a clone. I thought my whole life had been a lie. But I learned that it didn't matter, because who you are isn't about where you come from, but about what you make of yourself. *You* taught me that! What does it change if—"

"*Everything,*" the Magister said. He gestured, and the middle-aged man rose into the air, a paper and a pen appearing in the author's hands. The Magister stepped to the man's side and nodded at the items. "Now, Jonathan Porterhouse, we shall perform a small experiment, just like the Quanterians. You are going to describe me, the me you see before you, on paper. However, change one aspect of my clothing. A simple shift in color, perhaps."

Jonathan Porterhouse's nostrils flared as he frantically struggled for breath without his mouth, his eyes wide.

"What is this going to prove?" Bethany asked, her voice barely louder than a whisper.

"If nothing happens, then we'll know that these so-called writers have no control over us, or our world," the Magister said, turning to Bethany. "However, if my clothing does change based on the description that he writes . . ."

His eyes darkened, as did the room again. Somewhere lightning crashed, and Bethany didn't think it was from a storm. "Then we will have a problem."

CHAPTER 13

 ORING!" Owen shouted into the white blankness all around him. "This is so boring! Why can't something just happen already!"

He sighed and tried to bang his head against the nonexistent wall behind him. Nothing existed in this place, apparently. Not walls, not hunger, not time, and *definitely* not entertainment.

Or Dr. Verity for that matter. Which was weird. Shouldn't he have been here too? Had he broken out? And if so, why hadn't he left some sort of instructions so Owen could do the same thing? Being evil was one thing, but that was just inconsiderate.

"Still boring!" he shouted to no one. "Bethany, where *are* you? If you're off having fun with Kiel and the Magister without me, I'm never going to forgive you!"

Bethany, having fun? Okay, that wasn't likely, but given that she hadn't come back yet, she had to be doing *something* exciting with them. Assuming she was okay. Since they'd basically kidnapped her, the Magister and Kiel. After she'd been knocked out.

Owen frowned, suddenly worried. What if they stole her power, or banished her to a horrible dimension of just audiobooks or something? Or worse, what if they forced her to jump into stories to talk to all the cool characters? That'd make her crazy!

Nah, she had to be okay. The girl could grab aliens from Mars out of books if she had to. What was going to stop her? An old man and his awesome, incredibly cool teenage apprentice? No way. She was fine. She had to be.

When Bethany rudely didn't respond or come get him out of this nowhere nonprison he'd been trapped in, Owen banged his head a few more times, then tried walking around again.

The problem with walking into nothingness is that you honestly had no idea if you were getting anywhere. For all he knew, he'd walked ten miles and found just as much boring as the spot he'd left. He collapsed from boredom against the ground, and conveniently found another wall to bang his head against. Or the same one. Maybe the ground had just moved underneath his feet like a treadmill.

Would he grow old in here, until he looked like the Magister with a huge beard? Would his fingernails grow out like that guy in *Guinness World Records*? Could Bethany jump into *that* book and hang out with Fingernail Guy? . . . That'd be weird.

Was he missing his birthday? Had he already missed it? For all Owen knew, he'd been sitting here for years! Think of the presents he'd missed. Birthdays *and* Christmas!

"Let me out of here!" he shouted.

Nobody answered.

It was time to give up. There was nothing else to do, literally. Here he was, trapped in a book, but outside the book, and— wait a second.

If he was really still in the book somehow, maybe he could jump forward in the story, like books did when a chapter ended. It'd be like fast-forwarding time, chapter after chapter, until Bethany came back to find him. That was brilliant!

Except, how did you end a chapter?

Owen thought back to all the books he knew, and what he could remember about the ends of chapters. Most seemed to stop on some kind of ironic one-liner, or a cliffhanger. Cliff-hangers would be a bit tough in here, with no cliffs to hang off of, but maybe he could trick the book into chaptering by saying something horribly ironic, and then waiting for it to (*surprise!*) happen.

"Now would be a *horrible* time for someone to show up out of nowhere to come rescue me!" he said, then paused to see if it worked.

Time didn't jump forward, and no one showed up out of nowhere to rescue him.

This may not have been as good an idea as he'd hoped.

"You know what'd be funny? If Dr. Verity came back and kidnapped me! Who'd expect *that*!"

Nothing.

"I'd really hate if I fell asleep and it turned out this was all just a dream. . . ."

Nope.

"This seems like the most secure prison *ever*! NO ONE could break in here!"

Was that a sound? . . . Nope. Nope it wasn't.

Owen growled in frustration, then just started screaming various things. "Chapter Twelve! Chapter Thirty-Two! Chapter Seventy-Five, The Boy Who Was Rescued from the Boring Prison!"

Nothing happened.

"If anyone ever reads this," he said to no one, "I hope they find out just how dumb it was to jump into a book. Apparently, you just get thrown into jail and left to rot. Don't do it. Let me be a lesson. At least my life will have meant something!"

He paused to see if *that* had done anything, but no.

"Seriously, can NOBODY hear me?" he shouted.

"I can hear you," said someone. Out of nowhere stepped a person with no features, just a blank face and body, like an undressed mannequin. "And you can call me Nobody," the creepy no-faced person said.

Owen blinked. Now *that* would be the perfect place for a new chap—

CHAPTER 14

—ter. Except of course, there wasn't one.

"Who are you?" Owen asked Nobody. "And why would I call you Nobody, when clearly you're *somebody*? Not that you look like somebody, actually. You mostly look like an unpainted action figure."

"You talk quite a bit when you're nervous, don't you," Nobody said.

"My mom tells me that it's charming," Owen said, trying to sound indignant. "But you didn't answer my question."

"That's right, I didn't. You don't belong here, so I'm here to take you home."

"Why do you not have a face? Or anything else?" Owen backed away slowly. "Traditionally, when someone looks either evil or faceless, it means they *are* evil, and faceless, or they're a misunderstood good guy. How misunderstood would you say you are?"

"If you'd be more comfortable," Nobody said, "I can look a bit more . . . normal." With that, his body began to sprout clothing, hair, fingernails, and everything else one naturally took for granted when looking at a regular person. Two green eyes popped out right around where they should be, and the face split to grow lips and teeth and such. Not a moment later, a handsome, middle-aged man with bronze-colored hair stood in front of him, raising a now-existing eyebrow. "Better?"

"It would have been if I hadn't just seen it sprout out of your body," Owen said. "But that's fine. You can still rescue me."

The man's mouth curled up in a half smile. "I usually go formless when traveling between stories. It's easier that way. You wouldn't want to show up on an alien lizard planet looking human, after all." He gestured for Owen to follow him, then began to walk off.

"Wait, you travel between stories?" Owen shouted after him. "So you're half-fictional too?"

The man stopped abruptly and turned around, giving Owen a knowing look. "No, I'm not. I didn't realize she'd shared so much with you."

"She? Bethany? You know her?" Wait a second. Was this man actually her *father*? Had he really just found Bethany's father for her? What were the odds? Unless this was some kind of twist, and he actually wasn't her father, and everything he said was just to throw Owen off?

Or maybe he was *way* overthinking all of this.

The man smiled again, just slightly. "Let's be off. It's not safe out here, between stories. You can get pretty lost, and many never find their way back to the story they're from. You're lucky to have survived so long. Though I suppose that's because you aren't, strictly speaking, from a story. As far as you know, at least."

Huh. Cryptic. Classic trickster character. Those were always Owen's favorites, and that meant something interesting was happening. And right now, interesting was infinitely better than the boringness of the white, blank nothing. Plus, if this really could be Bethany's dad, Owen had to find out for sure. "So how'd you find me? You're not from the Kiel Gnomenfoot books, or I'd remember you."

"That's right," Nobody said. "But I'll have to take you back there first, to get you home."

"How? How can you get me home if you're not like Bethany?" Bam. Subtle.

Nobody just gave him the same half smile. "There are other ways to travel between the worlds. Now come on."

What did *that* mean? And why wouldn't he just say who he was?

"From what I could tell, two main characters just disappeared out of the book," Nobody continued, not looking back at Owen anymore as he quickened his pace, so Owen hurried to catch up. "If the last Kiel Gnomenfoot book were to come out right now, missing Kiel Gnomenfoot, questions would be raised. Questions no one should be asking just yet. That means someone needs to bring those two back."

"So?" Owen said. "Shouldn't you be talking to Bethany, then? Good luck finding her. She never came back for me. Like she should have, by the way. She left me here in prison!"

"Ah, here we go," Nobody told him, stopping in the middle of nothing. He reached out a hand and gently pushed.

The entire nothingness around Owen crumbled like he was on the inside of a sand castle as someone kicked it down, to be replaced by the Magister's study.

"Okay, that was kinda cool," Owen said. Nobody glanced around a bit, then walked over to the Magister's spell book. He stopped over the book, then pulled something out of the coat he had grown out of nothing, something that looked a lot like a hand mirror.

"Now," Nobody said, holding a hand over the spell book. "What I'm about to do isn't exactly magic. It is, but not in the way you'd think. But this spell book is a good way of accessing the power I need. It unleashes magic in *this* story, and I can use that energy to open a doorway. Not like Bethany does, but it'll get you home."

Home? A few minutes ago that's all Owen had wanted, but a few minutes ago he wasn't standing unchained in the Magister's study again. There was so much coolness everywhere, and he had to immediately say good-bye to it all? How unfair was that?

"There's not really a hurry, is there?" Owen asked, his eyes passing over Kiel's winged cat, Alphonse, who was currently curled up by the spell book. He hadn't even petted the cat's wings, which was supposed to be lucky. And what about all the weird magical experiments still bubbling merrily along, completely unwatched by anyone, which was probably a fire hazard, but still?

And then there was the spell book itself. Every spell that Kiel or the Magister had ever used, plus a bajillion that would never even get mentioned, all contained in that one book. And because of the whole tricking Bethany into using it, Owen hadn't even gotten to touch it, let alone learn any magic!

The hand mirror began to glow as Nobody recited words over it. Was this really it? Owen had saved the Magister, and now he'd just have to go back home? Bethany would bring Kiel and the Magister back, the story would go back to the way it was meant to, and so would Owen's life? What about meeting Kiel's half-robot friend, Charm, or time traveling or something?

The glow intensified, and Nobody held the mirror up toward Owen. On the other side, Owen saw his bathroom, and a kind of embarrassing dirty towel on the floor. Whoops.

"This was as close as I could get it, as you don't have a mirror in your bedroom," Nobody said. "Now, when you return to the real world, you can't speak about anything you've seen here. If you do, I'll come find you. Trust me, you don't want to see my formless face in a mirror sometime." He grinned humorlessly.

"You *are* just like Bethany," Owen said. "Neither of you likes anything fun."

Nobody ignored that. "It's time, Owen. I have to get you out of here now, then go locate those two missing characters before they cause any trouble in your world."

"No, *please*, not yet," Owen shouted. "Have you seen everything here? I only got to see a little of it, not all the best parts! Can't you just let me stay and hang around?"

"Charm is on her way, and the final book is about to begin," Nobody told him. "You must leave *now*."

"Charm's coming here? Now I can't go yet. I have to meet her!"

"You'd show up in the book, and I can't have that." Nobody held out a hand.

Owen's mind raced as he took a step backward. "But . . . but Kiel's not back! If he's not here when she shows up, the book will start out wrong. Someone has to be waiting for her, right? That's the whole point, that readers don't notice anything's different?"

Nobody gave him a questioning look. "What exactly are you suggesting?"

Owen didn't really know—he was making this all up as he went, but his eyes fell on the spell book, and suddenly an idea exploded like a lightbulb over his head. "There's a disguise spell in there!" he practically shouted. "Kiel's used it before! Use that on me, make me look like Kiel. I can do all the things Kiel would have until you bring him and the Magister back here. Then no one has to know!"

Nobody just stared at him for a moment. "There are so many things wrong with that idea that I don't even know where to begin. Still, you're not wrong. She is about to arrive, and I'm

not entirely sure how long it'll take me to return with Kiel."
He sighed. "Perhaps this might give me some insurance. If I
do this—"

"DO IT!"

"*If* I do this, you'll be completely on your own from now
until I can find a safe spot to switch you out for the real Kiel.
That might not be until the very end of the story, Owen. Do
you fully understand what that means? Whatever would have
happened to him will now happen to you, good or bad. And
you'd have to act *exactly* like him, or the story could progress in
a very different fashion. How well do you know these books?"

"SO well!" Owen shouted, realizing that wasn't exactly an
amount. "Tons! I know them by heart. I've read them all a
thousand times!"

Nobody sighed. "This is a huge risk, and I doubt it makes
sense—"

"Sometimes the impossible is the only thing that DOES
make sense!"

". . . Though it makes more sense than what you just said."
Nobody rubbed his eyes. "I would caution you—"

"I'm cautioned!"

Nobody gave him a tired look, then began to flip through the spell book pages until he found what he wanted. "So be it. Stand still, please."

"We're doing it?" Owen said as Nobody began to mumble something. "Are you casting—"

"Cast, past tense," Nobody corrected as Owen felt warm all over. "Look at yourself."

Owen glanced down in midsentence and trailed off. Instead of his normal clothing, he now had on a black cloak, a black shirt, black pants, and two magic knife-wands in two sheaths at his waist.

"What?" he said, barely able to contain his joy. "Are you kidding me?"

Nobody handed him the hand mirror. Now, instead of Owen's dirty towel and bathroom, it showed KIEL GNOMENFOOT standing in the middle of the Magister's study! "I've never been this happy in my entire life," Owen said, touching his face—Kiel's face—then pulling out his twin knife-wands. "This is the greatest thing anyone's ever done for me, or anyone, ever."

"I'm glad you approve," Nobody said. "Now, do you know what you're doing?"

"Doing?" Owen said, still distracted. He'd never seen such

an authentic costume before, which just made sense, since it was magic. Wait, did he know magic now too? He tried to think of a spell, but nothing sprang to mind. Apparently, his mind hadn't been disguised into Kiel's. Which wouldn't have made sense anyway. Oh well, there was always the spell book.

"Charm is just about here," Nobody said, walking back toward the wall that they'd emerged from. He gestured, murmuring some spell-sounding words. The entire tower glowed, then magically changed to look a bit more disheveled, as if someone had gone on a rampage through it. "Dr. Verity would have torn apart this tower if you hadn't interfered. Now, you as Kiel have arrived too late to save the Magister, so I'd suggest mourning when Charm arrives. She has the first six keys on her ship, but you'll need to locate the Seventh Key before Dr. Verity's armies of Science Soldiers destroy Magisteria. Finally, you'll need to face down Dr. Verity to stop him once and for all by unlocking the Source of Magic."

"Wait!" Owen shouted, shoving his wands back into their sheathes. "Dr. Verity was stuck in that same place I was, that blank place past the wall! What about him?"

Nobody gave him a look. "I already brought him back where

he was meant to go and wiped his memory of everything past the ending of the last book. The story must go on, even if that means setting villains free." He turned to leave. "I can't be present when the story starts. Charm is just about here, and that's where this last book begins. Remember, you came back to find the Magister missing, and presumed dead. That's all you know. The rest you'll find out as the book continues along. Don't mess this up, Kiel Gnomenfoot!"

"I won't!" Owen said. "I can't believe this. This is the greatest moment of my life!"

Nobody smiled. "Good luck, boy. You'll be fine. How hard can it be to play the hero you always wanted to be, after all?"

And with that, he disappeared into the same nothingness that Owen had just been trapped in.

"I'm Kiel Gnomenfoot!" he said to nobody now. "Me! Kiel Gnomenfoot!"

Alphonse, Kiel's winged cat, looked up with an unbelieving expression, then began to aggressively lick his paw as his wings curled in around him.

"No one asked you," Owen told the cat.

Footsteps outside the destroyed door to the study brought

him back to his senses. Owen glanced around, then suddenly realized what he was supposed to be doing. He'd read these books a thousand times. If Kiel Gnomenfoot had just found out that the Magister had potentially died, or at the very least was missing, he'd be completely crushed . . . but trying to hide it as much as he could.

Owen considered that for a moment, then fell to his knees, dropping his head into his hands. Only, instead of grieving, he was hiding a wide grin. This was so exciting! Kind of like acting, only this was playing a part in a story, instead of in a play or movie.

"Kiel?" said a girl's voice.

Don't get excited. Just because this is one of the coolest things you've ever been a part of.

Owen slowly lifted his head and glanced over his shoulder at the girl behind him wearing an all-black spacesuit, her right robotic arm and left robotic leg uncovered. Two ray guns were strapped to either side of her waist, and her human eye looked at him with pity. Her robotic eye, however, just looked at him like a robotic eye.

"We were too late, weren't we?" said Charm, daughter of the

now-deceased president of Quanterium, science genius, and half-robot best friend of Kiel Gnomenfoot. She looked around awkwardly. "I'm, uh, *sorry.*"

Right, Charm hated showing any kind of emotion ever since the loss of her parents! She never knew how to be nice to Kiel, and usually just yelled at him instead. Feelings made her nervous, and she hated Kiel's jokes, or so she said. The book made it out like she secretly liked Kiel and his sense of humor, though.

Which meant she now secretly liked *Owen*, and *his* sense of humor. Which worked out pretty well, because Charm was kind of cute for a half robot with a red eye.

Stop that. Play it cool. Owen took a deep breath to steady himself, then forced a grieving sigh. "I'm sorry too," he said as gruffly as he could. "It's all my fault."

"It was Dr. Verity?"

He nodded as seriously as he could.

"There's nothing more we can do here, then," she said, yanking him up to his feet with her incredibly strong robot arm. "I was going to wait in the ship, but sensors detected one of the Science Soldier transport ships surrounding Magisteria now on its way down here, so I figured I should warn you."

"Warn me?" Owen asked.

Something exploded just above them, and Charm flipped around, her ray guns in hand, pointing at the stairs.

"That we're about to have company," she said.

Okay. Yeah, this was totally like living out an incredible action movie, only a *million* times better. Too bad Bethany had to hate fun so much, or she could have been there with him, disguised as a desk or Alphonse or something.

"Let them come," Owen said to Charm, narrowing his eyes in what he hoped was a dangerous way. "I'm in the mood to take down a few robots."

Awesome.

CHAPTER 15

"*Write,*" the Magister told Jonathan Porterhouse.

Mr. Porterhouse, wide-eyed with fear, didn't move.

The Magister's eyes hardened, and he raised a glowing hand. For a moment it looked like he might attack the author, and Bethany could see the glow of magic reflected in Mr. Porterhouse's eyes.

But instead, the Magister lowered his hand, the glow dying. To her side, Bethany heard the boy in black quietly let out a huge breath he'd been holding.

"I have no desire to hurt you, Jonathan Porterhouse," the Magister said. He gestured, and the author began to sink into the floor. Mr. Porterhouse's face contorted like he was screaming, but no sound came out, given that he still had no mouth. "At least, not if you are innocent in this," the Magister continued. "If innocence is indeed a possibility. Consider your choices here, as I shall consider mine."

Mr. Porterhouse sank out of sight, his mouth reappearing just in time for his scream to be cut off as he disappeared, and Bethany shivered. "Where did you put him?" she whispered.

"He has no dungeon in this home," the Magister told her. "So the lowest floor shall have to suffice." He gave her a tired look. "I truly do have no wish to harm the man, if he is ignorant of his actions. In fact, I wish no harm upon anyone. But I have seen his library. Thousands upon thousands of stories lie within those books, and if each one contains a world like mine, existing solely to entertain your people . . ." He rubbed his forehead with his thumbs. "I cannot let this continue, Bethany. I *cannot.*"

Bethany shook her head. "I don't know what you're saying, but you can't just change it. There's nothing *to* change. What could you possibly do?"

"Nothing," the Magister admitted. "Not without your power."

"My . . . my power?"

"Magi, let's discuss this," the boy in black said, but the Magister ignored him.

"Your father comes from a world like mine," the Magister told her. "Did one of your writers invent him, too? Were his actions his own, or forced upon him? Don't you see, Bethany? If your father and his world were created to follow a story, then he had no freedom! His will was not his own!"

"I don't like where this is headed," the boy said. "Maybe it's time we all relaxed and took a deep breath—"

"Help me!" the Magister shouted at her. "Help me free these worlds from living according to another's whims. Give them back control of their lives!"

"What are you asking me?" Bethany said, taking a step backward.

The Magister held out his hand, and a Kiel Gnomenfoot book flew into it from a nearby table. "I'm asking you to use your power and deliver the people of these worlds into your own, like you have for Kiel and me. Free them, that they might no longer be controlled and can live their lives however they wish, subjected to no one's whim or story!"

What? Bethany's mouth dropped open. Bring every fictional character into the real world? That was *beyond* crazy!

"Magi, there would be chaos," the boy said quietly.

"And what do we have now, Kiel?" the Magister asked. "I

will not let myself be controlled! Not by Dr. Verity, not by Jonathan Porterhouse, not by *anyone*. How else do you propose to free us all, if not this? Destroy all writers on this world?"

"Of course not!" Kiel said quickly. "But—"

"I cannot let this injustice stand, apprentice. I cannot and *will* not."

As bad as things seemed before, this was twenty miles beyond that. Bethany concentrated on breathing in and out, desperate for someone, anyone to tell her that everything would be okay, that this wasn't happening—that she was dreaming or imagining it, or living out some kind of waking nightmare.

"There must be another way," Kiel said, holding his hands up for calm. The Magister sighed, dropping the Kiel Gnomenfoot book he was holding to his side.

And that's when Bethany realized that there might be a way out.

They were both right here, after all. With the book so close, maybe she could just grab it, then jump both Kiel and the Magister back into the story! At this point, even if they still knew they were characters, at least that was worlds better than unleashing every fictional character ever into the real world!

But to do that, she'd need to keep them talking, and paying attention to anything other than what she was about to do.

"You have no idea how many stories there are," Bethany told the Magister, her eyes everywhere but the book in his hand. "It would take us years to free all the characters. Centuries, maybe."

"Then we shall start this very moment," the Magister said, and laid the book down on a nearby table, then held out his hand to Bethany. "Help me. Help me right this enormous wrong. We shall free all the peoples of these worlds, and let them live their lives the way they wish, with no one telling them otherwise."

Bethany bit her lip and took a step forward. "Can I . . . think about it?" It was so close now, just a few feet away. She could almost jump for it at this point—

The Magister's eyes narrowed, and the Kiel Gnomenfoot book burst into flames, leaving nothing but a blackened spot on the table. *No!*

"I believe you may not be treating this request seriously," he said, his tone sliding down in temperature. "Perhaps you should take some time to consider it, along with Jonathan Porterhouse."

"Don't do this," Bethany pleaded, but her feet had already begun to sink into the floor. She gasped, trying desperately to stop herself, but the marble floor felt like quicksand. The more she struggled, the faster she sank. "Please! Let me go, and I can still fix all of this!"

"I could just siphon your power from you," the Magister told her as she descended. "Simply free these worlds myself. But then I would be no different from a writer, taking away your choice." His eyes glowed as he stared at her. "I will give you time to make your decision, and hope you choose correctly. For both our sakes."

And with that, Bethany's head sank into the floor, and everything went dark.

CHAPTER 16

All the years of boredom, math tests, gym classes, working at the library, and imagining exciting worlds that he'd never be able to visit—all those years had been worth it.

First of all, Owen was *Kiel Gnomenfoot*. That still made him tingle all over with awesomeness.

Second, Charm, *Charm*, was here, right next to him. Well, pushing a cabinet into the spot where the door had been previously with her superstrong robot arm, but still, close enough!

And third, he was about to fight robot soldiers. With *magic*.

"Ready?" Charm said, clicking her ray guns on in a tough, awesome way. "I'd prefer not to have to do all the work this time. Try to hold up your end of the fight, will you?"

"You take the ones on the left. I got the ones on the right," Owen told her, grinning. He took out his wands and aimed them at the door. Now what spell should he use?

Spells? . . . Uh-oh. He didn't *know* any spells. *Yet.*

"Actually, give me one minute," he said, and turned around to where the Magister's spell book sat halfway across the room.

"*What?*" Charm shouted, just as the cabinet exploded inward, covering them both in wood fragments. Laser beams blasted through the doorway, exploding all over the room and incinerating whatever they touched. None had hit the spell book yet, but it was only a matter of time.

That just confirmed exactly what Owen needed to do. Something *heroic.*

"Cover me!" he yelled, since that's the kind of thing that one yelled in this type of situation. "I'm going to grab the spell book and hit them with something huge!"

"WHAT?" Charm shouted again. She fired her ray guns frantically through the door. "Don't be stupid! You're not even using a shield spell!"

"Who needs one?" Owen told her, then ran in a crouch toward the middle of the room.

Lasers hit the floor all around him, some just inches away, but Owen barely even noticed them. All he could think about were the readers, the thousands of readers who were on the edge of their seats, watching him do something incredibly stupid and dangerous and not even get touched.

This must be making Bethany crazy!

"They're coming in!" Charm shouted. "I have to fall back!"

Owen glanced behind him at the door, where red eyes glowed from the smoke-filled hallway. Science Soldiers! He almost stopped moving, he wanted so badly to see what they actually looked like. But Charm shoved him forward, firing behind her as she ran.

"You useless magic-spewing pile of winged-cat droppings!" she yelled, smacking him with the back of her human hand. "This is what I meant by me doing all the work!"

If anything, she actually looked even cuter when she screamed like that. Owen flashed her a grin, then pushed himself the last few feet to the spell book, which miraculously had remained untouched, despite its pedestal being riddled with burn marks from the lasers. He yanked the book down and held a hand out over it, just as Kiel had always done. *Give me a powerful and impressively cool spell to use on the robots!* he thought.

A golden glow flooded through his body, like chicken noodle soup when you were sick in the middle of winter.

Owen almost gasped. It just felt so right. All his life, he'd been waiting for something like this, and finally, *finally* it was here.

"Stand back," he told Charm, then stood up in the middle of the laser fire. "SCIENCE SOLDIERS! I will return thee to the metal pits from whence you came!"

"Are you insane?" Charm hissed, yanking at his cloak to pull him down.

"Insanely awesome," he told her, then winked.

Kiel *always* winked.

Five Science Soldiers entered the room, their lasers firing everywhere. For just a second Owen stopped to marvel at how cool the robots were. They'd evolved throughout the series, starting as just plain metal humanlike robots, but by book two, Dr. Verity began inventing new types. There'd been the Science Spies, who looked exactly like humans, and the Science Police, metallic robots in uniforms who stood on every corner of every Magisteria town in book five, watching for any hint of magic or rebellion.

But these . . . these were Science *Soldiers*, the most dangerous of them all. Their entire bodies were weapons, bombs ready to explode as a last resort, taking out anything nearby. Their arms were basically laser rifles with hands, those hands each holding *more* laser rifles. And their eyes could see through anything but metal, scanning constantly for magical energy.

Honestly, they'd have actually been pretty scary if Owen hadn't known they'd never managed to hit either Kiel or Charm in any of the six books so far.

"I've got just the thing for you, my friends," he told them, raising his hands. "A little spell called Explosion of Fiery Greatness!"

"You said that was too *powerful*!" Charm hissed from right beside him. "You'll kill us both!"

"I've got this," Owen told her, then ran through the spell in his mind. "Hope you like your explosions ENORMOUS!" he shouted at the robots, the spell's energy coursing through him. He raised his hands, then released the power straight at the robots.

And then everything exploded into fire and chaos and awesome.

CHAPTER 17

*J*onathan Porterhouse's basement wasn't much of a dungeon. If the Magister had wanted them to suffer, he should have checked to make sure he wasn't dropping them into what looked like a movie theater, only with comfier seats. Three rows faced a large screen at one end, with a projection room at the other.

Bethany sat in one of the cushy chairs, her eyes on the floor, deliberately trying not to look at the clearly terrified Mr. Porterhouse, who sat two seats down from her, his eyes wide and locked on her. She wasn't sure exactly what to say: There wasn't a much more awkward conversation than trying to explain that an author's fictional characters had attacked him in his own house because you were half-fictional yourself, and your friend had wanted to meet them, but then they'd escaped using your power.

Except maybe explaining that now one of his characters wanted to free every other fictional character ever invented into the world, which might be fine if it were just Sherlock Holmeses or Gandalfs, but got a little questionable when you started talking about aliens, dragons, vampires, and other people-devouring characters.

"So," Bethany finally said. "I hear the books have sold well?"

"You have no idea how they end, do you?" Mr. Porterhouse whispered, his eyes flashing to the ceiling.

Bethany slowly shook her head. "I, uh, haven't actually read any of them."

For just a moment irritation passed over Mr. Porterhouse's face. "You haven't . . . *none* of them?" He shook his head. "Doesn't matter. The ending is what's important. The Magister . . . he's not a hero. At the end of the final book, Dr. Verity tells Kiel that the Magister planned on using the Source of Magic to destroy Quanterium, just like Dr. Verity wants to destroy Magisteria. They're both villains." He ran his hands through his hair nervously, his eyes flickering to the ceiling and back to Bethany. "Do you understand what I'm telling you? That man up there is crazy, and willing to wipe out a planet full of his enemies. We have to get out of here, *right now!*"

"What?" Bethany whispered as loudly as she dared. "You authors and your stupid twists! Look at what you've done!"

"I didn't know he was real!" Mr. Porterhouse hissed back.

"So he's just going to kill us?" She sat back in a daze, fear and confusion fighting each other in her head.

"I don't know!" Mr. Porterhouse whispered. "He's off book, so he could do anything at this point. All I know is what he was capable of in the story. And that was to destroy an entire world to make sure his people were safe."

"Yup, he's going to kill us," Bethany said with a short nod, then shook off her confusion and fear, at least enough to think. "Okay. We can't stay here—"

"Oh, really? We *can't*?"

She glared at the author. "Is there any way out of here other than the stairs? Since those lead back up to the crazy magician man?"

Mr. Porterhouse shook his head. "Not even a window. I don't like the glare when I watch movies on the big screen."

Perfect. At least there wouldn't be a glare when the Magister came down to blow them up or whatever. "How about a book? Anything at all down here?"

"Everything's upstairs in the library. I doubt there's so much as a piece of paper down here."

Bethany glanced around, growling quietly to herself in

frustration. Mr. Porterhouse wasn't wrong. Not only were there no books of any kind, there wasn't much of anything. Just the chairs, the movie screen, and the movie projector in the back, connected to a computer. Great, everything was digital. That didn't help when your weird book powers didn't work on a computer screen.

She just about gave up, then noticed a white booklet on the desk next to the projector.

Instruction manual. Hmm.

What would happen if *she* wrote something on paper, just even a simple sentence like *The monkey hated the elephant with a passion, and the elephant knew why*? Would she be able to jump into that paper? Was that enough of a story? Or did she even *need* a story?

She slowly, quietly, walked over to the manual, flipped it to a blank sheet at the back, then quickly looked around for a pen or something. As she was rummaging through the desk, the Magister materialized out of nothing, with an unhappy-looking Kiel Gnomenfoot at his side. Bethany froze, dropping her hands immediately to her side to hide the paper. Back in the chair, Mr. Porterhouse straightened himself up, his eyes wide with fright.

"I believe you have had enough time to think," the Magister said. "Have you come to the right decision?"

"Please—" Mr. Porterhouse started to say, only to have his mouth erased off his face once more. The Magister gave him a careful look, then turned back to Bethany, waiting for her answer.

Bethany quietly folded the manual over so the blank page was facing up, then slipped it into her back pocket, trying to look like she was thinking things over. "Yes, I have," she said, then slowly, very slowly, began to walk back over to where the Magister stood over Mr. Porterhouse.

There was no way this would work. *No way.* Not only had she never jumped into a blank page before, there was no reason to even *think* it might work. There wasn't a story there, after all. No fictional world to enter, just a bunch of blank nothing. Not only would it *not* work, and not only would it be humiliating when it didn't, but the whole thing was probably just going to make the Magister even more angry.

Still. Between humiliation and a crazy magician, she'd take humiliation.

She stopped next to Mr. Porterhouse and took a deep breath.

"You will help me free the fictional from their stories, then?" the Magister asked.

"Um," Bethany said, *"no."* Then she grabbed the author's hand and shoved the blank instruction manual directly at him.

Half of her expected his hand to rip right through the page, that there was no way this could work, and why even attempt something so risky, so dangerous?

But weirdly, the other half of her was actually *excited* to see what might happen. And that must have been the half that made her grin out of nowhere as everything turned a brilliant bright white all around her and the author.

They were in empty space! The blank page was just that: There wasn't anything here, but somehow, she could still jump into it. She almost laughed. It'd worked! How cool was that?

Any laugh immediately died in her throat when she noticed Mr. Porterhouse's death grip on her hand, staring at her with pretty much the same terrified look he'd given the Magister.

"It's okay," she said. "You're okay. I got you out. You're safe now." His eyes said he didn't necessarily believe her, but she didn't really have time to convince him. "We're going to be trapped in here if he burns that booklet, so I need to get back out. But don't worry, I'll come back for you. I just need to get the Magister and Kiel back into your books before they do anything crazy. So stay here, okay? I'll be right back." She paused. "And just so you know, this is all a kid named Owen's fault. You'll probably hear about him when he messes up your entire series of books. Don't worry, I'll get him back too."

Before he could stop her, she leaped out of the page and back into the movie theater, ready to grab the blank sheet of paper and run as fast as she could up the stairs. It wasn't much of a plan, but then again, the blank sheet hadn't been either, and that had worked. So maybe she had luck on her side for once?

She didn't. As soon as her feet hit the basement floor, a glow hit her full in the face. Magic raced into her mouth and down her throat, infecting her lungs, which immediately froze up. She gasped, making a rasping noise in her throat. *She couldn't breathe!*

As Bethany gasped for air, the Magister lifted his hand, sending her floating up above the marble floor. She clutched her neck, desperately trying to pull in oxygen.

"What are you doing?" Kiel shouted from somewhere below her. "Don't hurt her!"

"You have forced my hand, Bethany," the Magister told her. "Why can't you see how wrong these stories are? Especially considering your heritage? If you won't help me, then you dishonor your father *and* your abilities. Far better for me to use that power, if you refuse to."

The same cold, shivery feeling Bethany had felt when she first met the Magister coursed through her, and she knew that he was pulling her book-jumping power straight out of her, but that seemed less and less important as the sides of her vision started turning dark from lack of air, and she slowly began to black out.

CHAPTER 18

Owen woke up to find Alphonse, Kiel's winged cat, asleep on the Magister's spell book at his side. Silvery metal covered the floor, ceiling, walls, and every spot not taken up by a computer monitor or futuristic-looking chair.

"Excuse me," he said to Alphonse as he sat up. The cat gave him a dirty look, then closed his eyes again. Right beside the cat were some blackened marks, like the spell book had gotten singed in the magical explosion. Whoops. Owen frowned and rubbed at one of the spots, but it didn't come off.

Where was he exactly, anyway? He started to stand up, only to have the floor jump out from under him, slamming him into the wall. Just as quickly, the floor leaped in the opposite direction. "What is going on here?" Owen shouted at the floor. "Stop moving!"

"THIS IS ALL YOUR FAULT," the floor yelled at him. Or,

a speaker in the floor, probably. "GET UP HERE ALREADY!"

Up here? Owen gasped, grinning like an idiot. They were on the *Scientific Method*, Charm's spaceship! But how had they gotten here? And why was everything so shaky?

He pushed the winged cat off the spell book, then grabbed it to take it with him. The spell book seemed to pull away from him in an odd way, but he ignored that and made for the door, which whooshed open automatically, like on *Star Trek*, or less impressively, like at the library.

The ship pitched forward, sending Owen stumbling through the door and out into the nerve center of the ship. There he found Charm seated at the pilot's controls, frantically running her hands over transparent boxes of light hanging in midair in front of her.

That part was pretty cool, but what made Owen stop breathing for a second was the wall just past Charm. The *Scientific Method*'s viewscreen wrapped around almost half of the room, and from what Owen could see, it looked like they'd jumped out of Kiel Gnomenfoot and into *Star Wars*. More ships than he could count surrounded a green, yellow, and red planet, while laser blasts exploded on all sides.

"We won't live through this," Charm said without looking

at him, "but if we do, I'm going to kill you anyway."

"That seems . . . harsh," Owen told her, unable to take his eyes off the screen. "What's going on?"

"Right now? Lasers," Charm said, a bit unnecessarily as the ship dove forward, sending Owen falling straight at her. At the last minute, her robotic arm lashed out and caught Owen's cloak right before he slammed into the viewscreen. "Also, your spell destroyed the Magister's tower, along with a whole transport full of Science Soldiers."

Owen grinned. "Really? How many are in a transport?"

"You'll probably get to count up close in a few minutes," she told him, tossing him back into the room. "If I hadn't teleported us back to the ship right after you cast that spell, we'd both be buried underneath an entire tower full of rubble, if not disintegrated. But besides that, do you know what happens when a transport of Science Soldiers gets blown up on Magisteria?"

"Everyone cheers?" Owen said.

"You really are stupid enough to be Verity's clone, aren't you?" She hit a button, and Dr. Verity's image appeared on the viewscreen.

"Citizens of Quanterium," Dr. Verity said, standing in front of white columns. A blue flag with the image of a rocket ship taking off from a planet, Quanterium's flag, flapped in the wind at his side. "I come to you tonight to report that a Magisterian ship has broken our blockade and destroyed a Science Soldier transport. This is in no uncertain terms an act of war and must be addressed as such." He shook his head sadly. "I want peace as much as the rest of you, but the safety of Quanterium is my utmost concern, and I will not allow these magic-using criminals to do any more harm.

"I am officially declaring war on Magisteria. Our armies of Science Soldiers are on the move and will attack each Magisterian city within the next twenty-four hours. If the Magisterians truly wish peace, as they've claimed, then they will surrender and turn their criminals over to Science Police at once.

"This is a dark day for Quanterium, but I believe in our planet, our people, and our science. Together, we will overcome any who would reject the natural laws of the universe. May factual discourse guide you all."

The ship banked hard to the left as Dr. Verity's image disappeared, and Owen barely held on to a chair. "Wow," he said. "That escalated quickly."

"You seem to have that effect on people," Charm said. "So

now Verity's Science Soldiers from all those alternate dimensions where we found the Fourth Key are heading here to destroy Magisteria. His infinite robots outnumber the not-infinite Magisterians by . . . let's say an *infinite* amount. Usually that's a bad sign in war. You probably weren't taught math, though, so I understand why this is new to you."

"Ah, it'll be fine," Owen said, waving a hand. "That's why we're here. He said we have twenty-four hours. That's plenty of time!" And it would be. After all, this was the last book, and everything was going to end well, so what's the worst that could happen? The planet wasn't actually going to get attacked. This was just Jonathan Porterhouse raising the stakes, giving them a time limit so everything seemed more exciting!

Charm gave him a strange look, then turned back to the controls. "I can't open a wormhole while we're under attack." She jammed the controls to the left, and a laser blast blew past them, right where they'd just been. "And the longer we're out here, the more ships will arrive. So when we do get blown up, I hope you somehow go first."

"I'll handle it," Owen told her, and set the spell book down on the floor. Again, it seemed to pull away from his touch, which was weird. He didn't remember it ever doing that with Kiel.

"*No!*" Charm shouted. "No more magic! We barely lived through the last time."

"Oh, don't be such a baby," Owen told her. "We made it out okay, didn't we?" He touched the singed part of the book again, then shrugged. "But if it makes you feel better, I'll use something less explosive."

"*Kiel Gnomenfoot*, if your spell harms even one metal plate on my ship, I will eject you into the nearest sun. Over and over."

Owen ran his hand over the book, thinking, *Give me a spell that will keep these ships from seeing us.* That'd do it, right?

The magic filled him again, but this time it felt less warm and friendly, and more . . . not. He shrugged, then immediately cast the spell, using his magic wands to aim the magic right at the ship. "Invisibility, coming up!" he told Charm.

"*What?*" she said as the entire ship disappeared, leaving Owen, the spell book, and Charm all floating on what looked to be nothing. Charm gasped and frantically felt around for the controls. "THIS IS YOUR PLAN?" she shouted. "To make all my computers and sensors disappear? Whose side are you *on?*"

The *Scientific Method* began to slow down as Charm threw

146

her hands out, searching for the controls. Her hand hit something invisible, and the ship tilted left, just in time to save them from a laser that passed by.

Unfortunately, now that Owen could see what surrounded them, he realized that one laser wasn't their problem.

"That's a *lot* of ships," he said, pointing at the fifteen or so Science Soldier fighters that were flying right at them.

"I'm glad you finally noticed!" Charm shouted. "Now could you let me see what I'm doing so they don't shoot us to death?"

Owen immediately reversed the spell, and the *Scientific Method* faded back into view just in time for one of the laser blasts to slam into the ship.

Everything went sideways, and the wall nearest Owen exploded in flames and smoke. Foam shot from the ceiling to put the fire out as alarms blared throughout the ship. "We just lost half our life support!" Charm shouted. "One more hit and we're done. I need to open a wormhole, *now!*"

"I got this!" Owen shouted, and turned back to the spell book. *Give me something good, you stupid book! A spell that will actually stop those other ships!*

This time there wasn't even a cold, less friendly energy. This time the book didn't even open to a page. It just sat there, and weirdly, Owen got the feeling that it was glaring at him.

"Are you kidding me?" he said to the book, fear filling his stomach. "Give me a spell!"

The book didn't move.

"Well, they're locking on with their laser missiles," Charm said. "Now seems like a good time to tell you how I've hated you from the moment we met."

Owen glanced over his shoulder at her, then turned back to the book, breathing way too quickly. "Okay, I'm sorry! I'm sorry I got you burned, I'm sorry I called you stupid. Just please help us now, or we're all gonna get blown up!"

For a second, nothing happened. Then the book opened, and a cold, chilling energy filled Owen. He immediately let the spell out, not even caring what it did, and the spell book slammed shut, right on his hand.

"Ow!" he shouted, but the book just ground his hand harder.

"The Science Soldier ships . . . they're slowing down!" Charm said from the pilot's seat. "What did you do?"

Owen stood up, the spell book still holding his hand hostage. "I, uh, took them down. Hard." He tried to shake off the book as he stepped over to the viewscreen, just as curious as Charm was about what he'd done.

148

The attacking ships seemed to have changed color, glowing golden in the light of the nearby sun. Other than that, there didn't seem to be anything different about them.

"Obviously, I made them all, uh, gold now," Owen said, faking some Kiel Gnomenfoot arrogance, but inwardly, having no idea what had just happened. Gold? Why would the spell book have given him that spell?

"That's actually impressive," Charm said, raising her eyebrows in surprise. "If their missiles are solid metal, they won't explode on impact. Even if they hit, gold is too soft to damage my ship. And if they try to chase us, their engines would melt right through their ship. I might almost call that . . . clever."

"Well, it's all in a day's work for Kiel Gnomenfoot," Owen said, winking at her.

She stared at him for a second, then turned back to the controls. "Opening a wormhole. We'll be safe in a second. Then we can repair the life-support systems and get a move on."

Something large and multicolored ripped into existence in the middle of the nothingness right in front of them and sucked the ship right in. The ship stretched out, pulling every fiber of Owen until he wanted to scream, then let go, snapping him back like a rubber band as it spit them back out. They emerged from the other side of the wormhole into a nothingness that looked an awful lot like the one they'd just left, only this nothingness had no planets or attacking ships.

"It'll take them a while to follow us," Charm said, standing up from the pilot's seat. "Repairs are going, so we should have a little time."

"You don't need to thank me," Owen told her, grinning. Why had he been afraid, again? *Of course* they'd be fine. The book was written, and obviously Kiel made it to the end!

"Oh, don't worry about that," she said, and suddenly her ray guns were in her hands, aimed right at his face. "Instead, I'm going to shoot you. You have one minute to tell me who you are and what happened to Kiel Gnomenfoot."

CHAPTER 19

All Bethany could see was the ceiling as if she were looking at it through a telescope. Even as she struggled, something within her grew almost calmer as the ceiling got smaller and smaller, blackness folding in around it. Weirdly, it occurred to her that this must be tunnel vision, even as the tunnel of her sight began to collapse in on itself.

Then she slammed into the floor and suddenly could breathe again. She gratefully sucked in as much air as she could as her head pounded. What had happened?

"I said, *stop*," said Kiel from somewhere in front of her.

Everything in the room dimmed except for the Magister, who glowed from deep down inside. "What do you think you're doing, apprentice?" the old wizard said, his voice low and dangerous. "I would not have hurt the girl. But I need her power, and cannot take it while she defies me. You must understand what—"

The Magister abruptly went quiet, only to groan from a lot farther away than he had been. Bethany pushed herself up so she could see what was happening, and found Kiel holding double magic wands that looked like they'd been sharpened into knives. The wands pointed at the now crumpled form of the Magister where he'd just slammed into the far wall.

"*That's* going to cost me at chore time when this is all over," Kiel said. He turned to Bethany and winked. "Look, I get it. You're impressed with me, and probably dumbfounded. It happens. But don't just sit there. Maybe do something a little more useful than jumping into blank sheets of—"

He didn't finish his sentence; instead, he rocketed up into the ceiling, then down onto the floor, back and forth like a pinball machine.

"You will not raise your hand to *me*, boy!" the Magister said, stopping Kiel in midair. "After everything I have done for you? All the years of teaching and raising you as if you were my own?"

"This from the guy . . . who said none of that . . . was real," Kiel said to Bethany, cringing in pain. "Wouldn't that mean . . . all those years of being my guardian . . . didn't happen either?" He forced a grin, then aimed his twin wands at the Magister and mumbled something. Instantly, lightning launched from the tips of the wands directly at the older magician.

The Magister raised his hand, and the lightning absorbed right into his palm. "Always playing the hero, aren't you, Kiel? In your own mind, if nowhere else. But this isn't our world anymore, and things have changed. You're protecting a girl who has the power to save everyone and everything you know. She could end all the conflict back on Magisteria, end all the pain!"

"Weren't you going to do something?" Kiel asked Bethany, only to shout in surprise as hundreds of tiny imps appeared out of nowhere, holding his arms out to his sides to keep him from using his wands.

". . . um," Bethany said, and grabbed the blank page from the floor where it'd landed, then sprinted as fast as she could up the stairs.

"You're lucky I've got this!" Kiel yelled after her, struggling against the imps as they tried to pry the wands out of his hands. "Anyone else would probably be worried right now!"

How was he still making jokes while being attacked? That was *so* like a book character, to say clever lines while crazy things were happening. Bethany didn't waste her time responding as she pushed her way up the stairs, only to almost fall back down them as the Magister exploded through the floor, holding Kiel in midair as he turned to face Bethany.

"You cannot leave, Bethany," the Magister told her, his eyes glowing. "I must have your power!"

"Shouldn't you be . . . worrying more about me?" Kiel yelled at the Magister, despite not being able to move due to the imps. "I don't need . . . my wands to . . . beat you."

"Is that so?" the Magister said, and the imps finally pulled Kiel's wands out of his hands and dropped them onto the ground in front of the Magister. "And what magic have I taught you that could possibly defeat me?" He bent down to pick up the dropped wands.

Kiel half smiled. "Let's call it the magic of planning ahead."

One of the wands exploded in the Magister's hand, sending the older man crashing into a column in the middle of the room. The imps abruptly disappeared, dropping Kiel to the floor, which he hit hard with a loud groan. With the Magister distracted, Bethany sprinted for the library doors, then paused.

Owen would have helped Kiel here. It was probably the brave, heroic thing to do.

Like she was ever going to follow *Owen's* example.

With that, she leaped into the library to hide, leaving the door open just wide enough so she could watch what happened.

Kiel stood up, trying to catch his breath, and held his remaining wand aimed at the Magister. "This is all . . . making me seriously rethink . . . my apprenticeship," he said, then mumbled a spell. The marble floor shuddered, then rose up around the Magister, trapping the older magician in place.

The Magister's eyes lit up with blue fire, and the floor tiles exploded toward Kiel, who waved them away with his wand, then sent ice shards hurtling toward the Magister.

The shards slid around the older man, hitting the wall behind him.

"NO MORE!" the Magister roared, and Kiel suddenly dropped to the floor, his legs and arms flopping around uselessly, leaving the boy unable to stand, cast a spell, or even think. "This is but a Crisis of Confusion spell, Kiel, and you will eventually return to normal. But continue defying me and I shall take the magic from your mind altogether! We cannot continue living out the whims of these writers, living out conflict and hate for their entertainment!"

He stepped forward to kick Kiel's remaining knife-wand

from his hand, then gestured, wiping Kiel's mouth off his face like zipping up a zipper. Dark shadows grabbed each of Kiel's hands and feet and dragged him over to the wall, holding him in place.

"For the love I hold for you, Kiel, *please*, listen to me." The Magister, breathing hard, held out a shaky hand toward his apprentice. "Stop this, or I shall have to take steps. Be reasonable! You cannot defeat me with the magic I taught you myself."

Kiel closed his eyes, then slowly nodded.

The Magister gestured, and Kiel's mouth reappeared. The boy sighed, his eyes still closed. "You're right," he said. "I can't."

Then Kiel slammed his chin into his chest, and an impossibly bright light exploded like a sun in front of him, destroying the shadows holding him against the wall. The magician looked away with a cry as the light quickly faded, only to find Kiel standing just inches from him, holding a ray gun to the Magister's head.

The older man's eyes widened and his voice cracked with rage. "You . . . you would use *science* against me?"

Kiel shrugged, his eyes wild. "Charm gave me this ray gun and that flare for emergencies. I feel dirty even using them.

156

But, like you said, there's no way I'm going to defeat you with magic. Now *calm down* and maybe we can fix all of this before it gets even worse."

"There is no going back, Kiel," the Magister whispered. "Not to our world, not with the knowledge we now have."

"Yes, there is!" Kiel shouted. "Maybe that Porterhouse guy did create us. So what? You say he made us into who we are? Magi, *you* made me into who I am! You raised me, led me, taught me. You created the me that I am today, more than anyone else." He glared at the Magister. "Now look at you. Attacking innocent people? Threatening them, torturing them? This isn't you."

The ray gun exploded into a thousand pieces, and the Magister began to grow, magical energies exploding all around him in his rage. Ten feet, then twenty, and he cracked the ceiling of the room, his height still increasing.

"This doesn't look like calming down," Kiel said from below.

"The Magister who raised you never truly existed!" the magician roared, and his voice was as loud as thunder. "For his sake, and for the sake of all those trapped within every other story, I *will* have the girl's power!"

"Uh-oh," Kiel said quietly.

"Are you ready for someone else's idea?" said Bethany from his side, holding a book in her hand.

Kiel glanced over and shrugged. "It's not my typical strategy, but I'm flexible."

Bethany quickly whispered into his ear, then threw the book open onto the floor in front of them. As the Magister raged above them, casting some sort of elaborate spell, Bethany grabbed Kiel's hand, and the two of them leaped forward into the now-open book.

"NO!" the Magister shouted, realizing too late what was happening. He struck out and magical energy exploded from his hand, but they were already gone.

The book burst into nothingness, leaving behind just a blackened mark on the floor, the air still crackling with deadly magic.

The Magister settled to the floor, his eyes wide. "What have I done?" He touched the floor gently, the spot where his bolt had destroyed the book. "Kiel? What have I *done*?"

CHAPTER 20

"Who *are* you?" Charm said, her ray guns powered up and ready to fire.

How had she seen through his disguise? What was going on here? "I'm Kiel Gnomenfoot, Charm!" he said, holding his hands up in surrender.

"Are you?" she said, her weirdly cute robot eye staring right through him. "You haven't been the same since I found you in the Magister's tower. You're not acting like your usual self. The cat's ignored you completely, instead of hanging on your shoulder like it usually does. You're not worried about Magisteria being attacked." She frowned. "Also, that spell book is trying to eat your hand."

"What, this?" Owen said, frantically trying to shove the spell book off of himself. "This is just a difference of opinion!"

"*Scientific Method,*" Charm said to her ship, "scan him against all known records of Kiel Gnomenfoot, down to the quantum level. Show me the results on-screen."

The viewscreen changed from the empty space outside to an X-ray kind of image of Owen's body. He immediately dropped his hands to cover anything embarrassing, but it didn't seem to help. "Stop it!" he shouted, trying to stay calm but not succeeding at all. "I'm really Kiel. Quiz me. I can answer anything."

"There's no need," Charm said, her ray guns still aimed at him. "The scan will cover it."

His eyes flashed to the screen as his empty body began to fill up, like a countdown. "Remember when we found the First Key, back beneath twenty tons of dragon's gold, using that electromagnet of yours? You said that gold isn't magnetic, but the iron key would be. That's how we found it."

"The real Kiel never listened to what I said in his entire life," Charm told him. "Especially not about science."

"We went to the future! You ate a rat by accident! I had to use your arm as a wand once, in that alternate reality where magic was science! You get annoyed by everything I say, but secretly I make you laugh—"

"You do *what?*" Her eyes narrowed, and her fingers tightened on the triggers.

"I do! You hate to admit it, but I've seen it!"

"Name one time," she said as the viewscreen showed the scan just about finished.

Owen's mind raced frantically through the books. It was a huge part of their friendship, and came up at least once a book. Why couldn't he remember a single—

"The ruins of that magical school!" he shouted. "Remember? I said something like, 'I guess school's out,' and you snorted! Okay, it's not really a laugh, but it's pretty close, and I bet you thought it was funnier than you let on."

"You'd lose that bet," Charm said, just as the scanner chimed. "Looks like the results are in. Move even an inch, and you get rayed."

Owen watched her glance over the scan results, his eyes wide. Could he cast a spell? Not without the spell book, which still hadn't let go of his hand. But if he got called out as not being the real Kiel in front of everyone reading the book, it'd change the whole story, and Bethany would kill him.

Not to mention the fact that Charm might shoot him.

Charm raised her eyes from the screen. "This is interesting," she said. "Apparently, you're allergic to peanuts." Then she slowly lowered her ray guns. "Something's off. The *Scientific*

Method claims you're Kiel down to your core, but I'm not sure."

Owen let out a huge breath. "But it's science, so you have to believe it. The computer said so. I'm Kiel! I'm just acting weird because of, you know, the Magister. I'm sad!"

She gave him a careful look. "The ship's never been wrong before. But I'm going to keep an eye on you. And if you keep messing up, scan or not, I'm leaving you on some deserted planet until I find the Seventh Key. There's no more time for grieving. Get it together. We've got a war to win."

Owen dropped his hands, wanting to laugh or shout or just pump his fist in an awesome victory celebration. The scan hadn't seen through his disguise. Apparently, magic was a lot more thorough than he'd thought.

For a moment there, he'd actually been worried she was going to shoot him, and suddenly everything had seemed a lot less fun. But he had to remember that as far as the book was concerned, he really was Kiel Gnomenfoot. And that meant nothing really bad was going to happen to him. The hero always made it through.

"You did laugh at the school comment," he told her, his heart slowing back down to normal.

"Prove it," she told him, sitting back down in the pilot's seat. "Repairs are just about through. Are you ready to go on, or do you want to talk more about your feelings or something dumb?"

"I just miss him," Owen told her. "The whole thing just really threw me. It'd throw anyone. Even unfeeling half robots."

One of her hands rested on her ray gun again. "I can still shoot you, you know."

He smiled, hoping she was kidding. "I'm sure he's still out there somewhere. Maybe in some other world, watching over us, reading about our adventures, so proud that we're saving the world." Or maybe on his way back with Bethany and Nobody. What was taking them so long, anyway?

Charm snorted. "No one would bother reading about us. We never do anything exciting."

"We just saved ourselves from a whole bunch of attacking spaceships!"

She shrugged, turning back to her pilot controls in midair. "I guess we have different ideas of exciting. Now, where is this Seventh Key?"

"The Magister said that we had to go somewhere called the Original Computer, and that'd tell us more about it," Owen said.

"WHAT?" Charm said, spinning around. "No. Not the Original Computer. That's a *bad idea.*"

"Why?" Owen asked. "It can't be worse than almost getting blown up by Science Soldier ships."

"It can, and *will.*"

Owen shook his head. "That's where the Magister said to go, and he spent the last six . . . the last year looking for even this much information."

Charm growled in frustration. "This is *such* a bad idea. Promise me that you'll do everything I say *when* I say it while we're in there, or I leave you here. Got it?"

"Gotten," he told her. "Why is this place so bad?"

"You'll see," she said, then touched a panel in front of her, sliding something off of it. "Here." She held out one finger to him. "Put this in."

He bent forward and stared at the tip of her finger, where a tiny, almost microscopic square of metal lay. Owen touched one finger to hers, pushed down, and took the metal square up off her finger. "Um, what? *What* am I doing with it? Other than losing it?"

"Don't lose it," she told him. "Plug it into your brain stem, and we'll get going."

He blinked. "Into my who?"

Charm sighed. "Do I have to do everything for you? Here!" She turned him around until his back was to her, then pushed his hair up over his neck. "It's right . . . huh?"

"What's right huh?"

"You don't have a brain stem input." She grunted. "You people are so backward."

"Since when was I supposed to have a brain stem?"

"Brain stem *input*. And since you were born. How do you ever learn anything without just plugging it right into your brain stem for uploading?"

"It's a rough life," he told her. "So what was that thing *supposed* to do?"

"We have to get into the Original Computer," she told him. "And that means we need to become something that'll actually exist within it. That takes digital avatars. This chip was supposed to connect you directly to the ship's computer, which will download everything about you and spit out your avatar into the Nalwork."

"The what?"

"It really is like talking to a child, isn't it? The Nalwork? Short for interNAL netWORK? It's what connects the citizens of Quanterium to every computer on the planet."

Owen gave her a confused look. "Don't you mean INTERnal NETwork? The Internet?"

"The NALWORK. It's not complicated."

Even when she was annoyed, Owen just wanted to do things for her. Maybe clean her ray guns or give her an upgraded arm as a present or something. "Okay, the Nalwork. So how do I get in, then?"

She shrugged. "The chip's going to need to get into your brain one way or another. I guess we'll just have to do some surgery."

Owen laughed. Charm didn't. Owen laughed again, just to see if she needed some encouragement. Apparently, that wasn't the problem. He tried one more laugh, and she slapped his face.

"NO!" he said.

"Sit down," she told him, pushing him into one of the chair's seats. "Don't be such a baby."

"IT'S NOT BEING A BABY TO NOT WANT YOU DOING SURGERY ON ME!"

"I won't be the one doing it," she said, then tapped something in the air. The chair's arms spit out straps that covered Owen's wrists, then yanked them down, holding him still. He squirmed and tried to break free, but the chair wouldn't let him so much as move.

Since when did this kind of thing happen in the Kiel Gnomenfoot books? They were kids' books! Surgery? "Charm, let me go! I don't want this! We'll figure out another way to get into the Original Computer. Like, say, use a keyboard and a monitor, like a normal person."

"You sound like you're two thousand years old when you talk like that," she said, then touched the air again, and his chair went shooting backward toward the wall. It slammed to a stop right before it hit, and robotic arms popped out from the wall to hold his head in place.

"I'll magic you if you don't stop!" Owen said. "*Charm!* I can turn you to gold! I'm warning you!"

"Kiel, you have my word that if this hurts, I'll try to keep a straight face," she told him, then nodded at the robotic arms. "Do it."

The next thirty seconds were the weirdest of Owen's life. First, a fictional spaceship held him in place to give him brain surgery. Second, somehow, he didn't actually feel a thing, not after an initial pinch in his neck, which was probably some kind of shot to numb it. Despite all his screaming, the arms quickly released him, and he jumped up from the chair, frantically touching at his neck. "AAH!" he shouted. "There's a thingy there now!"

And there was! The ship had implanted some kind of thingy right into his neck!

"I'd hope so. That was the whole point," Charm said. "Now we can get going."

"That was the *worst* thing anyone's ever done to me," Owen said, pointing a finger at her accusingly.

She smacked his finger aside. "If it is, be thankful."

He made a face, gently touching the uploader thing on the back of his neck. "At least that's the worst part done. I guess it wasn't so bad. . . ."

"That?" Charm snorted. "That was the easy part! The worst part's coming next." And with that, she turned him around again. She touched the tiny circuit to his neck and pushed. Something clicked. . . .

And just like that, the world turned to digital billboards, millions of glowing people, and *TRON*.

CHAPTER 21

"I'm surprised that worked," Kiel said as Bethany took his cloak and folded it up. "If the Magister hadn't been so angry, he would have felt me use magic to teleport us away. We'll have to be more careful next time."

Bethany gritted her teeth. This jerk was a popular character? There was no way she was going to read those books now. "There's not going to be a next time," she told him, and held out a hand for his now-empty wand-holster belt.

It'd been a huge risk, telling Kiel to use his magic to teleport them away at the last second, making it look like they'd jumped into the book. Especially since the book was a blank journal she'd found in the library. There wasn't far they could have run in all that nothing if the Magister had used the bit of Bethany's power he'd stolen to follow them. But at least the trick seemed to have bought a little time to figure out how to deal with all this.

If there *was* a way to deal with all this. UGH.

"So here's my plan," Kiel said, now looking a bit more like a normal boy dressed in a black shirt and pants. Or at least like a normal boy dressed up like Kiel Gnomenfoot without the cloak and magic wands. "He's right. There's no way I can beat him at magic. He taught me everything I know. And he already took away the one bit of science tech-o-gee that—"

"Tech*nol*ogy."

"That Charm gave me," Kiel continued. "So the new plan is, we find some stockpile of ray guns or laser rifles or whatever it is you people have here. Something big and explosive and entirely made of science. Something that's been set up to specifically fight magic."

"That doesn't exist. Not in any way."

"You distract him with those science weapons, and I hit him with a forget spell." He sighed. "I think that's the best option. He's not a bad person, honestly. He's just . . . angry."

"Oh yeah? 'Cause I've got it on good authority that your teacher—"

"Magister."

"—was planning on blowing up the science guys. Once you found the source of whatever it was."

"The Source of Magic?" Kiel said, giving her a disbelieving stare. "He'd never do that. Who told you this?"

Bethany started to say, then shook her head. Kiel already knew way too much. "No one. I made it up. Sorry. But we're not doing any part of your plan, especially the parts that aren't possible." She glanced around the corner, holding up a hand to stop Kiel from following just yet. No one seemed to be looking their way, so she pulled him out onto the sidewalk from the alley they'd landed in. "The *real* new plan is: We take you home immediately, I find Owen in whatever prison you two left him in, then he and I come back and figure out a way to get your teacher—"

"Magister."

"—back home right after you," Bethany finished. "Then you can do whatever Forget Me Not spell you want on him. But that's it. There's no way I'm letting two fictional characters—"

Kiel winced. "Isn't there another way to say that? Fictional sounds insulting."

". . . Fine. Letting two *individuals* such as yourselves run around and get noticed. Do you have any idea what would happen if someone recognized you?"

"Nice Kiel Gnomenfoot costume!" said a teenage girl

walking by. "Where are your wands? You look like you could be in a movie!"

Kiel grinned and saluted her as she passed. "What's a movie?" he asked Bethany.

She sighed. "Nothing. Hopefully, they'll just think you're a fan or something. A lot of them probably come to this town, since the author guy lives here."

"More up there a ways," Kiel told her, pointing up toward the hills in the distance. "I did teleport us a safe distance away. Any closer and the Magister would still feel our presence."

"So which house was Mr. Porterhouse's?" Bethany asked him. The last thing she needed was to ring doorbells and ask if there were any crazy old men throwing spells around at home.

"Jonathan Porterhouse?" said someone else walking by, a man dressed in vintage clothes with black glasses. "It's that big mansion up on the hill." He pointed toward what looked like the biggest roof Bethany had ever seen, surrounded by trees. "It's cool, go check it out. He's got a fence up that was built to look like it was made from Science Soldier robots."

Kiel's face lit up. "That's genius," he said to Bethany. "Why did I never think of doing that?"

She glared at him, then turned to the stranger. "Thanks,

that's a good idea," she said to the man in the dark glasses. "Is there anywhere around we can find his books? Like a library or a bookstore?"

"There's Untitled Books just up the street," the man said, and pointed behind him.

"You've been a ton of help. Thank you," Bethany said, and dragged Kiel past the man.

"Cool costume," the man told Kiel as they passed, and Bethany gritted her teeth.

"If everyone's just going to recognize me, why can't I wear my cloak and belt?" Kiel asked as they passed a bunch of storefronts. "I feel weird not having them, even without the wands. And the belt has a few emergency spells in it, in case I use them up from memory."

"Because this is *not* happening, and I'm not going to let it not happen any more than it's *already* not happening."

"Your science logic is odd, but I'll take your word for it," he said, then stopped dead in his tracks. "WHAT. IS. THAT?"

Bethany followed his gaze, and almost dry heaved.

The entire window at Untitled Books was filled with a poster for *Kiel Gnomenfoot and the Source of Magic*. An almost life-size painted version of Kiel aimed his magic wands at what looked like zombified versions of robots, while at his back some half-robot girl shot ray guns at the monsters.

"This is my book?" Kiel said almost reverently, gently placing his fingers on the window. "I'm so . . . *handsome*! Look at me! Do you see this? LOOK!"

"Oooh, you do look just like him!" said a girl coming out of the store. "That's so cool!"

"Oh, really?" Kiel said, posing beside the poster. "I mean, I'm probably a bit better-looking, don't you think? The painting loses something a little. But I can see the resemblance, I suppose."

The girl laughed, so Bethany quickly stepped between them. "The sad thing is," she whispered to the girl, "he thinks he really is Kiel. It's something wrong in his head. We just came to the author's town to see if it might help snap him out of it."

The girl blinked, then flashed Kiel a worried smile and quickly continued on her way. Kiel watched her go, his face covered in disappointment. "That was evil."

"Good. Now come on, let's find the right book. You can think I'm evil all the way home if you want."

The bookstore had Kiel Gnomenfoot posters up everywhere, to Bethany's annoyance. As they walked in, the clerk looked up and grinned. "Cool cost—"

"No, it's not!" Bethany shouted. "It's just black clothing. He's not even *wearing* a costume!"

The clerk raised both eyebrows. "Oh, sorry about that. We do get a lot of Kiel costumes in here. I didn't mean anything by it."

Perfect. Now she was yelling at completely innocent strangers. "Sorry, I'm just in a bad mood," Bethany said, forcing a smile. "Where are your Kiel Gnomenfoot books, actually? My friend's never read them."

"Back on that wall," the clerk said, and Bethany grabbed Kiel's hand and strode off. "But we're sold out of most of them!"

"Sold out?" Kiel asked, pulling his hand away. "Do you get a lot of people interested in reading about this dashingly handsome Kiel person?"

"Oh, tons of kids," the clerk said. "Adults, too. It's a huge thing. I hear they want to make a movie, but the author says no."

"A movie?" Kiel asked.

"I know," the clerk said. "Why ruin a perfectly good book by turning it into a movie that can't possibly be as good."

"So true," Bethany said, dragging Kiel away. She whispered to him, "Could you *please* concentrate? Maybe they still have the sixth book. That's the only one I care about."

"We can't begrudge my fans their stories," Kiel told her. "I'd feel horrible depriving even one reader of hearing my adventures."

She struggled hard to not just drop him into the nearest cookbook.

The children's section covered the walls in one corner of the store, and Bethany quickly scanned the shelves for Porterhouse. *Kiel Gnomenfoot: Magic Thief* was there, as was *Kiel Gnomenfoot and the Tense Future* and *Kiel Gnomenfoot and the Infinite Reality*.

But that was it.

"NOOOOOO," Bethany moaned, searching the shelves just in case a book had been misplaced. No sixth book? Maybe she could just jump him into one of the others, and let him find his own way back to his present? He could just hide out for three or four books, couldn't he? She sighed deeply.

Kiel carefully pulled the first book off the shelf and opened the cover. "'The war had made food scarce on Magisteria, especially for orphans living on the streets,'" he read, then showed her the page. "*I* lived on the streets, and food *was* scarce! This is so accurate. It's just like being there."

Bethany slammed the book shut on his fingers, then pulled

it away from him and shoved it back onto the shelf. "What are we going to do?" she hissed.

"Not close any more books on my hand, for a start," Kiel said indignantly, holding his hands protectively.

Bethany fell backward against a nearby column and slid to the floor. "I . . . I just don't know how to fix this. I can't even put *you* back, let alone your teacher."

"Magister."

She glared at him. "Really? Could you maybe help instead of being . . . you?"

Kiel slid down the column beside her and patted her leg. "You're taking this all too hard. From the way you talk about it, we can jump back into the books at any point, right? And depending on the page, no time will have passed since I left. So what's the hurry? What's the big deal if I stick around for a little bit? Why do you care so much?"

She sighed, leaning her head back and closing her eyes. "Because none of this was supposed to happen! I'm just so tired of making mistakes. It seems like that's all I do. I shouldn't have trusted Owen. I shouldn't have brought him into the book. And I definitely shouldn't have gone back to his house." She rubbed her eyes. "And my mom? She won't notice I'm gone until tonight, since she goes to work before I get up, but when I don't come home? She's going to go crazy. She'll call the police, the FBI will come, I'll be on the news, and if I *do* come home? I'll never see the sun again. *So dead.*" She growled loudly and knocked her head against the column over and over. "That stupid Willy Wonka book! WHY?"

Kiel nodded, his face exuding deep wisdom. "I have no idea what any of that meant," he said. "But if this Willy person really did cause all of this, then I'm glad he did. Do you have any idea how much you've shown me in the little time I've known you? I'm practically a god here!"

"Nope," Bethany said absently. "Not even a little bit. You're a fictional character."

"That everyone loves! And please don't call me that." He grinned. "Besides, what's so wrong with you enjoying yourself? I saw the look on your face when you grabbed the Porterhouse guy and jumped into that sheet of paper. You were having fun."

She looked at him with wide eyes. "Are you insane?"

He shook his head. "I know what I saw. A crazy look in your eyes, a smile on your face. You were getting a thrill, admit it."

"Do you not realize what's happening here?"

"Eh," he told her, tossing a small ball of fire from hand to hand. "This is nothing. I've lived my entire life in a war zone. Seen some truly horrible things, too, even before Dr. Verity started his crusade against Magisteria. But guess what? I still smile. I still laugh. I still even have fun sometimes." He considered that. "Well, most of the time, honestly. If you're not enjoying yourself, what's the point?"

"The point is that you're trying to save the world from an evil scientist tyrant! How can you enjoy yourself when everything's going so terribly?"

He winked. "I'm multitalented."

She wanted to say something horrible and mocking—just as soon as it came to her—but her thoughts were interrupted by a noise like thunder. The entire building rocked, and the clerk at the front of the store shouted, "WHOA! Look at that!"

"Oh, come *on*, what now?" Bethany said, quickly jumping to her feet as books began to shake right off the shelves. She and Kiel made their way back to the front of the store and peeked out the window from behind the giant Kiel Gnomenfoot poster.

An enormous black-and-silver tower rose up from the hills outside the town, where Jonathan Porterhouse's house was supposed to be, shaking the earth as it grew into the sky.

Bethany stepped back, completely speechless. Kiel just nodded. "Okay, yes. That's the Magister's tower, all right." He threw a glance at Bethany and winced. "That's probably the kind of thing you *didn't* want to happen, isn't it?"

CHAPTER 22

The noise was incredible, with videos playing loudly everywhere. Lights of an impossible amount of colors popped in front of Owen's eyes, almost blinding him. But the craziest thing was easily the people. They were *everywhere*, and all of them were chatting with someone else, or commenting on something, or shouting a question. And other than glowing like they were made of light (which they probably were), no two people looked anything alike.

An entire world full of people of all shapes, sizes, ages, and genders had come to the Internet—or, well, Nalwork, apparently—and it was easily the craziest, loudest, most glowing thing Owen had ever seen.

Something touched Owen's hand, and he looked down to find Charm tapping a tiny glowing piece of paper into his palm. He took it and opened it up.

i hate this place, it said.

He laughed. "Why? I love it!" he tried to say, but his voice got lost in the din.

She shook her head, then showed him a glowing notepad in her hand. She concentrated on it for a moment, then ripped off a sheet and handed it to him.

you have to use the nalwork tools to talk privately. don't say anything out loud.

He nodded and looked around for his own notepad, then realized he probably just needed to think about one. He concentrated, and a notepad like hers appeared. He thought about what he wanted to say, then ripped off a sheet and handed it to her. so what now?

now we be careful. we're both wanted criminals. don't get caught.

He nodded as they moved around, trying to stay out of other people's way. Unfortunately, that wasn't easy as there were other digital avatars *everywhere*.

this is all anyone does anymore, Charm said in a note as they pushed their way through the crowds. it's so pathetic. people just sit on the nalwork all day, and robots do everything for them in the real world.

Owen nodded, his mind drifting off to the *real* real world. What was taking Bethany so long to bring Kiel and the Magister back? All she had to do was touch them and jump back into the book, right? Could she really be in trouble? Owen rolled his eyes. Her, get into trouble? She'd never do anything that fun.

He glanced back over at Charm, her hair pulled back into a ponytail, her red robot eye watching everything at once. Sure, she was a fictional character, but there was something just so . . . *blunt* about her. Honest. It was kind of nice, having someone just say whatever they were thinking.

Also, she was adorable, especially with her ray guns.

stop looking at me, her note said. you're making me nervous.

His eyes turned frontward, and he blushed. Fair enough.

She pointed at an advertisement for a new communications device that was no bigger than the chip she'd put into his head. they invented that centuries ago. now it just gets smaller and smaller. nothing new. at least magicians use their imaginations and come up with new stuff.

but magic doesn't last very long, he wrote back. at least this stuff exists for longer than a spell.

She shrugged. Quanterium has given up. in a lot of ways, not just by letting Dr. Verity take over.

Owen followed her through the throngs of people, stopping every so often for a crowd giving their opinion on something or other, or just a thumbs-up or -down here or there. All around them transparent tubes filled the only empty space, some of which had people shouting random phrases in them, then being whisked away. What were they doing?

Charm pointed at some nearby tubes. there. those will take us to the original computer.

what are they?

you'll see.

The crowds around the tubes were just as heavy if not worse than everywhere else, so it took a bit of time to get through. Charm gave him a few more notes along the way, explaining not to talk to anyone, not to say anything to anyone, and not to speak to anyone. Owen pointed out that those things all meant the same thing, but she just glared at him.

"Learn sixteen languages in just three seconds!" a robot shouted at Owen, loud enough to be heard over the crowd. "You, there, in the black cloak! Build your own holodeck! Buy

one time machine, get a second half-off, today only! Buy your girlfriend a matter transporter!"

Owen immediately blushed, and he stopped in place. "She's not my girlfriend," he said out loud.

Charm gasped, and somehow Owen heard it. In fact, as soon as he'd spoken, the entire Internet—Nalwork—had gone silent. All talking, all chatting, everything just completely stopped. Videos paused, the lights stopped blinking, and people in every direction turned to look directly at Owen.

Charm slapped her forehead with her palm, hard.

The robot's eyes flipped from a friendly blue to a bright red. "VOICE RECOGNIZED," it said in a much more monotone, less salesman-type voice, as if it'd been taken over by an outside force. "MAGISTERIAN CRIMINAL KIEL GNOMENFOOT IDENTIFIED."

"ruN!" someone shouted in a chat bubble. "he'S goNna kill us!"

"Magisterian criminals are so played out," someone else said. "It's all about the alternate-reality vampire Magisterians now. That's where the buzz is."

A third person just stood with some kind of camera, filming

the entire thing. "Thumbs-up if you hate magic!" he said into the lens.

"WHAT DID I SAY?" Charm shouted. "This is what happens when you respond to a Nalwork ad!"

"VOICE RECOGNIZED," said the same robot. "QUANTERIAN WAR CRIMINAL CHARM MENTUM IDENTIFIED."

"No talking," Owen whispered back to Charm, unable to stop himself from grinning at her.

She smacked him, her digital hand apparently still solid enough to hit him. "We need to get out of here!" she hissed. "NOW."

"What's so bad?" he asked as the crowd thinned around them, all but the one guy who kept his camera running. "What can they do?"

Tubes all around them began to slam shut, like prison cells locking. One by one, the Nalwork closed off their escape routes. "That," Charm said. "Now jump, or we're going to be stuck here until security shows up!"

"Security?" Owen said. "Like virus protection?"

"You better hope we don't need protection from viruses," Charm said, grabbing his hand and yanking him toward the only still-open tube. It began to close on them, but Charm jammed her robotic arm in and held the tube open. "GO!"

The man with the camera groaned. "Wait! Security isn't even here yet! I wanted to get that on film!"

Charm pulled out a digital ray gun and shot the camera. It exploded right in his hand, not harming his digital form at all. He glared at her, then gave her a thumbs-down. Weirdly, a tiny thumbs-down appeared on her shirt with a number one, right over her heart.

"That's . . . odd," Owen said, then got pushed into the tube. Charm jumped in a second later, letting the tube slam shut behind her.

For a moment they both just hung there in the middle of the tube, nothing above or below them. Owen gave Charm a look. "How do you make it go?"

"You have to tell it what you're looking for," she said, then looked up. "ORIGINAL COMPUTER!"

"SEARCH INPUT," said a computerized voice. "SEARCH COMMENCING."

And then Owen's stomach hit his feet as they shot up into the tube, faster than the speed of screaming.

CHAPTER 23

Everyone saw the tower. *Everyone.* There was no missing it. Bethany found herself outside the bookstore, not even remembering leaving. She looked around at all the people pointing and shouting about the Magister's tower, and couldn't speak, almost couldn't breathe, like she couldn't remember how.

"I'd never actually seen it from the outside before," Kiel said from beside her. "It's usually hanging off the bottom side of a cliff, so it's not the easiest thing to sightsee. The actual one, I mean." He paused. "Or maybe this is the only actual one, if the other one is made-up. You did make my life a bit more confusing, didn't you."

"I . . . I don't—"

"I know," Kiel said, patting her on the shoulder. "This isn't going to be fun for you. But look at the bright side. When things are as bad as they can get, what's there to worry about?"

She slowly turned toward him, fighting off the extremely strong desire to strangle him where he stood. "This . . . this is going to be *everywhere*. The news will cover it. The police are going to come. And your teacher—"

"Magister."

"—will not be too happy when those things happen!" Bethany's voice got louder and louder as she went. "And I can't even imagine what that means. I never even thought he'd do *this*! So how much worse is this going to get?" She grabbed Kiel's black shirt and pulled him close. "*You have no idea* how much more I can worry about."

Kiel took a step back, his eyes wide. "That was impressive," he told her. "But I really do think you're going about this all wrong."

Two news vans sped past them on the street, heading toward the mansion. Bethany just waved her hand at them, giving him a "See?" look.

"Forget that for now," Kiel said. "Do you remember when Charm and I were trapped in the future?"

Bethany shook her head impatiently. "I've never read your books, and *now isn't the time*—"

"And do you remember how—wait, what?"

"I've never read your *books!*" Bethany shouted. "I don't know what happened to you in book two, I have no idea what you saw in book three, and I couldn't care less about whatever went down in book five!"

"You're angry," Kiel told her calmly, "so I'm going to forgive what you just said. Anyway, when Charm and I were in the future—"

"What did I just *say?*"

"Our time machine had been destroyed by Dr. Verity's great-great-grandson, and we realized there was no way back," Kiel continued. "Things looked dark, and this was all after we learned that, well, my own personal future hadn't turned out so great either. But that's when I decided that sometimes you have to embrace the bad to find the good." He winked at her. "Think about it."

She slapped his arm over and over. "THAT. DOESN'T. MEAN. ANYTHING!"

"We got home, *Bethany*, because we realized that if we changed the *future's* future, someone would eventually come along to stop us. So we started messing up everything we could, and soon enough, along came the future's version of time police to fix things. As soon as they were distracted, we stole *their* time machine and used it to get back to the present!"

Bethany stopped slapping him to stare at him openmouthed. "Do you have any idea how little sense that makes?"

"So?" Kiel said with a grin. "It worked. And it worked because I embraced the problem and made it work for me. That's *real* magic."

"*No.* Real magic is when you make something happen that's physically impossible."

"Well, sure, that too. That's real magic. But this is real*er* magic."

"No, it's not that either. That word doesn't even exist."

"So in a way, that word is magic, by your definition." He winked again. "Now, do you want to argue some more, or do you want to fix this?"

She glared at him, then looked back at the tower. Fix this? *Fix this?* They'd passed "fix this" when Owen had started talking to fictional characters! This was so far *beyond* "fix this" that there was no fixing this at all!

A man stepped up next to them, dressed in a Hawaiian shirt and shorts, despite the coolness. He lifted his camera to take a picture, then grinned at Bethany. "You know, Jonathan Porterhouse keeps saying he won't make a movie, but I bet that's what this is. Looks like a set to me, doesn't it?"

"What's a movie?" Kiel whispered to her.

"No," she whispered back. "These people can't be seeing this! Can't you use a forget spell on all these people or something?"

"Won't work," Kiel told her.

"Just try!"

Kiel sighed and mumbled something, and pointed at the man in the Hawaiian shirt. The man's eyes went blank for a moment, and then he shook his head as if trying to clear out a fog. He turned to Bethany to say something, only to abruptly notice the enormous tower of black and silver up on the hill. "What the . . . ?" he said. "Do you *see* that?"

"It didn't work. Do it again!" Bethany hissed.

Kiel pointed at the tower. "He's just going to *keep* seeing—"

"DO IT AGAIN!"

"I can only do magic once without a spell book," Kiel told her. "Now, it so happens that I *do* have this spell written down in my belt pouches, mostly because—"

Bethany shoved his belt back to him and stamped her foot while she waited for him to find the right page in his pouch, while he made comments like "Huh, forgot I had this one," and "Ooh, that reminds me of . . . forget it." Finally, he pulled out the right page and glanced over the spell. His body began to glow, and he unleashed the forget spell again at the man in the Hawaiian shirt.

The man's eyes blanked out once more, and he shook his head, just like last time. This time, Bethany grabbed his shirt and pulled him around so he wasn't facing the tower. The man gave her an odd look. "Why would you do that?" He took a step away, then noticed the tower out of the corner of his eye. "What the . . . ?" he said. "Do you see—"

"NO!" Bethany screamed. "I don't! It's not there!"

Kiel grabbed her arm and pulled her away from the Hawaiian-shirted man as Bethany kept screaming about how the tower wasn't there. Finally, he raised a hand. "I'm this close to just making *you* forget all of this, if you don't calm down," he told her. "It'd make my life a lot easier, honestly."

"How are they supposed to not remember it if they keep seeing it?" Bethany said, her hands shaking. "You need to make the tower invisible! Like a big bubble all around Jonathan Porterhouse's mansion! You can do that, right?" She grabbed his shoulders and looked him right in the eye. "RIGHT?"

"You know, this isn't my world or anything," he told her, so calm it infuriated her, "but unless me being here somehow makes me much more powerful than usual, that's probably not going to happen."

"JUST ONE SIDE?" Bethany begged. "The side closest to town? Can you do that?"

He sighed, then looked up at the tower with an appraising look. "Well, I *am* pretty impressive, contrary to what I just told you. I'm sure I could handle at *least* one side. Probably two, if push came to shove—"

She shoved him, hard. "It came to shove when that tower popped up! DO IT! As tall as you can so no one sees it!"

Kiel gave her an annoyed look, then slowly spread his hands, chanting a spell. For a moment she considered making him go do his magic in an alley, but at this point, with the tower and all, a boy in a Kiel Gnomenfoot costume doing magic probably would just make this all look like a publicity stunt for the nonexistent movie.

Kiel finished his spell, and a bright light shot out from both his hands, weaving its way through the streets of the town and up into the hills. It poured over the tower (or at least one side, maybe two), and then abruptly, tower and light both disappeared.

Kiel, meanwhile, swayed like he was about to faint. Bethany quickly grabbed his arm and steadied him.

"I told you I'm impressive," he said, sounding completely winded. "Now I'm impressive *and* tired. When did magic get to be so exhausting? What's wrong with this place?"

"That was *amazing*," she told him. "Seriously, Kiel. Thank you."

He smiled, and she smiled back.

Then she slowly began to push the forget spell page in his hand up toward his face, so he could relearn it.

"No," he told her. "Rest now. Tired!"

"You can rest when you've wiped the memories of everyone in town who saw the tower," she said. "There's no time to wait! The people in those news vans will start filming soon, so we need to make them forget before the story becomes about how the tower not only appeared, but disappeared. Plus, who knows what the Magister is doing!"

"Wait, *what?*" Kiel said, his eyes widening as he caught up with what she was saying. "*Everyone* in town?"

"Not *everyone*," she told him, shoving him toward the

Hawaiian-shirted man, who now stared at Kiel with a look of shock. "No, actually, you're right, everyone is better. Let's do everyone."

"But I'm so *tired*—"

Bethany grabbed his hand and held it out toward the surprised man. "C'mon, you're Kiel Gnomenfoot! When bad things happen, you embrace them, or something!"

"You really *are* pure evil, aren't you," Kiel whispered, then read over the forget spell again.

Hawaiian-shirted man's look of surprise faded into a friendly smile as his eyes glazed over, then he shook out the fog and continued on his way.

"One down," Bethany said as Kiel dropped to his knees. "Who's next?"

CHAPTER 24

"A AH!" Owen shouted as the tube shot him and Charm straight up into nothingness, then twisted and jerked them around in a dizzying maze of other tubes and screaming billboards advertising cool science thingers.

"I need to clear our history!" Charm shouted into his ear over the noise of the ads. "The security system is going to catch up with us otherwise. This might scare you a little, so try to stay calm!"

"What does *that* mean?" Owen said, then screamed in terror as Charm shot at the sides of the tube just behind them with her ray guns. The tube instantly shattered, sending pieces of tube off to plow into various ads and other search tubes.

"That won't hide us for long," she said, putting her guns back in their holsters. "We'll need to be quick."

"Aah!" Owen told her, hugging her for dear life.

She pushed him off her, and they continued zooming along the tube separately—her looking impatient; him caught between terror and feeling like this was the greatest roller coaster ride ever, though leaning toward the first one, if he had to pick.

Just as Owen began to get used to the ride, or at least everything but his stomach did, the tube spat them out into what looked like a mass of zeroes and ones, the numbers actually breaking their fall.

Charm got to her feet before Owen did, then leaned down and yanked him up with her robot arm so hard he actually flew for a moment. "We're here," she said. "The Original Computer." She made a face. "It even smells out of date."

Owen sniffed loudly and nodded. There *was* an odd sort of sour-milk odor, weirdly.

"See all these?" Charm said, pointing at the zeroes and ones. "Can you believe computers ever actually ran like this? Binary? I mean, c'mon. We're up to centidecimal at this point in modern computers." She frowned at the streams of ones and zeroes. "It's like visiting prehistoric times."

Owen glanced around, seeing nothing but numbers. "So how do we find the location of the Seventh Key in all of this?"

"These numbers here don't mention anything about it," Charm told him, glancing around. "We could use an interface, but I don't see one anywhere. There should be one farther in, though. Come on."

With that, she led Owen off into the stream of ones and zeros, parting it like a curtain.

"What *are* these numbers, anyway?" he asked, dipping his hand into a bunch of zeroes. They felt cold to the touch, kind of like water, only less wet. Which was really all water was, but still. He reached for a one, then yanked his hand back as a tiny jolt zapped him.

"Ones and zeros are actually all a computer understands, at its core," she told him as they walked. "They're not even that, one or zero. It's actually just a different way of saying 'on' and 'off.' 'On' means there's electricity, and 'off' means there isn't. Everything else here is built off of those two ideas. On, off, one, zero. Get it?"

"So don't touch the ones," Owen said, and stuck his hand into another stream of zeroes, letting them flow over his hand. It actually felt kind of relaxing.

"Be careful," Charm told him, pointing at a different flow of numbers that looked exactly the same as the one he was touching. "That's the Original Computer's avatar software over there. Touch it, and you'll glitch us right into nonexisting."

"It looks exactly the same," he said, glancing between them quickly to see any difference.

Charm snorted. "So read the numbers before you touch them. Quanterian children learn to read binary in primary school."

Owen rolled his eyes. "Who cares if I *did* touch those specific numbers, the avatar software? What's the worst that could happen? We stop existing here and end up back in the ship?"

"I have no idea," Charm said. "But that's definitely not the worst that could happen. Enough of this. We're running out of time. Dr. Verity's armies are going to attack Magisteria in less than twenty-four hours, and we still don't even have the Seventh Key. I'm going to hack my own user interface, or we'll be here all day."

"Hack?"

She pulled something out of her glowing pocket and dropped it to the ground. The object instantly expanded into what looked like a desk, a chair, and a keyboard. She sat down and immediately began typing, and the air in front of her lit up like a computer screen. "One second," she said. "I have to make sure we're hidden."

"Hidden?" Owen asked, feeling like an idiot with all his questions. Though that's what Kiel always did whenever they were in Quanterium, so at least he was playing his role correctly.

"Hacking sets off alarms," Charm said, then nodded. Owen turned around to find a wall rising up to just about eye level in a wide circle around them. "There, I've set up a firewall. We should be safe now."

Owen touched the top of the maybe four-foot-tall wall in front of him. "Uh, really? This is hiding us?"

"Things don't work by sight here," Charm said. "Now stop talking."

"You need quiet?" Owen asked, looking out over the firewall. Something fluttered in the streams of ones and zeroes, and Owen stood up on his digital toes to get a better look.

"No, your voice just irritates me."

Fair enough. He glanced around at the number streams, but the flutter seemed to have disappeared.

"This is odd," Charm told him, typing away. "Yes, it's the very first computer. But there's history in here that goes back further than anything I've ever seen. Almost to the very beginning." Her eyebrows raised. "What? This isn't right. It says that magicians originally came from Quanterium."

Something caught Owen's eye far to the left, and he circled around. "Who cares? Concentrate on the key."

"It says that there used to just be one planet," she said. "Not two. That's plainly false. Are all computers just failing on me today?"

"Planets don't just pop into existence," Owen agreed, slowly moving around the wall. What was out there?

"Unless you magicians did something unnatural again," Charm said. "It can't be right, though. Magicians never lived here. Magic and science together? They'd have killed each other. Trust me, I think about that every day I'm with you."

Owen grinned, throwing her a look. Magic and science working together *was* sort of the entire point of the Kiel Gnomenfoot books. She didn't notice his look, though, and kept typing.

"Here, something about the Source of Magic. It says the first magic-user and the president of Quanterium jointly locked it away in the Vault of Containment. They each made three keys to lock the door, then together formed a Seventh Key, to ensure that neither scientist nor magician could separately open the door."

"So what'd they do with it?" Something flickered in the corner of Owen's eye again, and he turned back to the firewall.

"Charm, I think I saw something," he said, his eyes locked on the spot.

"Good for you," Charm told him without looking up. "There's lots more about the first six keys. That's useless. We have those."

Something glitched in a different stream, and Owen shook his head. "Seriously, come look!"

She growled in frustration, then stood up and leaned forward to look over the wall. "You know what I see? You wasting my time."

"There," he said, pointing at a new glitch. "Did you see that?"

Charm squinted, then stepped back, her hands on her ray guns. Without a word, she ran back to her computer and typed something in, then turned back to the wall. "All right, this isn't good," she said quietly. "If they are what I think they are, then the command I just typed in will make them reveal themselves."

Owen pushed himself up to his tiptoes and looked out, expecting to see streams of numbers.

Instead, the numbers glitched into what looked like old, clunkier versions of Science Soldier robots. And they extended as far as the eye could see.

"Um?" he said.

"The alarm couldn't have worked so fast," Charm said, backing into her computer, then sitting down and typing frantically. "And the security systems didn't follow us this soon either. The soldiers must have been left here as a trap, to protect the location of the Seventh Key."

"Why aren't they shooting?" Owen asked as the now-visible robots began to silently march forward toward the firewall from every direction around them.

"They're not actually robots, any more than you're a real person in here," Charm told him, not looking up as she typed. "They're viruses."

Computer viruses that looked like robots? Awesome! "Those just affect computers, though, right?" Not that he was scared or anything, but the robots *were* pretty big.

"Right now, you *are* a computer," she said. "These viruses infect by touch. Here you're just as digital as they are, so they'll overwrite whatever data they find."

Owen sighed in relief. "So then we'll just get sent back to the ship or something. That's not so bad."

"You don't get it," Charm told him, her voice more panicked than he'd ever heard it before. "What do you think happens if they overwrite your brain here, Kiel? It'll get uploaded back into your head that way, as the robot virus. So anything in your brain—if there *is* anything in your brain—gets written over until the virus is all that's left."

Owen swallowed hard. This book was turning out to be *much* darker than the last few. "At least we're safe behind this firewall," Owen told her. "Right?"

The first robot virus reached the firewall and extended a hand to touch it. The entire wall trembled like a leaf in the wind.

Charm's forehead furrowed. "Of course."

Owen let out a huge breath and smiled.

"We're completely safe until the wall falls, which won't be for at least a minute, maybe two," Charm continued. "Now, what did I say about you talking?"

CHAPTER 25

Bethany walked Kiel up to the front gate of Jonathan Porterhouse's mansion, her shoulder under his arm. The boy magician dragged his feet with every step, and his eyes had glazed over at some point, probably when he'd decided to stop casting his forget spell on individuals and to just do one big spell for the entire town.

From the outside, the mansion looked even nicer than it had from within. As promised, a silver fence surrounded the building, designed to look as if it'd been made from discarded robot parts. Mostly just arms and legs, but every few feet a head would pop up, like a warning to any robot thieves.

"We're here," Bethany told him, and laid him down gently on the ground.

"*Science Soldiers,*" Kiel said, pointing at the fence, still a bit unfocused. "Serves them right, becoming a fence. I hate those things."

"Not surprising, if they wanted to kill you," Bethany told him, trying not to grit her teeth. Yes, the tower was invisible, and yes, they'd dodged a bullet with the townspeople forgetting they'd seen it to begin with, but the tower was still there, and the Magister was still doing . . . whatever it was that he was doing. They'd started hearing some kind of odd roaring noise as they'd gotten closer, at which point Bethany had panicked, stopped letting Kiel walk on his own, and basically half carried him the rest of the way.

Making a tower invisible was one thing, but she doubted there was an equivalent spell for making loud roars disappear.

"Wait, who are you again?" Kiel asked her from the ground. "So sleepy!"

"You're hilarious," she told him, then gestured at the gate. "Can you magic this open?"

Kiel groaned loudly. "Are you joking! Just push on it or something! I've never been this completely drained before. What is *wrong* with your world, anyway? Why is magic so tiring here?"

"The real world doesn't like when people do impossible

things," Bethany said as she tried the gate. It didn't budge—completely locked up. That made sense, given how many fans probably came by to see the house. "Nope, no go. Your turn."

"So very evil," Kiel said, and flopped over onto his stomach, then slowly pushed himself to his feet. "Can't you just pop the fence into a book or something? I seem to be doing all the heavy lifting around here."

"Please just hurry," Bethany told him, shifting from foot to foot. Another roar, and her heart jumped. "Seriously, Kiel, they can hear that down in town. Whatever the Magister is doing, we need to stop him!"

"Story of my life," Kiel said, then put his hands on the gate, groaning as he touched the metal. "You have no idea how much I hate using magic on science. It makes my stomach hurt." He closed his eyes, leaning most of his weight onto the fence, then mumbled a spell.

The gate began to glow a bright red, then slowly creaked open, Kiel stumbling with it. Bethany quickly pushed past him, then grabbed his shirt and yanked him inside too, kicking the gate closed behind her. "C'mon!" she yelled, pulling on his arm.

He just glared at her, too tired to even speak at this point.

But at least he shuffled forward, letting her drag him to where she remembered the tower had been.

As they reached the base and passed through Kiel's invisibility spell, Bethany's stomach dropped again. The tower was just so huge! Even if they brought the Magister and Kiel back into his book, how would she explain *this*? "How long do your spells last?" she asked Kiel.

"Just until I fall asleep," he said.

She immediately slapped him, and his eyes flew open. "HEY!" he yelled.

"Don't fall asleep!" she hissed. "What about the forget spells? Are those going to go away too?"

"No, those are more of a permanent . . . thing," he told her. "Effect. Whatever you want to call it. This not-seeing spell is . . . it's changing what people's . . . their eyes see, and—"

She slapped him again.

"STOP IT!" he yelled. "I'm awake!"

"You didn't sound it," she whispered. "Now be quiet. The Magister might hear us!"

A roar so loud that it hurt Bethany's ears echoed through the entire tower, and Kiel glared at her. "Really? You think he's going to hear us over *that*?"

"What is that?" she asked him, her voice shaking as badly as the rest of her.

"Sounded a bit like a dragon," Kiel told her, then shrugged.

"A DRAGON?"

Kiel took a step back and glanced up at the tower. "Oh, yeah!" he said, pointing. "See? It's right there!"

Bethany's eyes widened, and she stepped back too. There, at the very top of the tower, two red, reptilian eyes glowed down.

Then, even worse, a second pair of eyes, these golden but just as reptilian, blinked on the ground to their right.

"Uh-oh," Kiel said quietly. He stepped backward, grabbing Bethany's shirt and pulling her with him. "Maybe we should, uh, back up a few feet."

"Tell me you've fought dragons before," Bethany whispered to him.

"Of course I have!" he said indignantly. "I'm Kiel Gnomenfoot, hero to your people! I've handled . . . well, *a* dragon before. Not ever two at once, but how hard can it be? Twice as hard? Three times? One of those." He stepped forward, then sort of swooned. "Whoa, how are the dragons making the ground spin? The fiends!"

The dragon on top of the tower spread its wings wide and

expelled a huge spout of fire straight into the sky, while the dragon at the bottom of the tower slinked out into the sunlight, its eyes focused on Kiel.

Wait a second. These weren't just some random dragons, created from magic. These were dragons from *books*! The golden one on the ground looked like the Dragon King from *Dimension of the Dragons* while the other had to be an Albino Red from *The Mystery of the Missing Dragon Tamer*.

This wasn't the Magister using magic. This was the Magister using *her* power to free other fictional creatures!

"This is *so* bad," Bethany whispered, backing away from the golden Dragon King as it shuffled toward them on its sixteen feet. "He's releasing fictional—"

"Don't call them that," Kiel pointed out automatically.

"He's releasing *fictional monsters* into the world!" Bethany screamed. "And I don't have any books to throw them back into!"

"Psh," Kiel said, turning to look at her. "Let me handle this. You just sit back and pretend you're reading a real, live Kiel Gnomenfoot book, while I go do the hard stuff."

The ground shook again, just like it had when the tower appeared, and the tower's front doors exploded open. Then a hand the size of a small car pushed its way out of the tower.

"Hmm, is that a giant?" Kiel asked. "That adds a little difficulty, but nothing I can't—"

Little red eyes flashed all over the tower, crawling from every window. For a second the sunlight on the silver lines in the tower blinded Bethany, but it quickly cleared, revealing the outside of the tower covered in tiny goblins made almost entirely out of teeth.

"Oh, and now there are . . . those things," Kiel said. "Okay, I *may* not have this."

And that's when the golden Dragon King snapped out, grabbed Kiel's cloak in its teeth, and swallowed him whole.

CHAPTER 26

"Isn't this where you'd normally say some inane comment meant to be funny?" Charm asked as the hordes of robotic computer viruses began to pick away at the firewall.

It was, wasn't it? But somehow the idea of having his brain overwritten by robots made everything seem less fun. "I don't know," he said. "I guess it just doesn't seem like a laughing moment."

Charm actually turned to look at him. "Whatever's wrong with you, I hope it stays that way."

Ugh, he kept forgetting to act more Kiel-like. Why was he so worried about the robot viruses, anyway? There was no way they'd be in serious danger, not at this point in the story. They had to make it through to the end, after all. These robot viruses were just an empty threat designed to make it *look* like they were in danger, probably until the very last moment when

Charm would come up with something and save them.

That thought made Owen feel a bit better, and he gave the marching horde a condescending look. Stupid robot viruses. *Nice try.*

"Why don't we just search our way out of this or something?" Owen asked, feeling a bit better but still preferring to be back on the ship as soon as possible. "Use those tubes to escape?"

"The Original Computer is way too old for that," she said, throwing a look over her shoulder at the robots staring at her from the top of the wall. "We have to go out the way we came in. That's the only input *or* output."

Owen turned back to the firewall. "We're not going anywhere without taking out a *lot* of robots." In fact, were there even more than before? And less of the ones and zeros. "Hey, I think they might be multiplying."

"Of course they are," Charm snapped. "They're taking over the computer. Should only be a matter of time before everything in here is the virus. That's why I need you to *be quiet* for the foreseeable future, if I'm going to find the Seventh Key's location before it's overwritten."

As Owen watched, a few robots touched one of the remaining streams of ones and zeroes, and the stream sort of blipped, then glitched into an exact copy of the robot.

"Why is this taking so long?" Charm shouted. "There shouldn't even *be* this much memory in the computer!"

"I could start attacking them or something," Owen said, looking around inside the firewall for a computer rock or something to throw.

"No weapons," Charm said. "In here, all a ray gun will do is connect you to it, giving it a way to overwrite you. The only thing that'd work on those viruses is an antivirus program, and I didn't bring that kind of gun. The firewall's the only protection we have."

The wall shook harder, all the way up from the foundation. Charm glanced over her shoulder and frowned.

All this wall shaking made Owen less confident in his whole *we're fine, the book won't kill us this early* theory. "Can't you make another firewall or something?" he said, backing away a bit. "Before this one falls down?"

"I could, if you want me to lose the Seventh Key's location forever," Charm said, typing frantically.

"Yeah, but we're not going to be able to use that if they overwrite our brains, right?"

No, *stop*. That wasn't going to happen. They were going to be fine! Owen repeated this to himself over and over, before a completely out of nowhere idea derailed his train of thought.

What if because he wasn't *actually* Kiel, Owen had done something just slightly . . . different? And that slight difference ended up throwing the entire plot off, meaning he and Charm were going to suffer some kind of horrific, awful, grotesque death that was never meant to happen in the story?

No. *No.* That couldn't happen. Jonathan Porterhouse would never put them in a situation that they couldn't get out of.

That *Kiel* couldn't get out of.

Uh-oh.

"We need to get out of here, Charm," Owen said, backing away from the shaking firewall. "They're going to break through any second. I *really* don't want to be a robot."

"So *do* something," Charm said. "Cast a spell and distract them."

"I don't have my spell book!"

"MAKE ONE!"

"MAKE—?" Owen shouted, then stopped midyell. Make

one? Could he? He concentrated on his hand, thinking about a spell book instead of a notebook, and . . .

And a tablet appeared in his hand with the words spell e-book scrolling across the screen.

Wow, seriously?

Still, any port in a stormy sea, or whatever that phrase was. He swiped the screen on, then paged through the spell e-book. *I need something that will work on a virus,* he thought at it.

Nothing appeared.

Ugh. What was the problem now? This spell book hadn't existed long enough to hate him. He quickly swiped through spell after spell, finally stopping on a Balls of Flame page. Good enough. He tapped the screen, feeling that warm glow he'd felt the very first time he'd learned a spell, then quickly cast a fireball right at the viruses over the firewall.

The robots glitched as the fireball passed through them, then immediately cleared up and began their infection of the firewall again.

"Magic isn't *working*!" Owen shouted at Charm.

"It's a digital realm!" she shouted back. "Find something that'll work *here*!"

"Like what?" *Don't panic, don't panic, don't panic.* It was going to be fine! Next spell . . . nope. Not that one either. Or that one . . . wait. "Frozen in Time?" he asked Charm.

"You want to stop the robots in time? We still can't touch them, and since they're everywhere, that doesn't really help us escape!"

"That's the best I'm finding!" Owen yelled, frantically flicking through spell after spell.

"GOT IT," Charm shouted, and shoved her palm in his face. There, inside her hand was a glowing light. "It's right there, downloaded to my avatar: the last known location of the very first magician, the one who created the magic keys. All we need to do is upload this to the *Scientific Method*, and we'll be one step away from the Seventh Key."

"Great?" Owen said. "That's helpful if we ever get out of here!"

"Let me see if I can program something," Charm said, sitting back down, only to jump to her feet as the computer glitched, morphing into one of the robot viruses. "Kiel, they're in!"

Owen grabbed her arm and yanked her away from the robot, back toward the wall. The robot marched toward them, its hand outstretched. They tried to keep away from it by circling around the firewall, but there wasn't that much room inside the wall to begin with.

"There has to be something else that works on them, other than antivirus ray guns!" Owen shouted at Charm.

"They don't have any kind of physical presence in here. They're just lines of code," Charm said, her fists held out in front of her like she might punch the robot. "Even the firewall is really just dead space to keep the code from passing over it."

There had to be something. If they really were viruses, maybe a healing spell? He quickly found one, then cast it at the robots. Each one glitched for a second, then grew a foot taller.

"This is the worst you've ever been at magic!" Charm shouted at him. "When did you get so bad?"

"I'm doing my best!"

Computers! There had to be something else about computers, something that maybe Kiel wouldn't know, but who cared? Right now, he'd use anything he could get! "What was that you said about memory?" Owen asked, the robot inside the firewall getting closer and closer with every circle. "Computers need that to run things, right? The memory's where the programs actually run?"

Charm snorted. "How'd you know that?"

"You probably told me before. Who cares! It's true, isn't it?"

"It's a bit more complicated—"

"So that's a yes. I've got an idea." He flipped quickly through the spell e-book until he found the spell he was looking for. "Okay, this is a horrible idea, but I'm desperate. The internal logic of this place might finally work *for* us."

"What spell are you casting?"

Bits of the firewall began to crash in around them. The robot inside stopped, laid a hand on the wall, and began infecting it from the inside. The wall immediately began to glitch out of existence.

"Amnesty of Amnesia," Owen said with a wince, holding up the spell e-book to show her. "A forget spell."

Charm just stared at him.

"It's magic, it'll work!" he said. "Magic is about doing the impossible. And right now, if those programs need memory to run, then let's take that memory away!"

"There are *so many* logical issues with what you're saying right now that I don't even know where to—"

The firewall glitched completely, crumbling away into nothingness. Now unstoppable, the Science Soldier robot viruses advanced, marching in unison right at them.

"Cast it!" Charm shouted, backing into him.

Owen quickly absorbed the spell as the robots advanced. The magic filled his body, warming him from his hair to his toes, then exploded outward, filling the entire universe of the computer.

The robots didn't stop.

"It didn't *work!*" Charm shouted.

"Give it a second!"

"We don't *have* a second!"

The nearest robots extended their arms, their hands just inches from Owen and Charm.

This was not how Owen wanted to die. In fact, he didn't want to die at *all*. But definitely not in a book somewhere, being brain-erased by robots. He'd much rather die from having too much money and too big a house a thousand years in the future.

"It can't end this way," Charm said. "I won't accept it. No robot is taking over my body, and Dr. Verity is *not* going to win." She gritted her teeth so hard, veins popped in her digital head. And then she stepped in front of him, her eyes shut, her arms stretched out.

"Stay behind me, Kiel!" Charm shouted. "The viruses overwriting my brain should buy you an extra ten seconds or so. Use them!"

"NO!" Owen shouted.

The nearest robot's hand reached out to grab Charm, and she flinched, closing her eyes.

Which meant she didn't see all the robots glitch out of existence, one by one.

When the last one had disappeared, Owen reached out and tapped Charm so she'd open her eyes. As soon as he touched her, she punched him with her robot arm, sending him flying.

"OW!" he screamed in pain, and her eyes opened.

"Wait," she said. "That was you? What happened?"

Owen started to say something, then just pointed up at the huge hundred-foot-high letters in the black-and-green sky, blinking like a digital clock after the power went out.

"ERROR," they said. "OUT OF MEMORY."

CHAPTER 27

"$\mathcal{K}$iel?" Bethany said blankly, her mind refusing to work. That hadn't just happened. A fictional dragon from *Dimension of the Dragons* hadn't just swallowed Kiel Gnomenfoot. Fictional dragons didn't eat fictional heroes from fictional books, not in the real world. Not even in fictional books, because heroes were main characters, and that kind of thing just didn't happen to main characters!

She weakly backed away from the Dragon King, who was licking his lips. Dragons, a giant, goblins, not to mention magic towers and good-turned-evil magicians . . . This was a dream! That was the only possible explanation. This was all a dream because she'd said no to Owen and felt guilty!

The had-to-be-a-dream Albino Red dragon caught sight of her from the air, then dove down, its talons spread in anticipation.

The roar of the attacking dragon tore through her body, and almost without thinking about it, she leaped out of the way a moment before those enormous claws ripped through the earth where she'd been standing.

The dragon screamed in rage, then pulled back up into the sky again, circling around for another pass. The golden Dragon King finally noticed her as well, and began to gallop toward her, all sixteen legs moving at once. And the teethy, creepy little goblins kept swarming off the tower.

RUN! her mind screamed at her. *Get out of here! This is real, you idiot! Whether you want it to be or not, this is real and you're going to get eaten, just like Kiel! If you die, Owen will be stuck in that nowhere prison forever!*

She pushed herself to her feet and began to run from the Dragon King, only to throw herself out of the way of the diving Albino Red again as the goblins raced after her in an ever-growing swarm. Where was she supposed to go? For now, this was all behind the invisibility curtain, but if she ran away from the tower, the entire town would see what was happening.

Wait, the invisibility curtain. Wasn't that supposed to have disappeared if Kiel had . . . fallen asleep? Wasn't being eaten worse than sleeping?

She dodged an Albino Red dragon strike, only to get tossed to the ground by one of the Dragon King's sixteen clawed feet. It roared, raising its head over her to attack.

And then it froze, an odd expression on its face.

"I . . . hate . . . being . . . eaten!" shouted a muffled voice. And then, slowly, the Dragon King's jaws began to push apart, revealing a very slimy, very annoyed Kiel Gnomenfoot. "You have no idea how many times this has happened," he told Bethany in disgust. "You always forget the smell." With that, he leaped out of the dragon's mouth a step ahead of the jaws snapping closed, landing right beside her on the ground. "I'll tell you what: Nothing in the world wakes you up like the smell of a dragon's stomach. *Nothing.*"

Bethany just stared at him as he gestured with both hands, and new magic wands appeared in them. He quickly aimed one at the golden dragon, which shrank to the size of a mouse. The other wand shot some sort of magical energy into the sky, wrapping the Albino Red's wings around its body and sending it crashing to the ground.

"Kiel?" she said. "You're alive?"

"Forty-two," he said with a grimace. "That's how many times I've been eaten. Well, forty-three now." He grinned. "Don't let me have all the fun here, Book Girl! Get in on this!"

Despite the dragons, the tower, the Magister, the giant, everything . . . Bethany just had to smile. "You are *insane*, Kiel Gnomenfoot."

"That's why everyone loves me," he said with a wink. "Now do that fiction thing you do! It'll be fun!"

"I don't have any books!"

"Weren't there a whole bunch in that house right there?" Kiel said, then ran over to the crashed Albino Red dragon, which was trying to right itself. Kiel climbed onto its back and kicked its sides with his heels. "Up, dragon! I need a better view of things."

The dragon roared and snapped its jaws at him, but immediately stopped, a red glow surrounding its head. Instantly the dragon calmed down, then leaped back into the air, a laughing, still slimy Kiel on its back.

Bethany watched him take off for a second, then gasped as a wave of goblins came barreling toward her. She turned and sprinted in the opposite direction, toward Jonathan Porterhouse's mansion, just hoping the front door was unlocked.

It wasn't, but when she turned around to find another way in, three goblins leaped at her, missed, and hit the door instead. The door collapsed inward, giving her a way in. "Thanks," she told the goblins as she jumped over them, feeling a weird surge of energy, like she'd had too much caffeine. Where was this coming from? This was the worst thing that'd ever happened to anyone ever, and part of her was *enjoying* it!

The entryway still had a large blackened spot where the Magister had blown up the empty journal he thought they were jumping into. She skidded around the spot, then ran as fast as she could for the library. There wouldn't be time to find the correct books that the dragons, goblins, and giant all came from, and it was altogether possible that the Magister had those in his tower anyway, since he'd freed the characters to begin with. Still, with as many books as the library had, there would have to be enough good ones to find something useful.

She threw open the doors of the library and came to a complete stop.

The shelves were empty. Of the thousands and thousands of books, Bethany saw just two scattered on the floor, forgotten.

The magnitude of what that meant hit Bethany like a rock, and for a brief second she considered just lying down and giving up. Then she remembered the teeth of the goblins chasing her and she slammed the door instead, focusing on the remaining two books.

She quickly grabbed her only options and spread them out on the library's desk in front of her.

This had to be a joke.

Twenty Thousand Leagues Under the Sea and a large leather-bound copy of *Emma,* by Jane Austen. A book about a submarine fighting a giant squid and one about an English matchmaker in the 1800s. . . . Seriously?

The library doors burst open, and a horde of goblins scrambled through, coming right at her, their spittle leading the way. She ducked behind the desk, but they leaped over it, arms outstretched for her.

"FINE, you get nineteenth-century romance!" she shouted, then smashed the nearest goblin over the head with *Emma.* Another one jumped at her, and it got some Jane Austen too. "Who's next?" Bethany shouted, smashing goblins in the face over and over with the book's cover. "You? You want some of this too?!"

The goblins circled around her, surrounding her. They swarmed up and over her arms, pulling her down to the ground, teeth everywhere. She kicked and growled, then turned to her other weapon, pulling random pages out of *Twenty Thousand*

Leagues. Instead of jumping in, though, she just stuck a hand in, then pulled out whatever she could feel.

A gush of water like a fire hose exploded from the first page, right into the nearest group of goblins. Bethany scrambled back to her feet, then pushed her hand into a second page, pulling out more of the ocean. Then a third page, and a fourth.

Soon the entire room was filled with a good inch or two of water. Though each page immediately stopped shooting water as soon as she dropped it, the force of the ocean spitting out of the tiny pages was enough to send almost all of the goblins flying. There were little unconscious toothy goblins everywhere, and the few remaining ones were easily cleaned up with a little *Emma.*

Bethany dropped to the wet floor, breathing so hard she thought she might faint. Was this what it was like being fictional? Doing crazy things just to keep yourself alive? Not even caring about the consequences? She glanced around at the former library, now aquarium, of Jonathan Porterhouse's mansion. There were even a few fish flopping around.

Fictional fish. This was all so very, very odd.

Finally, Bethany took a deep breath and stood back up,

grabbed her two weapons, then went back out to see how Kiel was doing.

As she emerged outside, something enormous with laces slammed into the ground just in front of her. She looked up, then up, and up some more, to where a giant easily as tall as the tower held Kiel and his dragon tightly in a fist, keeping either from moving.

"Oh, hi!" Kiel shouted down. "I hope you found something good in there, because things took a slight turn out here. Nothing I can't handle, of course, but I'll let you help if it makes you feel better!"

CHAPTER 28

"You were going to sacrifice yourself for me," Owen told Charm as they walked toward a deep, black, ominous-looking cave on the side of the tallest mountain in all of Magisteria. "Back in the Original Computer. You tried to—"

"I wouldn't have, if I'd known you'd bring it up again," Charm told him. "Can we stop wasting time?"

"You like me, don't you," Owen said, inwardly grinning. Sure, it was Kiel she actually had tried to save, but still.

She glared at him. "Every minute we waste, more Magisterians suffer. Keep that in mind the longer you spout on about nonsense."

"Okay," Owen said, stopping in front of the cave. "But next time we almost die, warn me before you try to jump in front of any ray guns for me. I'll just duck instead."

Charm narrowed her eyes, both human and robotic. "Trust

me, it won't happen again." She turned toward the cave and shook her head. "Why don't your people ever just live in nicely lit places? It's always towers or castles or dank, dark caves."

"You're asking the wrong person," Owen said, peering into the nothingness.

"According to the Original Computer, this is it, the last known location of the First Magician," Charm said, checking a wrist computer to be sure. "So all we need to do is find him and ask where the Seventh Key is. How hard can it be?"

A chill ran through Owen as he remembered Charm saying those exact words in the previous books. "Could you not do that anymore?"

"Do what?"

"Ask 'How hard can it be?' Have you not noticed a pattern, whenever you say that?"

"No."

"What'd you say before the dragon's lair?" Owen said, counting off on his fingers. "Or right before the trip to that alternate, evil dimension? Or in the future? Or the nothingness at the end of the universe? Or with the ice giants, the ruins of that school for magic—"

"I'm a positive person!" Charm shouted at him, her robot eye shooting him a death look.

"No, you're not," Owen said, unable to keep from smiling at her. She was just so cute sometimes, what with her tough robot half and her tough nonrobot other half.

She snorted. "Who cares! Why is it so wrong to say, anyway?"

"Because you're *asking* for bad things," Owen told her, still grinning. "That's how this works. You say 'could be worse,' and things suddenly are. It's called irony, and authors—I mean, the universe loves it."

Charm snorted. "You magicians. You act like there's someone out there watching us." She waved her hand up at the sky. "No one can see us, Kiel. And no one's going to use what I say against us just because it'd be some kind of ironic situation. Try thinking logically for once."

Owen shrugged. "Fine. *You* go first, then, Ms. Positive Attitude. Just wait and see what eats you."

She held up her twin ray guns. "Bring it on." She turned to the cave, then paused. "Though we could use a little light." She took out three miniature light balls, then tossed them into the air. The balls glowed with illumination and floated into the cave.

All three then immediately crashed to the ground and went out.

"Right," Owen said. *"How hard can it be?"*

She smacked him. "This is a *magic* cave. It's probably got some antiscience something or other. This is why you're along, for times when the laws of nature get thwarted."

"Thwarted?" Owen said, then brought up a spell in his head. This time, he was actually ready. Light of My Life had already been looked up, memorized, and was ready to go. The spell filled him with warmth, then passed through him to light the immediate entryway of the cave. It wasn't much better than the light balls had been, but at least they'd be able to see what they were tripping over.

"After you," Charm said, gesturing for him to go first. "It's your spell. If you die in front of me, I promise to shoot whatever killed you really hard."

"That's sweet," Owen said, but led the way in.

The original magician had picked an odd place to live, if he was still here. The walls, ceiling, and floor all looked . . . unnatural. It was as if the cave had been built to *look* like a cave, not just formed over the centuries. The stalactites were just too perfect, and too evenly spaced out, while the path was just a bit too smooth.

"Something's wrong," Charm said. "If science really doesn't work in here, my arm and leg would have gone dead. There's more going on than we can see." She put a hand on the wall. "I think it's more localized than that. Some sort of strong electronic pulse could have disrupted the light's hovering ability near the entrance. But what would be the point of that? The only thing that'd need such a strong power source would be some sort of . . ." She paused. "Oh."

"Oh?"

"Nothing."

"What's nothing? Don't do that."

"Just thinking that some sort of energy bars coming down over the entrance to the cave might produce an effect that would have killed my lights. That's it."

"Energy bars."

"Yes. Energy bars."

"Like bars. Made of energy. Say, for a prison. To keep someone or something trapped inside."

"Or outside," Charm said with a shrug, still pushing her way through the cave.

Owen grabbed her arm, his heart racing. "So you're saying this is a trap?"

"Probably," Charm said. "It wouldn't be the first one. Who cares? If it is, we fight our way out. That's how this works."

Owen swallowed some choice words for her, then forced himself to continue, visions of the virus robots in the Original Computer floating through his mind.

His light spell didn't do much to illuminate more than a few feet in front of them, and did even less behind them. Glancing back, Owen couldn't see the entrance, despite it being broad daylight outside. For some reason his mouth felt really dry, and he wanted nothing more than to run back out the way they'd come and never return.

Hopefully the book was almost done, because this was *not* turning out to be as much fun as he'd originally thought. There was much less awesome magic and science, and *way* too much almost dying. Had the books always been this dangerous?

And even if they had, where was Nobody, anyway? Wasn't he supposed to be bringing Kiel and the Magister back? And seriously, what had happened to Bethany? Was she ever going to come back for him? Or had she decided to punish him by leaving him in the book to die some horrible death in the cave? Was she reading the seventh book right now, laughing at him?

Or worse, was she in trouble, and couldn't help him even if he needed it, just like he couldn't help her?

Nobody said Owen might be stuck in the book until the end. Fine. He'd just live out the rest of the story as quickly as he could, then hopefully find Nobody or Bethany waiting for him. And if Bethany *was* in trouble, then all the more reason to get things wrapped up here so he could get back and find out.

None of these thoughts were making him feel better, so Owen clutched his irritated spell book closer to his chest and tried to put them out of his mind.

It felt like years before they actually found something, though it was probably just months. Or minutes. One of the two. But gradually they began to notice odd breaks in the cave. Here or there, instead of rock, there'd be just a hint of something metallic, as if the rock were some sort of fake covering. Owen knocked on the rock, and it felt real, but why was there metal behind it? And metal, in Magisteria? They always used wood or stone in their buildings. Metal was far too scientific.

"Look," Charm said, pointing just ahead into the darkness.

"There's something behind that wall right there." Owen followed her to the spot, and carefully, slowly reached out to touch what felt like glass.

"Is that . . . a screen?" he asked.

"A computer monitor," Charm told him. "It hasn't had power in years, looks like. But I'm starting to think this isn't the First Magician's home. I think it's some kind of Science Prison."

"For who?" Owen said. "Him or us?"

"Let's not ruin that surprise," Charm said, powering up her ray guns.

Agh. Why couldn't this part of the mission just be easy and not potentially kill them?! Didn't readers want to have a nice chapter of nothing bad happening?

The walls crumbled worse the farther they went, until finally the cave stone stopped altogether, and Owen's light spell revealed steel floors, walls, and ceiling. Huge, old computers lined the floor, stacked on top of one another as if they had no better use. Broken glass bottles and tubes were everywhere, with burn marks around some of them, as if someone had destroyed a laboratory.

But the worst thing of all was the bodies.

"NOPE, I'M LEAVING!" Owen shouted when he saw the first one.

"Calm down!" Charm said. "It's just a Science Soldier!" She kicked the robot lying on the ground with a missing head. "See? Robots! What's there to worry about?"

"There are, like, fifty of them," Owen said. "What took them out, Charm? And what will that thing do to us?"

"The enemy of my enemy isn't my enemy," she told him, then stepped over the robotic bodies to move on, her ray guns held high.

"That's not how that phrase goes," Owen whispered after her, then hurried to catch up.

The robotic bodies grew more frequent until they just about blocked the tunnel forward. Charm began to yank the robots off of one another, trying to clear a way, then gave Owen a questioning look. He sighed, then helped her carry Science Soldier remains out of the way, just enough so they could climb through.

"We're going to die here, aren't we?" he said as they carried the last body away.

"Whatever happened here, happened years ago," she told him. "Look at the layer of dust. There's no way whatever did this is still here."

Owen groaned loudly. "What did I tell you about jinxing us?"

"You never used to be this nervous," Charm told him. "Stop worrying. Logic is logic, whether it sounds positive or not. There's just no chance that something would have destroyed all these things, then left them for this long. It wouldn't make sense."

Something clanked behind them, and they both froze.

"Do you see what you did?" Owen whispered at her.

"It's just the robots settling," Charm told him. "Stop being paranoid."

He gave her a dark look. "You know that we just effectively blocked our own way out by moving those bodies, right?"

"Of course I knew that," she said, clearly lying. She gave him an irritated look, then pushed him farther into the cave. "It'll be fine. The First Magician will probably be just like the Magister, nice and friendly."

A few steps past the pile, and Owen stopped so quickly that Charm plowed right into him, knocking both of them to the ground.

The light wasn't good, but it'd been clear enough to show Owen exactly how much of the First Magician was still around to be nice and friendly. Owen raised his gaze from a skeleton foot, to a skeleton leg, then up to the skeleton's completely bony body, seated on what looked to be a throne entirely formed from circuit boards or something. The skeleton held some sort of magical wand in one hand, and wore a metal bracelet that looked almost like Charm's computer watch on the other.

"Or, he could just be dead," Owen said, strangely relieved. "Looks like we're not going to find out much from him."

Charm stared at the body for a moment, then shook her head. "Nope. You can do this."

"Do what?"

"Bring him back." She pointed at the spell book under his arm. "You know. Magic."

Owen blinked, then blinked again. "Um . . . what?"

CHAPTER 29

Slight turn?" Bethany screamed up at Kiel. "I thought you had this!"

"I do!" Kiel shouted. "Just not quite as quickly as I'd hoped!"

The giant shook Kiel and the dragon up and down, then threw them both straight at Bethany, who gasped and covered herself with her two books.

A powerful wind almost knocked her off her feet, and she looked up to find the dragon frantically flapping four new pairs of wings, along with its original two, in order to right itself. All six of the wings glowed red from Kiel's magic as the dragon came to a halt just a foot above Bethany's head, then launched back into the sky.

"I told you!" Kiel yelled. "I have this handled!"

The dragon climbed so quickly that it shot right past the giant's head, flying too high for the giant to actually reach. The giant roared in anger, bent its massive legs, then did maybe the worst possible thing it could do: It jumped right into the air. All ten million pounds of it.

The entire world slowed down as Bethany's mind exploded. When that thing landed, not only would the town be destroyed from the impact, but people would feel the tremor for *hundreds* of miles. Not to mention that everyone anywhere close was just going to be completely buried in rock and goblins.

All the blood drained from Bethany's face as she dropped *Emma*, then sprinted forward, right to the last place in the world she should be going.

The giant strained to grab Kiel at the top of its jump, its massive hand just missing the dragon. Even free of the giant's hand, though, there wasn't much Kiel could do about the giant crashing back to the ground.

But maybe Bethany could.

She stopped directly under the giant's now plummeting feet and opened her remaining book.

There was no way this would work. *No way.* She was going to die, and so was everyone in town. This could *not work*.

She did it anyway.

The giant came crashing down right on top of her. Bethany

raised one hand into the air and dropped *Twenty Thousand Leagues Under the Sea* onto the ground beneath her, stepping onto a page. Then she cringed and waited for the giant to hit.

The moment the giant touched Bethany's hand, they both went plowing right into the pages of the book, exploding into the middle of the book's ocean.

The force of the giant's fall sent both monster and Bethany rocketing into the deep, dark depths of the water, but Bethany didn't wait around. Without even bothering to figure out which way was up, she immediately jumped out of the book and back to the real world, her clothes soaked, but about as uncrushed as she possibly could have hoped.

Just to make sure, she frantically patted down her arms, legs, and head, then shrieked in absolute joy.

"KIEL!" she shouted. "Did you see that? I did it!"

"Bethany?" Kiel said, landing beside her with his dragon. "You may want to—"

"I just beat the giant!" she shouted. "ME! After it jumped up to catch you, I took the entire thing down! It's in the middle of a fictional ocean now! I can't even believe that worked!"

"Bethany?"

"Wow, my heart is racing!" she said, one hand on her chest.

"I should have died! We *all* should have died! That was so amazing!"

Kiel grabbed her by the shoulders, then slowly turned her around.

There, right in front of her, stood the Magister. And behind him were far too many fictional fantasy monsters to count. Griffins. Unicorns. More dragons. Trolls and witches and enormous wolves and knights and huge blobs of monster and too many other things that Bethany didn't even recognize.

"Kiel," the Magister said, and Bethany couldn't tell if he was happy or sad to see his apprentice. "I thought . . . I believed . . . I am glad you have returned. Both of you. You must now be ready to admit the error of your ways, then?"

"Not exactly," Kiel said. "It's time to go home, Magi, and put everything back the way we found it here."

The Magister raised a hand toward Kiel, then dropped it, closing his eyes. He shook his head, and when his eyes opened, any trace of happiness at Kiel's presence was gone. "No," he said, his voice low. "We will not be returning to that world. It never truly existed, just as none of these creatures' worlds did. And to those who would control us, rule us, I say the time has come to take our lives back." His eyes hardened. "I don't understand what sort of power the people of this world have, to create us from nothing, then dictate our lives. But I will do everything I can to make sure that comes to a stop right now."

"What do you mean?" Bethany said, holding her copy of *Twenty Thousand Leagues Under the Sea* out like a sword. "What are you going to do?"

The Magister turned to her. "First, as I promised, I'll free all fictional creatures I can find. I've explained the way things work to my friends, here. And they'd like to speak to their creators, much as I'd still like to." He held out a hand. "Give me Jonathan Porterhouse, and no harm shall come to you."

Bethany swallowed hard. "What for?"

"He will accompany any and all other writers into a fictional world, where they will be free to live or die as they can." He spread his hands. "It is the only way to ensure an end to their power, and seems the fairest way to imprison them. After all, it is no more than they have done to us."

Bethany's eyes went wide. "You can't just send everyone into books! Do you have any idea what would happen?"

"*Do you know what happened to me?*" the Magister roared. "Fighting a war for the freedom of my people, only to find none of it is real? Let the writers of this world decide if their dystopian futures, their dangerous magic, their monsters and stories of terror are so entertaining once it's their *own* life or death they're living out!"

Her legs shaking, Bethany took a step forward. "I'm not going to let you do this," she said quietly. "I can't."

"Bethany, don't," Kiel whispered to her, but she shook her head.

"There's nothing you can do that I can't undo," she told the Magister. "So go ahead. Steal my power some more. I'll just find a way to put everything back where it belongs, and will keep at it as long as I live."

"I understand," the Magister said. "Then I suppose you leave me with no other option."

"NO!" Kiel shouted, but it was too late. The Magister gestured, and Bethany immediately crumpled to the ground, unmoving.

CHAPTER 30

W hat's the problem?" Charm said, waving her robotic hand for Owen to hurry up. "We don't have much more time!"

"Give me a minute," Owen told her, trying not to look at the skeleton sitting on the computer-circuit throne. Kiel had mentioned wanting to bring his parents back to life using magic (before he found out he was a clone of Dr. Verity, of course), but the Magister had always forbidden it, saying that such dark magic led to horrible results. "It's dangerous, this kind of magic."

"So is letting Dr. Verity destroy all of Magisteria because we didn't find the last key." She checked her watch. "In just under ten hours, by the way."

Owen gritted his teeth. "Fine! But if this goes badly, then I'm blaming you."

"This went badly about a year ago, so blame me all you want." She moved away to watch back down the cave tunnel the way they'd come in. "I still don't understand why the First Magician would be here, in a cave made with computers and metal. It doesn't make sense. The bars weren't down. He wasn't imprisoned."

"Maybe you can ask him in a minute," Owen mumbled, running a hand over the spell book. The book started to snap at him, but he'd gotten used to dodging it now. Even with the hostility, it was nice to have the actual book back in his hands; the e-book version just didn't feel right. "I know you and I don't get along," he whispered to the book. "And that's fine. But right now, I need a forbidden spell to bring a dead person back to life for a few minutes. Notice I said need, not want, 'cause I don't *want* to do this any more than you want me to. So can we just agree that this is a horrible idea, and get on with it?"

The book's harsh glare turned to surprise, but it still didn't move, at least not at first. Finally, almost reluctantly, the book slowly flipped open toward the back, revealing pages of black paper and bloodred writing.

Um. There'd *never* been any mention of black pages and red writing in the Kiel Gnomenfoot books before. Nope. Not one.

The spells herein are forbidden to all but the most powerful magicians, the first page read. *Without the utmost power and control, these spells will turn on you and destroy you as well as your surroundings. Be warned. Be AFRAID.*

Okay. This was *such* a bad idea.

"What's taking so long?" Charm asked him, one foot on a Science Soldier body. "Do you need me to hold your hand?"

For the briefest of moments, the idea of her holding his hand derailed all his thoughts. He shook it off and showed her the black pages. "The book says we're messing with power beyond our control. Just so you know." He tried to grab the page to turn it, but for some reason, the paper resisted his touch, and he had to use his fingernails to pry the page free from the rest of the book.

The picture on the next page tied his stomach into knots.

"Um, maybe not that one," he said quickly, swallowing hard.

"Seriously, we don't have time, Kiel," Charm said. "Find a spell and bring the dead back to life already!"

The next spell was worse, followed by one he couldn't even look at, so he kept turning pages until he found a spell showing a person rising from a coffin. Conquer Death, the spell said, but that was about all he could read off the page. The spell itself was written in some other language, not even the fun nonsense words like the rest of the Kiel Gnomenfoot spells.

No, these words sounded *dark*.

This was so weird. Why would these spells be any different from the others? Wouldn't Jonathan Porterhouse have written them all the same?

"Krtttlqqqfbapr," Owen said, trying to work his way through the first syllable of the first word. Weirdly, he felt nothing this time. No warm *or* cold feeling, just strangely . . . empty.

A sudden chill made Owen shiver, like the entire cave dropped a good twenty degrees in temperature.

"Did it just get colder in here?" Charm asked, glancing at him and rubbing her arms. Great. He hadn't imagined it.

The next word came out, and the light spell he'd cast earlier flickered, struggling to remain lit. The shadows all around them seemed to grow taller and somehow *hungrier*.

Well. Things definitely seemed to be taking a very horror-movie-type turn, didn't they?

Instead of waiting, Owen just shut his eyes, recited the last word, and finished the spell as quickly as he could.

And just like that, his light spell fizzled out, leaving them in complete darkness.

For a second, nothing happened, and Owen and Charm both waited, holding their breath in the dark. Then a pair of sickly green lights lit up the darkness, right about where the First Magician's skull had been.

"Finally," Charm said.

"So, so bad," Owen whispered.

The light in the skeleton's eyes expanded, flooding that sickly green shade out to surround the First Magician's bones. The light wrapped itself around the body, then faded into ripped skin, fading organs, and other unpleasant things.

"Um, Mr. First Magician sir?" Owen squeaked, his voice somewhere at the bottom of his pants.

The green eyes didn't respond.

"Oh, Kiel," Charm said quietly. "Please don't tell me you just made him a zombie." Owen noticed that the green light reflected off her ray guns, which she'd pointed at the former skeleton.

Green Eyes shuddered once, then again. Finally, his formerly skeletal arms moved, and he pushed himself to his now flesh-ish feet. The decaying hands pointed somewhere generally in Owen's direction, and they began to glow green like his eyes.

Then the energy flickered out from his fingers to explode throughout the cave.

"DOWN!" Charm yelled, shoving Owen to the floor. She shot her ray guns at the magician, but the blasts just bounced off that green light and back into the cave.

"What's he doing?" Owen whispered, his voice hoarse.

Behind them, metal began to creak and moan, almost like a living thing. Voice boxes crackled with static. Rock scraped against robot.

The First Magician's green eyes turned down and stared directly at the two of them.

"I *might* have zombified him," Owen admitted.

"That's not all," Charm said, nodding over her shoulder. Owen threw a glance behind them, where all the broken Science Soldiers now had glowing green eyes, at least the ones that still *had* eyes. Even those without eyes had begun picking themselves up and were shuffling mechanically toward Charm and Owen.

"Okay, great," Charm said. "Now the robots are zombies *too*.

That's not even possible. This really went well. *Nice job, Kiel.*"

"YOU were the one who told me to make him live again!" Owen screamed at her.

Charm started to shout back, then looked up just in time to see the zombie First Magician's hand light with green fire, then fire that magic directly at them both.

CHAPTER 31

A birthday party. Four candles on the cake. Bethany watched, dreamlike, as a bunch of little kids screamed and yelled, while a woman and a man corraled them all toward the table.

In front of the cake sat a little girl with bronze-colored hair, wearing a bright-blue dress and a huge smile.

"Daddy, watch!" she shouted, bending her head over the cake.

Then she pitched face-first straight into it, sending frosting, candles, and cake flying everywhere.

The man laughed, long and loudly as the girl in the blue dress pulled her head out of the cake and laughed too, wiping the frosting off her face with both hands, then shoving those hands into her mouth.

"That's not how we eat cake!" the woman said, but smiled in spite of herself. "What about the other kids?"

"You heard her, kids!" the man said. "Go for it!"

One by one, the kids shoved their faces into the cake, taking away mouthfuls as they retreated for the next kid in line to have a turn. Cake and frosting ended up on every surface in the dining room, while the girl in the blue dress clapped her hands loudly. "I love my party!" she shouted.

Bethany walked through the room unnoticed, no one touching her, even as the kids ran around her, mere inches away. It was as if she weren't there at all, a presence that no one could see or touch.

She squatted in front of the girl in the blue dress.

"I'm Bethany," Bethany said to the girl, everything feeling unreal and foggy. "What's your name?"

"Bethany?" said the man, and Bethany turned. As did the girl in the blue dress.

The man held up a pile of wrapped gifts. "Who's ready to open some presents?"

"PRESENTS!" the girl in the blue dress yelled, and ran past Bethany toward the living room.

"Get them out of here," the woman told the man. "I'll . . . well, I was going to say clean up, but I think we're past that now."

"This should distract them for a little while at least," the man said, carrying the presents into the other room.

"No," Bethany whispered, but wasn't sure exactly why. What was this? Why did it seem so familiar?

"You know how this story goes, Bethany," said a deep male voice, a voice she recognized. Bethany looked around, but she was alone now, apart from the woman. The man and all the kids had left to open presents in the other room.

"I don't," Bethany said, fighting to clear her head. "Who are you? Where . . . where is this?"

"This is your home," the voice said. "You are living out the story of your life. A mistake was made here, a mistake that will haunt you for years to come."

"I'll . . . I'll change it," Bethany said, and took a step toward the living room, not knowing what the mistake was, but feeling like that's where she ought to be. "I'll fix things. Whatever went wrong, I'll make it right."

"Will you?" the voice asked, and suddenly Bethany froze, unable to move. She struggled against whatever invisible bonds held her, but they tightened even more in response.

From the other room the girl in the blue dress yelled in

surprise and happiness. All the other kids shouted too. Something about a gift.

"This is your life, Bethany," said the deep voice. "Yet you are not in control here. You have no power. Your life happens here, now, at *my* will, and you have no power to change it."

"No," Bethany whispered, and something in her mind screamed that she'd been here before, seen all of this. Years and years ago . . . The memory was so hazy, though. Why couldn't she think?

"What is it?" the man in the other room asked.

"A book!" shouted the girl in the blue dress.

The woman in the dining room next to Bethany froze in place, then dropped the plates she was holding back to the table. "No," she whispered, just like Bethany had.

"How does this feel, Bethany?" asked the deep voice. Time seemed to slow down as Bethany watched the woman start to run to the other room, her mouth open like she was screaming something.

And then Bethany was moving with her, too slowly to do anything, too slowly to change anything, just fast enough to reach the doorway to the living room at the exact same point as the woman, as her mother. . . .

The empty living room. Empty but for a few wrapped gifts, a couple of toys, and a book lying open on the couch right in the middle of everything.

"NO!" her mother screamed, and she ran for the book, time speeding up again.

"NO!" Bethany screamed as well. "Not again! This isn't happening again!"

"Come back!" her mother screamed at the book, her voice breaking. She scraped at the pages desperately, as if she could reach through and pull someone out. "Please, no, come back, Bethany, my little girl!"

As her mother screamed, Bethany turned away, unable to watch and more angry than she'd ever felt in her life. "Why are you showing me this?" she shouted at the voice. "Why are you *torturing* me?!"

"You have to see how it feels to live a life out of your control," the voice told her. "A life that chooses *for* you. A story controlled by another, putting you through horrible things for the entertainment of others. This is what you would have for me, and for my people. Do you see now, Bethany?"

"This is some sort of lesson?" Bethany shouted as her mother fell to the couch, sobbing, the book clutched to her chest. "You put me through this just to make a point? How could you!"

"Perhaps I did," said the voice. "But the lesson isn't over."

Abruptly, a tiny hand reached out of the book.

Bethany's mother shouted in surprise and grabbed the hand, pulling it and the body that followed out of the book. It was one of the children from the party, with another following right behind. Another, then another child climbed from the book, some crying, some seemingly happy.

Finally, the girl in the blue dress climbed out, a huge grin on her face. "Did you see, Mommy?" the girl asked excitedly. "Did you see what I did?"

"Where is your father, Bethany?" her mother yelled, holding the girl tightly by the shoulders. "Please, tell me where he is!"

"Perhaps stories might still be changed," said the voice of the Magister, "when writers are no longer in control of them."

The little girl's face grew determined, and she leaned back into the book, her arm completely disappearing, only to grunt and pull back out.

And holding her hand tightly was a man's hand, a hand that

then grabbed the edge of the book and pulled. And there, just moments later, stood her father.

Her mother cried out, grabbing the man and hugging him tightly.

"Let's not give her any more books for now," her father said, and hugged little Bethany and her mother closely.

CHAPTER 32

Charm's robot arm slammed Owen backward, smacking him against the wall as the First Magician's green magic bolt exploded right in the spot Owen had been lying. "We're in a little trouble here!" Charm shouted, tossing a ray gun at him. "No more magic, just shoot them!"

The First Magician aimed green magic at both of them, and Owen ducked as Charm took a hit in her robotic arm. The arm shuddered, then turned on Charm and began to clutch at her throat, as if it had a mind of its own.

Charm shouted in surprise, then shot her arm off at her elbow, letting it fall to the ground. The robotic arm hit hard but kept coming, clawing and scraping its way at her until Charm shot it over and over with her ray gun.

This is a horror book. What had changed? There'd *never* been any horror in Kiel Gnomenfoot, but now it was coming out of the walls! Was this meant to happen in the story, or was it because Owen had done something different than Kiel would have?

If Bethany was okay and he lived through all of this, he'd gladly sit for hours while she told him how stupid he'd been, and how right she was about everything. *Hours.*

A moaning Science Soldier zombie grabbed for him, and he yanked away, firing his ray gun at the creature. Holes exploded in the robot's chest, but it didn't stop coming until Charm dropped a computer monitor on its head.

"Watch out!" he shouted at her as the First Magician turned to them again. Owen aimed his ray gun at the zombie, but Charm pushed the gun off course before he could fire.

"Don't kill him! We need to know where the last key is!"

"I don't care!" Owen shouted at her. "That almost got us killed in the Original Computer, and it's *definitely* going to kill us here!"

Charm just stared at him. "Wait. It's the same trap. The same one, Kiel! Someone set these up to protect the Seventh Key. The viruses were the science version, and this is the magic version!"

"So?"

"Magic saved us last time, so maybe science will work here." She felt around in her pocket and pulled out a tiny field medical pack, then tensed, like she was looking for an opening to move.

"What are you *doing*?" Owen shouted at her, shooting his ray gun at the robot zombies behind her.

"Fixing this," Charm said, pulling open the med pack with her teeth and shaking something out into her remaining hand.

The zombie blasted green magic at them, and this time Owen couldn't move fast enough. The blast hit the spell book under his arm, and the book began to shudder and shake. He quickly dropped it to the ground, where it began to drool and slobber, using its cover to drag itself over toward Charm.

"AAH!" he shouted, shooting the spell book over and over until it stopped.

Well. That was it for any more spells, then.

"I'm going," Charm said, jumping past him and the now-dead spell book, weaving in and out so the First Magician zombie couldn't get a fix on her. "Cover me!"

Owen just gritted his teeth, his eyes everywhere at once. The zombie robots were about to overwhelm him from behind, but every time he tried to shoot them, the First Magician almost zombified him. And now Charm was actually running straight at the undead creature? With a first aid pack?

The First Magician raised his hands together, forming an enormous ball of the same green magic just as Charm reached him. "Hope this works," she muttered, then smacked the item from the med kit right into the zombie's chest. It stuck there, a white square of plastic with a big red button on its front. Charm slammed her hand on the button, then jumped away.

Thousands of volts of electricity jolted into the zombie's chest, and the green ball of magic went careening off into the back of the cave somewhere. The First Magician toppled over, still shaking and shuddering, while Charm just grabbed her ray gun with her now-free hand and aimed it at him warily.

The shaking stopped, and the magician didn't move again.

"I thought you said *not* to kill him!" Owen shouted at her, finally able to turn his attention to the shambling robotic zombie horde shuffling toward them. For every robot he shot, two more zombies rose from the ground, replacing their fallen comrade.

Charm kicked the First Magician. "Huh. Thought that'd work."

"Work? Shooting him full of electricity?"

Charm stared to reply, then leaped backward with ray gun raised as the First Magician began to cough, then slowly pushed himself up to a sitting position. "Ah," he said in a dusty and rarely used voice. "Guests!"

"*Shoot him*, he's awake!" Owen shouted, and turned his ray gun on the First Magician.

"Don't!" Charm shouted. "He's going to be okay. I restarted his heart."

"You *what*?!"

"Ah, the robots," the First Magician said with a frown. "I'd forgotten about them. I never did like robots much. What say we do away with them?" He gestured, and green magical energy swept out, playing like lightning through each of the zombie Science Soldiers. As the magic touched them, the robots immediately dropped to the ground, unmoving.

Owen looked at Charm, who grinned for maybe the first time ever. "Science wins again," she said.

"Excuse me for a moment," the First Magician said, waving

his hand over himself. "I just want to tidy up a bit." A long white coat grew out from his clothes like a living thing, covering his tattered outfit and decaying skin. Glasses pushed up from his face, and sensible brown shoes from his feet, along with a pair of brown pants. All in all, he looked like nothing more than—

"A scientist?" Owen blurted out.

The First Magician raised an eyebrow. "Well, of course I was. Once. But that's not important right now. You're probably here to ask me about the Seventh Key, I would suppose?"

"I'm Charm Mentum of Quanterium, and this is Kiel Gnomenfoot of Magisteria," Charm said. "And yes, we're looking for the Seventh Key. The current leader of Quanterium, Dr. Verity, is about to destroy Magisteria with an army from alternate dimensions. We need your help to open the Vault of Containment so we can use the Source of Magic against him."

The zombie nodded. "Ah, I can see why you would need the Seventh Key, then. Are the two planets still really at war? Seems like yesterday we invented magic, left Quanterium, and formed Magisteria, just to stave off that kind of problem."

"Invent magic?" Charm asked.

"Form a planet?" Owen said.

The First Magician started to say something, then seemed to almost faint. He grabbed for the circuit-covered throne, while Owen rushed forward to help him. "I don't have much time," the zombie said. "I used the science in this cave to keep my body preserved, in the hopes that someone would come along and use the throne's circuitry to reanimate me." He looked from Owen to Charm. "I suppose you two found a different way."

"Kiel's fault," Charm said. Kiel gave her an indignant glare.

"But I think we've reached even the limits of science," the Magician continued. "This body is just too old. As for the key, I must pass my secret along before I sleep once more, if the danger is so great. Everything was arranged to ensure that neither Quanterian nor Magisterian could ever find all seven keys without the other's help." He smiled gently at Charm and Owen. "You two seem to be exactly what I'd hoped for."

Charm snorted. Owen just shook his head. The First Magician probably wouldn't be thrilled to learn that one of them wasn't a magic-user so much as a kid from the real world who'd been magically disguised to *look* like one.

"The Seventh Key doesn't actually exist, not anymore," the Magician said, then keeled over in pain. When Charm tried to help him, he shook his head. "We destroyed it after locking the vault. But it *can* be re-created. The magic of the vault ensures that only a person with a truly selfless intent may open it, and that's where the final key comes in. Re-forming the key requires a heart that wishes to open the door for others, not for him or herself."

"That's a little metaphoric," Charm said, flashing Owen the look that she gave him whenever magic impossibilities came up. "How *exactly* do we remake the key?"

"I just told you," the First Magician said, then coughed hard. "The heart of a selfless individual. Remove the heart from the body, and the key will emerge from the heart itself."

"Wait . . . what?" Owen said. "*Actually* remove the heart? Wouldn't that kill the person?"

"Of course," the First Magician said. "But what selfless person wouldn't be willing to die for their cause?"

Was he *joking*? Heroes in books didn't die! Sometimes they thought they might, and were willing to, but they never actually did. That'd be a horrible ending. There must be some twist here. There had to be!

Charm seemed lost in thought as well, finally turning to Owen. "Actually, that explains some things."

"Explains?" Owen asked, barely able to concentrate on what she was saying. "It doesn't explain anything!"

"Remember back when we went to the future to find the Second Key?" she said. "Remember how we saw all those historical stories about you dying? They all said you died after losing your heart." She awkwardly patted him on the shoulder. "We thought that meant you gave up. Guess it wasn't metaphor *there*, either."

CHAPTER 33

"Happy birthday, Bethany," her father said, removing his hands from her eyes.

Bethany gasped. "A Pegasus?" She ran toward the pitch-black winged horse with eyes blazing red and hooves sharp as knives. "You got me a Pegasus!"

"Be careful!" her father yelled after her. "Those hooves can cut through steel, and he's a man-eater!"

"I will!" Bethany yelled, then ducked under the creature's snapping jaws as she ran, only to throw her arms around his neck and swing herself up and around onto his back. "No reins?"

"Do you need them?" her father yelled.

"Nope!" she shouted, and nudged the startled Pegasus in the side. "Let's fly, boy!"

The winged horse had never had a rider on its back and didn't exactly know how to react to Bethany being there. First, he tried bucking her, which didn't so much as budge her. Next, he took off, and tried to fly close enough to trees and underhanging rocks to scrape her right off his back.

"I know all these tricks, boy," she said, yelling in his ear over the rushing wind. "A centaur taught me everything anyone could ever know about riding horses. But do what you have to. I can wait!"

From the ground her father waved over and over, while her mother stood shaking her head in disappointment. Bethany laughed loudly, knowing that her mother had probably said no to her father getting Bethany a fictional creature for a pet, and that her father had just gone ahead and done it anyway. Sneakily.

As her new Pegasus began to slowly realize that Bethany wasn't going anywhere, and that maybe cooperation might be better, things began to smooth out, and the ride grew a bit less exciting.

That wasn't going to work.

"Yah!" Bethany said, and nudged the creature in the side again. "We're not gonna do boring on our first ride! Let's go find Hercules or something and help him fight monsters!"

"No getting involved in other people's stories!" her mother yelled up from the ground. "I'm tired of having to fix them!"

"I won't!" Bethany lied, then grinned.

As the ground pulled away, Bethany could just barely make out Mount Olympus through the clouds. Lightning played within the city of the gods, and for a moment, she wondered if she could ask Zeus for a lightning bolt, just to borrow.

"Bethany," whispered a voice, a man's voice.

She glanced around, but saw no one. Was one of the gods speaking to her? Or even better, was her Pegasus telepathic? She'd always wanted to—

"Bethany," said the voice, stronger this time. It seemed familiar, and yet not one she could place. Where had she heard it?

"Bethany, you need to break out of that story," said the voice. "This isn't your life."

"Who is this?" Bethany said, her voice getting carried away by the rushing wind as the Pegasus glided toward Olympus. Lightning began to flash through the clouds as rain whipped against her face.

"Nobody important," the voice said. "But I know who you are, and I know that all of this is just a story, not your actual life."

"What . . . what do you mean? Just a story? Of course it is!" She glanced around. This wasn't her life, it was a book of Greek myths. Who *was* this—

"The Magister put you in a story, Bethany," the voice said. "He had Jonathan Porterhouse write you a new life, a life with the father that you never actually had. You need to let it go and come back to reality."

"There's no such thing as reality," Bethany murmured, trying to remember who the Magister or Jonathan Porterhouse were. "That was the first thing my father taught me. The fictional world is just as real—"

"Of course it is," the voice said. "But this story isn't yours. You need to be living the story you're meant to, not one that the Magister created to make you happy. Leave this behind and come back out to reality."

The rain and lightning and man-eating Pegasus didn't bother her, but for some reason, the voice's words sent a chill down her back. "No," she whispered. "I'm not leaving."

"Bethany!" the voice shouted. "If you don't come out, the Magister will sentence your entire world to live out fictional stories!"

"NO!" she shouted this time. "I have my father back, and

I'm not leaving! This is the life I was supposed to have. This is the life I didn't mess up. I don't care what it is, I'm taking it and you can't make me leave!"

"You're right," the voice said. "I can't make you. But that's not your father, Bethany. Not the real version. And there are people counting on you. The Magister has Kiel, Bethany. And Owen is still trapped."

The names formed images in her mind. A boy, a boy who knew magic, and his former master, the Magister. They'd . . . they'd escaped from their book, because of . . . because of Bethany, and a friend of hers. Owen.

OWEN!

The realization almost knocked her right off her horse. How long had she been here? How long had Owen been trapped in the Kiel Gnomenfoot books? And how could she let the Magister run loose in the real world?

"Kiel needs your help," the voice said. "As does Owen. Come back for them."

"I . . . I don't know!" she shouted over the wind. The lightning and rain crashed all around her now, and she could barely see. "I need to see my father. I need to . . . I need to say goodbye, just for now. Tell him that I'll come back."

"He's not your father, Bethany," the voice said.

The Pegasus below her turned its head and bit down on her hand, hard. She screamed, and the winged horse bucked hard. She slid right off its back, off into nothingness as rain and thunder pounded all around her.

"Bethany!" the voice shouted.

"NO!" she said, even as wind whipped past her so fast she could barely breathe. "I'm not leaving! I'm not leaving without saying good-bye!"

The clouds whizzed by, revealing a lush green land that rose alarmingly fast. Above, the Pegasus dove straight for her, his mouth open, his razor-sharp hooves ready to strike.

"NO!" she shouted again. "I can't . . . not again!"

But the voice didn't respond as Bethany tumbled down and down, everything falling apart.

CHAPTER 34

Owen sat by himself, his head on his knees, staring off into the blackened, charred remains of the Magister's study, not speaking, barely moving.

He wasn't sure how long he'd been there, just sitting. It was hard to tell time in a place that didn't believe in the science behind clocks. Though those clocks probably would have been destroyed in the explosion that Owen had caused anyway. Ruined just like everything else.

A light appeared in the dimness, and Charm stepped out of a teleporting beam, then slowly walked over to Owen, who didn't look at her. Kiel's winged cat, Alphonse, appeared right after her, then took to the air, sniffing all around as he flew. Owen watched as the cat settled on the remains of a high cabinet, then moved one glowing paw in a circle. Food magically appeared in a bowl in front of him, and the cat happily began to eat.

"What are you doing here?" Charm asked him, sitting down next to him. Owen noticed out of the corner of his eye that she had a new robotic arm. Apparently, her ship didn't just do brain surgery.

"Waiting," he told her.

"For what?"

"To go home."

She looked all around. "This isn't home?"

He shook his head. "You should probably leave."

"I can't. You know that. All of Magisteria is about to be destroyed in just a couple of hours, and—"

"I can't do this, Charm," Owen said quietly. "I don't belong here. I never did. She was right, and I should have listened."

"She?" Charm asked quietly.

"This friend of mine," Owen said. "I thought this was going to be fun. We'd go on adventures. I'd cast magic spells and fight Science Soldiers and take down Dr. Verity. My friend told me it was a mistake, but I didn't listen. And the worst part is, I might even have put her in danger, and it's too late to do anything about that. I have to leave. I have to go home."

"I'd do it myself, you know," Charm said, turning her head back toward the burned study. "Give up my heart, if it weren't

278

made of metal and plastic. So you wouldn't have to."

"You're a much better person than I am, then," Owen said, looking away.

"That's not why I said that. I meant that if I could take this choice away from you, I would. It's not fair. You've given up almost everything to save your world, and now it's asking for what little you have left."

Owen squeezed his eyes shut, wanting to punch something. No, he hadn't. He'd done this on a whim, wanting to play Kiel Gnomenfoot instead of doing the smart thing and heading home with Nobody! At least then he could have made up for his original mistake by helping find Bethany and bringing the Magister and Kiel back. Instead, he'd chosen to stay, knowing that by not helping, it'd give him more time to be the hero.

And now, when people actually did need him, all he wanted to do was run home.

Part of him wanted to scream and yell, kicking floors and punching walls. It wasn't fair! This wasn't his fight. He didn't know any of these people. Were they even real? And if so, was there even going to be an attack, or was that just what they as characters were told so the story could move along? What was real here?

Part of him thought those things. But the rest of him knew better. The people of Magisteria might be fictional, but they were as real as Charm was, sitting there beside him, trying to be there for him when all he wanted to do was run from his mistakes and from Kiel's future. And he'd chosen this to be his fight when he hadn't left with Nobody. He hadn't realized it at the time, but not knowing didn't change what had to be done.

"Whatever you decide, I'll understand," Charm said, pushing herself to her feet. She paused. "But in the meantime, I have something for you."

He glanced up to find her holding a familiar-looking box, one that increased in size as he took it. "It's the magic box you gave me when we found the First Key," she told him. "You should have it back. Just in case."

He took the box but didn't open it, not even sure what had been in it when it'd first turned up back in the original Kiel Gnomenfoot book. "Thanks."

"I'm going to go back to the ship," she said, standing up. "Even with a robotic heart, maybe there's still some way I can stop Dr. Verity. I'm not going to give up. You . . . you do what you need to."

He watched her move away and ready the teleporting beam. "Charm?"

"Yes?" She stopped before pushing the button.

"Since when were you comfortable being all emotional like that?"

Her eyes narrowed, and she started to yell something, then stopped. "Honestly? It's been you. Without all that arrogant bragging and those clever jokes, I actually don't hate you." She grinned slightly. "At least not as much."

Then she clicked the button and disappeared in the same light that had brought her.

Owen dropped the magic box, gritted his teeth, and let out a growl of frustration. "I don't want to die!" he shouted to no one except Alphonse, who looked up for a moment, licked his lips, then went back to eating. "It's not supposed to be me. I just . . . I just wanted to go on an adventure. Is that so wrong?"

No one, nor Nobody, answered.

Owen looked across the destroyed study, the room that he'd destroyed himself. Yes, Kiel should have been here, and he *would* have been, if Owen hadn't tricked Bethany into coming in the first place. None of this would have happened, and

Owen would still be safe at home, reading about Kiel sacrificing himself for his entire world.

Magisteria, all those people . . . They didn't have a hero anymore. Not when they needed one. And it was Owen's fault.

He glanced up at Alphonse noisily eating his magically
created food. The cat looked up again, then leaped into air, his
wings gliding him over to Owen, where he landed on Owen's
shoulders. The cat began to purr, pushing his head up against
Owen's, his wings wrapping around his body comfortably.

With a sigh Owen opened the magic box Charm had left
him. Inside was a teleportation button, which would bring him
back to the ship. She must have left it just in case.

Owen reached up and scratched Alphonse's neck. "This is
the dumbest thing I've ever done," he told the cat.

The cat just purred in response.

"I really hope there's a big funeral," he said.

Right as he pushed the teleporting switch, he glanced down
and noticed one last thing in the box as he disappeared in a
beam of light.

There, at the very bottom of the box, lay a robotic heart.

CHAPTER 35

Bethany's Pegasus dove straight for her as the ground rushed up to meet her. She screamed, then at the last possible moment jumped out of the story and into complete darkness.

"NO!" she screamed, feeling all around her. Where was she? Was she dead? And if so, why did it smell so bad?

"Bethany?" Kiel said from a short distance away. "Is that you?"

Her heart beat fast, too fast, at the sound of his voice, and she took a deep breath before answering. "Yeah, I . . . I think so. Where are we?"

"The tower's dungeon," Kiel said. "I assume, anyway. It's a bit hard to see in all of this darkness. Definitely smells like it, though."

She felt around, and little bits of hay stabbed into her fingers. "We're in jail cells?"

"Basically. I'd watch where you put your hands, by the way. The hay isn't just for sleeping on."

Ugh. "I . . . I was in a story. A voice told me that the Magister had Jonathan Porterhouse write me into one. Was that you, the voice I heard?"

"Um, not that I know of," Kiel said. "I saw the Magister push you into some pages, but I didn't know you could hear anything in there. What did this voice say?"

Bethany paused, then shook her head in the darkness. "It's not important. Can you magic up some light or something? We need to get out of here."

Kiel went silent.

"Kiel?" Bethany said. "Are you okay?"

"He took my magic," Kiel said softly. "Just like he said he would. The Magister used the forget spell on me, and suddenly I can't remember any spells at all. I can't so much as make one finger glow." He sighed deeply. "I think you might have been right, before. About the Magister, and how he'd use the Source of Magic to destroy Quanterium. I never thought he'd be capable of it, but look at what he's doing."

Bethany's eyes widened. "So we're stuck in his dungeon with no magic and no books?"

"Not unless you count the story pages you were just trapped in. Can we go back there?"

Bethany's shoulders drooped. "No. It wouldn't do any good. So that's it, then. We're done."

"Not quite. There is *one* thing we can still do."

Bethany slapped the hay-covered floor in frustration. "What? Give up now before we're tossed into whatever horror novels Jonathan Porterhouse had hanging around his house?"

Kiel paused. "Okay, I guess that's two things. Horror books, or my idea. It's a bit simpler than yours, honestly, but yours sounds more exciting!"

Bethany sighed. "What's your idea, Kiel?"

She heard him rustling around on his side. "I may have forgotten my magic, but the Magister must have forgotten how I took care of myself before I met him."

"Did it involve teleportation spells?"

"Ha, no. Not many of those on the streets of Magisteria. Remember the title of my first book?"

Kiel Gnomenfoot: Magic Thief? And then it hit her. "Wait, you're a magical thief. You can pick the locks and get us out!"

Something clicked from the general direction of Kiel's voice. "The word 'thief' is really no nicer than 'fictional,' but yes.

Hay's not the greatest lock pick in the world, but it'll do."

"What took you so long, then? Why didn't you escape before?"

"And leave you behind?" Kiel snorted. "Trapped in a story filled with monsters and horribleness? Never."

The image of her father and mother in the middle of Greek myths popped into Bethany's head. "That was it, a total nightmare," she said quietly. Clicking noises sounded from somewhere in front of her as Kiel began to unlock her cell as well. If it hadn't been Kiel's voice, whose was it? It couldn't have been a dream. Could Jonathan Porterhouse have written the voice into the story to wake her up?

Hinges creaked just in front of her as Kiel opened her cell. "Ready? We can stay longer if you'd prefer, but the stench is starting to get to me."

"Where are we going, then?" she said, not moving. "You don't have your magic left. I don't have any books. Even when we had *both*, the Magister completely destroyed us. Now we don't even have a chance."

Kiel sighed, and she heard him sit down beside her. "I'm going to make a suggestion that you're not going to want to hear."

"And what's that?" she said, barely even caring.

"You're supposedly half from this world, and half from mine, right?"

"Half-fictional."

"I *really* don't like that word. But fine. If you're half-fictional, stop acting so realistic all the time and embrace it! *Be more fictional*, Bethany."

Bethany froze in place, then began to laugh, harder and harder, until she laughed herself into a coughing fit. "Be more fictional?" she shouted. "*That's* your advice? When the Magister is about to toss all of humanity into stories that will probably kill them, and release every fictional character ever out into our world? Be more fictional?"

"Think about it. All this time you've been reacting to admittedly crazy things as they come. That's no way to win, Bethany. Why not try getting ahead of the craziness with a little nuttiness yourself? Embrace the impossible! Find the magic within! BE MORE FICTIONAL."

"Get ahead of the craziness?" she shouted at him. "How?! This is all my fault. *That's* why I'm dealing with it as it comes! I can't go back and not make the mistakes I've made, so I'm trying to fix them."

"And you're constantly failing, because you *can't* fix the past. It took me a year—or six books, I guess—to realize that. It's about time you did too if we're going to have any chance here."

"So, what, I should stop thinking anything through and just do whatever comes to me at the time? How about I let all the fictional characters out first, so the Magister can't? Or shove people into books to save them?"

"Why not?"

"Because that's a horrible idea! It's the exact opposite of what we're trying to do! Putting people into books—"

And then she stopped.

"Uh-oh," Kiel said, tapping her on the shoulder. "Did I break your mind?"

"Shut up," she said, a plan forming in her head. "You might not be entirely one hundred percent wrong here. Maybe there's something to be said for taking a few stupid risks."

"A few stupid risks is my middle name. It's a family name, from my father's uncle."

"We have to find the Magister," Bethany said, ignoring Kiel as she jumped to her feet. "But first I need to find where he's keeping all the books he took from Jonathan Porterhouse's library."

"That's it!" Kiel shouted. "Are you going to release some

crazy monster to attack him? Honestly, that's what I'd do. Something huge, toothy, and immune to magic. Seems like the smart thing to do, given—"

"No, and stop talking. But I do have a specific kind of book in mind, so I might be a while. And that means I need you to do something for me."

"I am at your command, of course," Kiel told her. "Though remember, I've got no magic, so maybe something nice, easy, and safe."

She frowned. "I need you to go distract all the fictional monsters outside and make them chase you back in here. Round them all up and bring them to me."

"Even *better*." And despite the dark, Bethany knew Kiel was grinning.

CHAPTER 36

This won't be easy," Charm told Owen, her hands flying over holographic maps in the middle of her spaceship. "First, we'll need a way to teleport down to Quanterium, breaking through the planet's shield system that blocks teleportation rays, which they put up after we found the Fourth Key."

"I'm okay not getting there right away," Owen said, watching the stars fly past out the window.

"Second, we'll need to make our way through Quanterium to the Presidential Palace, through Science Soldiers from a million different dimensions. And we'll be entirely on our own, since anyone who might be willing to overlook the fact that we're criminals is probably on the Nalwork anyway. Which brings up another issue: With everyone on the Nalwork, we'll stand out just by walking around, no matter what our disguise."

"Well, my spell book was destroyed, so I don't have any magic to disguise us anyway," Owen pointed out.

"Which takes away any chance of surprise that we had," Charm said with a frown. "Still, you invade a science planet with the magic you have, not the magic you want. Once we reach the Presidential Palace, we'll need to make our way down to the very bottom floor, where the Vault of Containment is hidden."

"Are we sure that this mythical, magical weapon actually does anything?"

"All magical weapons are mythical. And no."

Owen sighed. "I see what you're doing. You're focusing on how we're going to die so you don't jinx us, like back at the First Magician's cave!"

She shrugged. "If that helps you."

Ugh. Despite Charm's estimation of their odds, Owen was actually pretty sure they'd make it to the vault. Dr. Verity had always enjoyed a dramatic confrontation, and what would be worse than letting Owen and Charm get right to the vault door before stopping them? That had to be the spot where the final confrontation would take place, and Owen would . . . He'd have to give up his . . .

Anyway.

Alphonse moved around on his shoulder, the cat's wings rubbing up against his head. Owen absently scratched Alphonse's neck, and the cat purred. "Charm, if things go badly down there . . ."

"I'm sure they will," Charm said without looking up.

"Because of your positive attitude, right. But if something happens to me, I want you to take . . . what you need and finish the job. Okay?"

She turned around and gave him a curious look. "No."

Owen's eyebrows raised. "No?"

"That won't happen," she said, standing up. "I don't have any misconceptions about what we're about to get into, Kiel. Trust me on that. But I will get you to that vault. Doesn't matter how many Science Soldiers Dr. Verity lines up between us and that door. You'll get there and unleash the Source of Magic. I promise."

He smiled, just a bit. "How can you possibly promise that, with everything we're about to face? It's not exactly a fair fight."

She shrugged. "*None* of this is fair. It isn't fair that you're a clone, or what happened to my parents and sister. It isn't fair that so many of your people are suffering, or that the people of

Quanterium ever allowed Dr. Verity to take over. It's *not* fair, Kiel. Believe me, if anyone knows that, it's me." She took a step toward him and laid her human hand on his arm. "You're about to give up your heart, to save the world. I can't imagine anyone who wasn't named Kiel Gnomenfoot ever doing that."

Owen forced a smile, very aware of her hand on his arm. "That doesn't mean we'll win."

"It means you already did." She paused, then made a disgusted face. "What have you turned me into? I had a whole speech planned about how I'd make *sure* you got there, no matter what, and you make me go and say something like 'you already won'? Ugh!"

Owen laughed as she shook her head, smiling in spite of herself. She was right, though. This wasn't the same Charm from the books. Something *had* changed.

Not that it mattered, though. She didn't even know who Owen really was. The girl who grinned at him with the awesome robotic eye really did believe he was Kiel Gnomenfoot, not Owen Conners. Why couldn't he just tell her, now that it was so close to the end? What would it change?

"Can I . . . tell you something?" Owen said. "A secret?"

She sighed, swatting his arm. "If you have to."

It'd be so easy. Just say it, and she'd know!

But she'd also *know*. She'd know that the Kiel she thought she knew was actually some stranger. She'd know that the boy she was about to get into the fight of her life with was someone she'd never really met before. A boy who'd lied to her from the moment he met her, and even now couldn't tell her the whole truth, that she was a character in a book.

And worst of all, she'd lose all hope that they might actually make it through this.

"I'm really happy to have gotten to know you," he said finally, and quickly hugged her.

She gave him a surprised look, but accepted the hug, if a bit awkwardly. And for a moment things didn't seem so bad.

And then something hit the spaceship, and the two were thrown into the wall hard enough to almost knock Owen out.

"What was that?" Charm shouted, pushing Owen to his feet and running back to the piloting computer as the ship tilted forward, falling out of control toward the planet below.

"I think we were hit," Owen said, trying to shake the fog out of his head and grabbing for the nearest chair to steady himself with the tilted floor.

"Missiles from Quanterium!" Charm yelled, holding on to the pilot's chair. "We're going to crash in less than a minute!"

Before Owen could answer, a bright green hologram shimmered into place in the middle of the ship and turned to address them both.

"Ah, children," Dr. Verity said, his hologram crackling as the ship began to hurtle to the ground. "I take it you have the Seventh Key and are on your way to open the Vault of Containment, then?"

Owen gave him a cold, hard, Kiel-type look, or as hard a look as he could give while desperately holding on to a chair to keep from falling forward. "So what if we are?"

Charm shook her head violently at him, but Dr. Verity smiled. "Indeed. I considered letting you reach the vault, as that seemed like the most fitting and enjoyable place to end all of this. Let you believe you'd won, then pull the rug out from under you. But then it occurred to me. Why take the chance? Isn't it far safer to just do away with you here, now?"

"So you shot us down?" Charm shouted.

Dr. Verity shrugged. "Seemed a bit pedestrian, I admit, but it did the job. Speaking of doing the job, though: Just to make sure, this hologram will morph from soft to hard light when I finish speaking, then explode." He smiled. "As I said, just to make sure."

"Kiel, the keys!" Charm shouted, and leaped for the spot where the first six keys were hidden.

"It's been a true pleasure, using you as my scapegoats," Dr. Verity told them. "You really have made this whole starting a war against Magisteria *so* much easier for me. And for that, I owe you big." He paused. "Let's hope this is a big enough way to say thanks!"

And then he exploded.

CHAPTER 37

The tower seemed higher than it had any right to be, considering it'd just been created out of thin air within the last day. Bethany climbed as silently as she could, hoping that the Magister wasn't using magic to listen for intruders.

Each room she passed, she stopped to check for books. The Magister seemed to have re-created his tower exactly, so instead of anything useful and literary, most rooms were filled with magical experiments, weird time changes where everything happened backward, or worst of all, the room of ten thousand smells. (The less said about that last one, the better. Jonathan Porterhouse apparently liked his magic quirky.)

She had the location spell still, of course. It could probably locate the perfect thing to use against the Magister, just as easily as it might find her father. But after seeing her father, even the version in the Magister's fake story . . . she couldn't. Not her one chance to find him. With everything happening, she had to hold on to this one thing, keep this one thing safe, for herself. No matter what.

After exploring fourteen floors up from the dungeon, Bethany finally opened the door to what looked like a room the size of a closet, only it turned out to extend farther than she could see. And every single inch was filled with books.

"Finally," she whispered, and walked inside, leaving the door just a bit open so Kiel would know where to lead all the fictional creatures the Magister had freed already.

She walked into the room full of shelves, pushing her way past random piles of books on the floor, as well. Now that she was here, how was she ever going to sort through all of these? Somehow, not only did she need to find a weapon to use against the Magister, but she also had to take care of all those monsters in one fell swoop. Assuming Kiel made it back with them all.

What was she talking about? He'd been eaten alive by a dragon, then walked out of its mouth making jokes. If anything, he'd be here *sooner* rather than later.

In spite of everything, Bethany smiled to herself. *Be more fictional.* Somehow, Kiel actually made things fun, even in the worst of all possible situations. Which they were clearly in.

She passed through the shelves, scanning the titles as fast as she could. Every so often she'd pull a book down, making a pile for later use, but nothing she found would do much against a horde of mythical creatures.

Wait. They *were* all creatures from myth and fantasy. Where were the monsters and aliens from science fiction? Maybe unconsciously, the Magister was still avoiding science. No matter how much he hated the idea, part of him was still the same character from the Kiel Gnomenfoot books.

A roar from below brought Bethany back on track, but at least she had an idea for what to use against the Magister's army. And now that she knew what she was looking for, the search went much quicker. Two shelves later, she found something that might do just fine.

After a quick jump into and back out of the book, she was back on the stairs with a pile of books, taking them two by two as loud footsteps pounded up a few floors below. "This way, you made-up idiots!" Kiel yelled. "Catch me if you can, which you can't, because you're so poorly written!"

She stopped three floors up from the library, then froze, trying hard to hear the moment Kiel reached the library door. He must have found it, because she heard him yell, "In here! First one who eats me gets a punch in the gut from the inside!"

And then Bethany heard the enormous crackling of electricity she'd been listening for, followed by complete silence.

Poor Kiel. Still, he should be fine, at least for a few minutes. She waited, just to be sure there weren't any stray fictional creatures still wandering around, then turned and continued up the tower.

Carrying a pile of books made the climb to the top take even longer than she'd have thought. Thankfully, all the noise below hadn't seemed to disturb the Magister, as the enormous wooden door at the very top remained closed. It occurred to Bethany that this was the exact same door Dr. Verity had opened what felt like years ago at this point when she and Owen had visited the sixth Kiel Gnomenfoot book.

And now she was Dr. Verity, coming to face the Magister. Ugh.

As her hand touched the doorknob, she heard a voice from inside, and froze. "You're not from this world, boy," the Magister was saying. "No more than I am. But they control you here. They force your every action to suit their whims, mostly for their own entertainment. They invented us because magic never existed in their world, so they had to invent it just to feel whole."

"But this is my world," said a young voice with a British accent. "At least, it feels . . . similar."

As she listened, Bethany carefully flipped through the books she'd brought and ripped out specific pages, stuffing each into her pocket.

"Open your eyes, boy," the Magister said. "Don't you see? Don't you see what they've done?"

"If what you say is true, then *why* would they do this?" the boy asked. "And where would they find the power, especially without magic?"

"I haven't yet learned that answer, but I will. And you shall stand by my side when I do. I have a power source, locked in the dungeon below. With that power, I can free all oppressed characters from every story ever written. And then, with their former entertainers united against them, we'll send this world's people into the stories they wrote for us. We'll be free to live on their world, as we should have been from the beginning!"

"But many would be hurt, maybe killed," the boy said. "How can you think that's—"

"Those who would control the fates of others deserve no

less," the Magister said. "But if you need further proof as to these people's treachery, I offer you this."

The door flung open, and Bethany stumbled into the room.

"This girl," the Magister said, pointing at Bethany. "It was *her* power I used to bring you here. Cast a spell on her mind, my new apprentice. Force her to tell you the truth. The others come from other worlds, but she was born here. She will know. *Make* her tell you."

The boy, wearing a gray shirt and pants that looked like they came from the middle ages, gave Bethany a doubtful look. "I don't use my power like that." He frowned. "At least, I don't *want* to. Part of me wishes I did, but . . . but that part isn't in control."

The Magister smiled. "You can be whoever you want to be once they're gone, my friend. That is the *beauty* of freedom, and all it takes is seizing it!"

"He might be right," Bethany admitted, standing up. "I can't honestly say that . . . Wait, what's your name?"

"Merlin," the boy told her.

Bethany's eyes widened, and she lost her place for a second. *Merlin?* But she quickly pulled herself together and continued. "He could be telling you the truth, Merlin. Not about freeing all the characters from stories, or trapping people in books—that part is insane. But writers here do somehow see into your minds, see your thoughts and your worlds, see other time periods and histories." She shook her head. "Do they make them up? Are they just witnesses to a different reality? I don't know. I don't know that *anyone* knows."

"That can't be!" the Magister roared. "The writers *must* hold us in their sway! You believe the people of Quanterium would try to wipe out all of Magisteria if they weren't being controlled somehow?"

"I think that people do horrible things when they're frightened," Bethany said quietly. "And I don't just mean the people of Quanterium. Go back to your world, Magister. Leave this place in peace, and we can forget any of this ever happened. Literally. We'll use a forget spell, and you can go back to being a hero, a mentor, a teacher, whatever your world needs. Whatever *Kiel* needs."

"Kiel *betrayed* me," the Magister said.

"This isn't you," Bethany said. "Not the real you. You're someone that people here look up to. Someone they wish taught them, even though they don't even believe you exist. Think about that. Think of what that means, that kind of inspiration, that kind of wonder. How do you think they'd feel if they saw you now?"

The Magister narrowed his eyes. "Do not test me, girl of two worlds. I tried to give you a world of happiness, but you rejected it. I still need your power, and it's just as accessible if I leave you in my dungeon instead."

"Hear that, Merlin?" Bethany said. "That the side you want to be on?"

Merlin dropped his head into his hands. "Part of me . . . yes."

Bethany swallowed hard. Right. Merlin had some evil blood in him, if the stories were true. Which they were, if he was here. "Um, okay. Then listen to the other part. The part of you that you *want* to be, not the part of you you're afraid you are. Embrace that half." She forced a smile. "Embrace the fictional, Merlin."

"You would return to your book, living out their stories?" the Magister told Merlin. "You'd prefer that life to one where we live in freedom?"

Merlin stood up and looked the Magister right in the eye.

"There must be another way—" he started to say, then immediately disappeared.

"So be it then," the Magister said, then turned back to Bethany, his eyes furious. "You seem to be making a habit of turning my apprentices against me, girl. I have grown tired of this game. It's time to end it."

"What did you do with Jonathan Porterhouse?" she asked, eyeing him warily.

"I left him in a book, as I promised," the Magister said. "First he wrote you a new life story for me, and now he will spend the rest of his days seeing if he can write his own. He cannot be left to control my world with his writing anymore!"

"Which book? There are thousands downstairs!"

The Magister glared at her. "The titles were meaningless to me."

Bethany gritted her teeth. "He could die!"

"I . . . would hope not," the Magister said. "But if so, would my world not be the better for it? And what about your friend Owen? Don't you wish to know where *he* is?"

Bethany's eyes widened. "What did you do with him?"

"This was not my doing, I assure you," the Magister said, then held up a book that Bethany had seen the cover of earlier that day, in a poster as big as a wall. "*Kiel Gnomenfoot and the Source of Magic,*" the Magister read. "An advance copy, I'm told. It seems your friend didn't want the story to go on without its main character." He glared at her. "Perhaps Jonathan Porterhouse neglected to mention that he murders Kiel at the end of this book? And now your friend Owen plays at being Kiel, following his story. This sort of thing cannot continue!"

"No," she whispered. *"Give me that book."*

The Magister snapped, and flames burst into his hand, setting the book ablaze. "There are more," he said calmly. "Down in the library, as well. Porterhouse had an entire box of them. But those will burn just as easily, my dear, if you continue to defy me." He wiped the remaining ashes from his hand and raised an eyebrow. "So what now, Bethany? You have no protectors, no magic on your side. You've left behind your happiness, the only thing you wanted, and for what? To have your say here?" He shook his head. "Perhaps there really *is* no escaping our stories. It is not too late to help me. Kiel might listen to you. Join me, and together we will end these authors' power once and for all!"

Bethany couldn't stop staring at the ashes of the Kiel

Gnomenfoot book. Owen was trapped in there, and going to . . . die?

All of the fear, the worry, everything she'd felt the last day or two suddenly just disappeared. No more guilt or panic about books or changing their stories. Owen? The same Owen who'd looked at the Everlasting Gobstopper with so much excitement, who'd told her about the locating spell for her father? The Owen who loved Kiel Gnomenfoot so much that he'd messed up the entire series just to be a part of it?

"Protectors?" Bethany said softly. "Magic? You think I need those things to face you? A made-up character? Everything you were was in those books. Out here, you're nothing. A shadow. A *fiction*."

Her mother, her father, everything just faded away in front of an all-consuming anger. *Be more fictional,* Kiel had said.

"You should not speak to me that way," the Magister said, his voice low and cold.

"You talk a big game," Bethany said, glaring at him with pure hatred. "Let's see what you've got, Mr. Imaginary Magician."

His eyes widened, and both his hands rose. "So be it, then.

The dungeon it shall be for you, and this time, there will be no happy ending to your story!"

"Only if you catch me," she whispered, holding up a page of a book that she'd taken from the library. "Come and get me, old man."

And with that, she dove in.

CHAPTER 38

Owen opened his eyes to pain. Pain *everywhere*. He groaned, trying to figure out why he couldn't move most of his body. Everything was smoky, and the air just felt hot, way too hot.

"Charm?" he said, his voice croaking from the smoke.

And then he noticed why he couldn't move.

Charm lay on top of him, eerily still.

No. Oh please, *no*.

Most of her body had been blackened by the explosion, and she was missing her robotic arm and leg. "Charm?" Owen said, almost pleading, and gently tried to lift her off of himself. She weighed far more than she looked, and he could barely move her enough to slip out from under her.

All around them were the remains of popped plastic bubbles, what had to be some kind of protective crash mechanism.

Somehow, Charm had saved him both from the crash *and* the explosion.

"Charm?" he whispered, gently touching her shoulder.

Her robotic eye opened slowly, but didn't focus on him. "Kiel?" she whispered.

"Yeah, it's me," Owen said softly. "You look . . . good."

She tried to smile, but only half her mouth seemed to work correctly. "My robotic parts . . . They usually send damage reports. I'm not even . . . getting those. I . . . I don't think I can move."

"You're going to be okay," he lied. "Seriously. You'll be fine. You just need to rest."

"I can't move," she said, and the light in her eye began to fade. "Kiel . . . you have to go. Go now. Get out of here."

"I can't just leave you here," he whispered.

"You *need* to," she said, her robotic eye fixed on him, finally, even as it grew dimmer. "The Science Soldiers will . . . be here any minute, if they're not . . . here already. They'll find you. . . . They'll capture you!"

Owen glanced around at the carnage from the spaceship crash and thought he made out more than a few robotic casings. "I think we have a few minutes."

"*Go*, Kiel," she said, and the light in her eyes began to flicker. "Take the keys. They're in my pocket. I got them . . . from the ship. Get to the vault. Stop Verity. *Please.*"

He started to argue, but the light in her robotic eye went out as she fell unconscious, and he just nodded instead. "I will. I'll . . . I'll go. I'll take care of all of this. And I'll come back and find you, when I can. Okay? Don't worry about anything. I've got it."

He wiped his eyes, then grabbed the six keys from her and pushed himself to his feet, his entire body screaming in pain. The sounds of Science Soldiers' metal footsteps began to echo through the rubble, and he realized he really *didn't* have any time. There had to be a hiding spot around here . . . but what would hide him from the robots' scanners? He remembered that their scanners could penetrate anything other than metal, but there was nothing left of the spaceship big enough to hide him, and—

He glanced down at the rubble and realized that maybe hiding wasn't the best idea. Maybe he needed a disguise, instead. And not one made from magic.

The first Science Soldier to arrive, a commander, clanked its way to the crash site and found Charm's unconscious body, as well as Owen wearing the outer shell of a beat-up Science Soldier like a costume, standing over Charm with a laser rifle held at the ready.

"REPORT, 4329918," the commander said.

"SPACESHIP CRASH-LANDED, SIR," Owen said in his most robotic-sounding voice. "CRIMINAL CHARM MENTUM THE ONLY SURVIVOR."

"SURVIVORS HAVE BEEN ORDERED TO BE TAKEN TO THE PRESIDENTIAL PALACE FOR INSPECTION BY DR. VERITY," the commander said. As more soldiers made their way into the crash area, the commander gestured for them to pick up Charm and carry her away. Owen began to follow, but the commander stopped him.

"REMAIN IN SURVEILLANCE MODE AT CRASH SITE, 4329918," the Soldier said. "DR. VERITY ORDERED A THOROUGH REPORT. USE ALL AVAILABLE SCANNERS AND CHECK IN WHEN COMPLETE."

Owen started to protest, then realized that robots weren't exactly known for arguing. "SCANNERS DAMAGED WHEN THE SPACESHIP CRASHED INTO MY UNIT, COMMANDER," he said, flinching under the Science Soldier helmet that he'd yanked circuitry out of in order to fit his head. "NEED REPAIRS BEFORE ANY FURTHER SURVEIL-LANCE CAN TAKE PLACE."

The commander paused, tilting his head as if considering this. Or scanning Owen. Uh-oh. Owen slowly, subtly readied his laser rifle, just in case. But the commander just nodded. "SEE TO REPAIRS AT THE PALACE, THEN RETURN FOR SCANNING." With that, the commander turned and marched away.

Well. That was easy. Robots might not argue, but they were pretty easy to lie to.

Owen fought the urge to sprint after the soldiers carrying Charm, and instead walked robotically after them toward the large troop transport that'd take them all back to the palace. He climbed in with the rest of the unit, each sitting frozen in their assigned seat as the transport began to move. Charm had been set on a stretcher that floated in midair within the transport, so at least she wasn't getting hurt as the transport bumped over the wreckage from the crash.

Soon the ride smoothed, and Owen noticed that they had hit the empty streets of Quanterium. He'd read about the city in the books, of course, but the sight of it almost took his breath away, though that could have just been his lungs still feeling bruised from the crash.

Blue electrical energy crackled everywhere within transparent walls and beneath glass bridges over streets, filling each building with power. The buildings floated off the ground at varying heights, with trees and grass planted in perfect measured squares all around them.

Everything, everywhere was perfect. Quanterium had no sickness. Every known disease had been eradicated centuries ago, according to the books. No one was hungry, as food was created by specialized machines from the CO_2 they breathed out. And with the Nalwork as a distraction, who needed money?

All in all, Quanterium would have been a paradise, if not for the robotic armies roaming the streets and the tyrant who was about to destroy a planet full of magic-users.

As Owen watched, the buildings grew more and more elaborate, though he noticed that they were all basically the same design, just with more or fewer features. There wasn't much creativity here; everything had a similar look, as if the magic-users had taken all the imagination with them when they left Quanterium. Everything just felt so similar. Everything, that was, except for the Presidential Palace, which they now approached.

Carefully cultivated gardens surrounded the palace, kept in untouchable condition by a coating of plastic over all the plants, frozen in time at the peak of perfection. No animals or birds roamed these grounds, though, and no people sat on the benches that popped up every few feet.

Instead, Science Soldier units paraded up and down the glass pathway to the palace. As they drew closer, more and more soldiers appeared. When his troop transport finally ground to a halt, Owen looked out to find thousands of other transports on every side of him, each one filled with Science Soldiers. Some were gigantic, hundreds of feet tall, probably from a reality where everything was huge. Others floated along like bumblebees. Here, there were humanoid-looking robots, and there, lizard-shaped ones.

The armies of an infinite multiverse, that Dr. Verity had gathered to wipe out Magisteria.

Owen nodded to himself, then stood up with the rest of the Science Soldiers.

For Charm's sake, for Bethany's sake, to make up for his *own* mistakes, it was time to finish this story already.

CHAPTER 39

The Magister roared in anger at Bethany's disappearance, then leaped right into the page after her. He landed easily on a world with three moons and one burning green sun. All around him, people gave him looks as they went about their business, all wearing clothes so fine and weightless they could have been made of clouds.

"What is this place?" the Magister asked.

Then something hit him hard enough to send him plowing through a nearby building.

"*This* is Argon VI," Bethany said, standing over him with a hard look and her fists raised. "A world light-years from Earth."

The Magister, a bit surprised he wasn't hurt, started to murmur a spell, so Bethany picked up a hovering car and slammed it into him over and over. "You see," she said as she hit him, "Earth was about to explode . . . for some reason or another, I forget. A couple of scientists decided to save their baby daughter, Gwen, so they put her in a rocket and sent her here."

She picked the Magister up by his robes, swung him in a circle a few times, then launched him into the air.

He came down miles away in a desert, and Bethany landed just behind him. "You wouldn't know, but it's the reverse of something called Superman," she said. "Argon VI has less gravity than Earth, so it makes Earth people superstrong." Then she punched him into the sand up to his shoulders. "And the green sun apparently gives you the power to fly. I don't entirely get it, but that's *EarthGirl* for you."

The Magister stopped his struggling for a moment. "That would mean that we both share these powers, then?"

Bethany grinned. "Yup." She punched him farther into the ground, far enough so that sand poured in on top of him, blinding his eyes. When the Magister finally dug himself to the surface using his new-found superspeed and strength, Bethany was gone.

"You can't hide from me, Bethany!" he shouted into the nothingness. A quick retrieval spell sent a page from another book flying into his hands, and he leaped in after her.

This time he emerged right in the middle of a crushing waterfall.

The Magister quickly cast a flying spell, which kept him steady beneath the torrent of water. Unfortunately, he still couldn't breathe as thousands of gallons poured over him. Just as he tried to cast a breathing-under-water spell, two men plowed into him, sending him falling down into the river below.

A little ways downriver, the Magister floated to the surface, one of the men on his back. The other appeared to have hit the river too hard to survive, not having the benefit of a semi-floating magician to land on.

"Sherlock Holmes was supposed to die, falling off that waterfall," Bethany said from the shore as the Magister floated by. "It was a whole thing with his nemesis, Moriarty. But you just saved him. Millions of readers will thank you. He's *very* popular."

And with that, she leaped into another page, which floated away on the breeze.

The Magister dragged himself out of the river and grabbed the page with another spell as quickly as he could. The farther ahead Bethany got, the more of these traps she could lay for him.

He poked his head in more carefully this time, to see what awaited him. . . .

Only to quickly pull it back out as a dragon's mouth snapped shut around the spot where his head had just been.

The Magister caught his breath, then murmured a spell of protection and pushed in again. The dragon bit down once more, only to stop in place as it hit a blue bubble of magical safety. "Tell me where the girl went," the Magister asked the surprised dragon in its own language.

"The key is gone. Why must you torment me!" the dragon shouted, and sent a flame that could melt rock exploding into the blue bubble.

Even as the Magister realized where he was, the heat from the flame began to seep through the protective spell, and he soared into the air to get a better look, the flying spell he'd cast previously still in effect. Below him were vast piles of gold, enough to fill an ocean.

The dragon's tail plowed into his protective spell from behind and sent him careening into the gold hard enough to send incalculable riches spraying. Though he wasn't hurt, the Magister was starting to lose track of where he was, let alone where the girl might be hiding.

Enough was *enough*!

"STOP!" he commanded, unleashing the full power of his

magic on the dragon. "I do not want your key. My apprentice already took it, did he not?"

"Yes, the Gnomenfoot!" the dragon shrieked, writhing in pain from the force of the Magister's magic. "Please, let me be! I just want to be left alone, now that I've failed in my protection duty!"

"Tell me where the girl went," the Magister demanded.

As the dragon opened his mouth to speak, something yanked on the Magister's foot, pulling him down into the piece of paper that he'd been unknowingly standing right on top of.

He found himself floating in nothingness, surrounded on all sides by metal spaceships, much like the ones in Dr. Verity's fleet, only larger and more dangerous-looking.

As he quickly cast a spell to ensure he could breathe, one of the spaceships sent out an enormous orange glowing light, streaking toward the largest of the other spaceships. The targeted spaceship sent out a light of its own, with both on course to collide right where the Magister floated.

One glow hit another just feet away from him, and the entire universe began to explode.

"BETHANY!" the Magister shouted into the nothingness, his voice not traveling at all in space, even as his magical spell of protection quickly peeled away beneath the force of the bomb. Everything turned to bright white, and the Magister closed his eyes, awaiting his end.

Except nothing happened.

He opened his eyes, and found himself on a white plane of nothingness, surrounded by arrows, lines, and numbers.

"You're lucky," Bethany said from behind him. "I thought about leaving you there in that last one. It's pretty intense science fiction, and they don't mess around with their endings. If I remember right, that bomb started a second big bang. Even *your* magic wouldn't have survived that."

The Magister pushed himself to his feet, and instantly attacked, casting the spell Paralyzed With Fear straight at Bethany.

Bethany, however, just smiled.

The Magister's mouth dropped in surprise, and he quickly cast another spell. Nothing again. "What is this place?!" he shouted.

"I found this in the books you took. Probably from Jonathan Porterhouse's school days. This is where I'm leaving you. You can't do any harm here, since your magic won't work. And if your magic won't work, that means you can't keep stealing my power. And that means you're not jumping back out after me."

She shrugged. "Should have looked before you leaped, I guess."

"Where have you brought me?" the magician demanded. "Why does my magic no longer work?"

She grinned wider. "The entire point of this place is that there's no such *thing* as magic. Everything here? All the graphs and numbers and equations? It all adds up to you not going anywhere. Maybe I'll let you out someday. *After* you pass a test, to show what you learned."

"You can't do this!" the Magister shouted. "You're no different from the rest of your kind, taking my freedom while you laugh. Enjoy yourself, girl! Enjoy yourself at my expense!"

Bethany's grin faded, and she sighed. "Here's what you don't understand about the fictional world," she told him. "I don't know if authors watch what you do on some kind of television in their brain, or make the stories up purely from their imaginations. But we don't read about you because we're bored, or just to amuse ourselves. We read about you to be *with* you, to walk in someone else's shoes, to experience another life. Some of those lives are hard, and others are easy, but we're with you every step of the way. We read about people in impossible situations because *we're* dealing with horrible things ourselves, in *our* lives. And you going through your story helps us with ours, no matter how yours ends. Though I do think we both like a happy ending, don't we?"

"That doesn't give you the *right*—"

"Think about it this way," she said. "You thought of yourself as alone for so many years, fighting against Dr. Verity. But there were hundreds, even thousands of readers on my world who lived it with you. Who felt every victory, every defeat, and want more than anything for you to win. Who cried, actually cried when they thought you died. Those are the people you're trying to make suffer, the ones who've been on your team this entire time. Just something to think about."

And with that, she leaped out of the page from Jonathan Porterhouse's old school math book about multiplying fractions, leaving the Magister to scream alone into nothingness.

CHAPTER 40

The Science Soldiers pushed Charm's floating stretcher through the halls of the Presidential Palace, and Owen followed, trying not to stare at the wonders around him. Water flowed against gravity in energy fields that transported it to the higher floors. Lights exploded at atomic levels, miniature nuclear bombs that continually formed new atoms, then split those, creating perpetual light without using any energy.

And then there were the holograms.

As far as Owen could tell, the palace was filled with people, unlike the city outside, yet no one was real. Everyone used the same kind of hologram technology that Dr. Verity had used on their spaceship, going about their business while their body stayed home. It was almost like the Nalwork, just with fewer ads.

The Science Soldiers walked right through the holograms, at least the ones who didn't pay enough attention to step out of the robots' way. Just to test, Owen ran a hand through a hologram of a man in what looked to be a formal uniform of some kind. The man gave him a strange look, and beneath his helmet, Owen blushed. Whoops.

The robots continued on into the palace, finally arriving at the largest, most expensive-looking of all the rooms Owen had seen so far. This seemed to be some kind of audience chamber for the president, and it was empty of people, holograms, and soldiers. The clank of robot feet on glass floor seemed extra loud as the Science Soldiers walked Charm toward an extremely large desk made of brown metal, sculpted to look like wood.

The chair behind the desk turned, and Dr. Verity pushed to his feet, a wide smile on his face. "Welcome, soldiers," he said, and gestured for them to line up before him.

The soldiers immediately moved to stand at attention, Charm's unconscious body floating just in front of the line. Owen quickly took a spot at the end of the line and tried his best to stand as still as possible in the same pose as the rest.

"Commander, report," Dr. Verity said, stepping in front of Charm's body. "I see you found the missing daughter of the former president."

"AFFIRMATIVE," the commander said in its monotone

voice. "CRIMINAL CHARM MENTUM WAS LOCATED IN THE CRASH SITE OF THE SPACESHIP PREVIOUSLY LICENSED TO HER FATHER, THE FORMER PRESIDENT MENTUM, NOW DECEASED. SPACESHIP IS NOW UNUSABLE, DUE TO—"

Dr. Verity waved his hand. "I don't care. What about the boy?"

"NO YOUNG HUMAN MALE WAS LOCATED—"

Dr. Verity smiled. "Oh, yes, he was. There was indeed a young human male located at the crash site. But we can get into that later. For now, there are more important matters to discuss." He reached down and touched Charm's cheek, shaking his head sadly. "It didn't need to come to this, Ms. Mentum. You never should have survived the first attack on your family, honestly."

Owen gritted his teeth to keep still while Dr. Verity turned his back and sighed. "And now you've gone and injured yourself even further, which surprises me. I figured *you'd* survive the crash over the boy. But . . . could it be? Did you protect him?" He began to laugh, then patted her shoulder. "Oh, my dear girl. What a waste!"

"ORDERS, SIR?" the Science Soldier commander asked, but Dr. Verity just waved his hand again.

"I'm not finished, Commander. You see, things are about to change. My armies are even now beginning their attacks on Magisteria. And without the Magister, those pathetic magic-users will have no one to organize them, to lead them against my antimagic robots from all realities." He stopped, as if considering things. "Still, those spell-eaters will do their best to defend themselves, casting their disgusting magic and such. Why waste the time and energy to fight them? Why not just use our new weapon?"

"WEAPON, SIR?"

"Why, the very same one that Kiel Gnomenfoot hoped to use against me, Commander. The one he journeyed all the way here to find. You see, the fabled Source of Magic has been locked away under this palace for thousands and thousands of years. When the first magic-users left Quanterium, they hid the Source inside the Vault of Containment to keep it safe. Here, on a world of science!" He snorted. "Truly disgusting that it's been here so long. But I've developed a weapon—a bomb, really. It's quite simple. It takes the power of the Source of Magic, recognizes any quantum connection between the Source and those who have ever used magic, anyone in all of history, and *destroys* them. Rather dramatically, too, I'd imagine. I'm hoping they'll be burned from the inside, personally." He smiled. "Billions will die, of course," he said. "Throughout space and time. But magic will quite truly be no more. And it will all be thanks to the majesty of science!"

A bomb?! That's what this had all been about? Everything Kiel and Charm had done, seven books of finding keys, and it'd all been a manipulation, a trap on Dr. Verity's part? And now here Owen was with the first six keys, and a heart for the seventh, delivering them right to Dr. Verity? He had to escape before the doctor found him!

Dr. Verity stopped and glanced at the Science Soldier. "No questions, Commander?"

"NO, SIR."

"Obedience," Dr. Verity said, clapping his hands. "I love obedience! The fun part of all of this, though, Commander, is that I shouldn't have been able to do any of this. You see, those clever little magic-users thought of everything. They knew that we pure, true-hearted scientists might someday want to destroy their precious Source. So they ensured that only a scientist working with a magic-user could possibly locate all the keys to open the vault." He grinned. "But what self-respecting Quanterian would ever associate with a Magisterian? I needed a magician if I had any hope of getting into that vault." He made a face. "Given that I was once one of those horrible creatures myself, thousands of years ago, I know how things worked there."

Dr. Verity gave the commander a look, and when the robot didn't say anything, the scientist hit a button. The robot jolted, then asked, "WORKED, SIR?"

"Science builds upon what exists, Commander. Just like logic. But magic . . . dirty, horrible magic creates something where nothing once existed. And magic so infuses Magisteria now that it's changed how life there works." He shook his head. "There, those with nothing inevitably become the most important. Orphans. Forgotten children. The least among the least. Magisteria takes those downtrodden and builds them up, just like magic does." He looked disgusted. "You should see their greatest heroes. All came from nothing. It's almost a cliché there now. But when one understands the reasoning why, then one—*I*—can work with it. All I had to do was drop a child into one of their cities, produce a threat, and sit back waiting for my hero. Nothing could have been easier!"

He hit the button again, and the commander jumped. "HERO, SIR?"

"But I needed a trustworthy child," Dr. Verity told the robot. "One I could count on to follow through and eventually see things my way. And since I trust no one but myself, I had no choice: clone myself. And it worked! My old friend the Magister found the little me and taught the boy everything he'd need to know to deliver me my keys. And do you know what, Commander?"

"NO, SIR?"

Dr. Verity leaned forward, then looked around as if to check if anyone was listening. Then, he whispered, "I think that boy might have even found the last one, the Seventh Key. The one that was destroyed!"

Dr. Verity waited for a reaction, but got none from the Science Soldier. Finally, the doctor sighed and shook his head. "You're a terrible audience, you know that?"

"YES, SIR."

"Good," Dr. Verity said. "Now, if only there was someone *else* here to listen to me go on and on like this. Someone who thinks he's disguised, tricking me into letting him run free in the Presidential Palace so he can go open the vault and use the Source of Magic *against* me."

. . . *Uh-oh.*

"Kiel?" Dr. Verity said, and the other Science Soldiers all took one large step back. Owen quickly did the same, but far too late.

"Oh, Kiel, let's not play this game anymore," the doctor said, picking up a laser rifle almost three feet long from the desk and aiming it right at Owen. "Please, you're insulting my intelligence! And if there's one thing I absolutely won't stand for, it's an insult to my intelligence."

Owen winced and pulled off his mask.

"Ah, there he is!" Dr. Verity said, beaming. "The apprentice magician. The one destined to defeat the big bad Dr. Verity. The clone himself, ready to take a shot at the real deal!" He winked. "You *are* quite intimidating."

And then Dr. Verity shot Owen right in the chest with the laser rifle.

"Well, at least you were," the doctor said. "Commander! Have your soldiers search his body for the keys." He grinned widely. "It's time I got to play with a weapon of *magical* destruction!"

CHAPTER 41

"A shrink ray?!" Kiel shouted at her.

"It worked, didn't it?" Bethany asked, frantically looking through the shelves. "Stop complaining and help me look!"

"A shrink ray," Kiel repeated. "You do understand that when you shrank down the monsters, you hit me as well? Meaning they could still easily eat me? Not to mention the insects that used to be normal-sized but now were spiders the size of small horses?"

"You're fine," Bethany said, pulling a book off the shelf, then tossing it away. Where *were* they?

"A shrink ray," Kiel said, shaking his head. "I was almost eaten for a forty-third time!"

"Forty-fourth," Bethany said absently. "And aren't you the one who told me to be more fictional? To take more risks? Don't you *like* danger?"

"Well, yes," he said indignantly. "Though it is a *bit* less fun

332

without magic, I can't lie. What'd you do with all those monsters, anyway?"

She nodded at a large overturned bowl in the middle of the library. "Rounded them up and threw that over them," she said. "They're kind of cute, at that size."

"Not if you're that size too," he said, tapping the bowl. "Aww, look at the little blob monster! Blub blub blub!"

"We'll put them back where they belong as soon as I find the last Kiel Gnomenfoot . . . the last *you* book." She'd seen copies of the series when she was in here last. She'd even taken a copy of the first book, which she'd used in her chase with the Magister. But where had it—AH! "*Kiel Gnomenfoot and the Source of Magic!*" she said, yanking the book off the shelf. "This is it!"

"Shouldn't it be blank without me in it?" Kiel asked, giving the book a confused look.

Bethany quickly opened to the one of the final chapters. "No, because Owen somehow turned into you and lived out your story." Of course he had. Why had she assumed that just because Owen was trapped outside of space and time he still couldn't get himself into trouble?

"*No one* turns into me," Kiel said, looking offended. "I'm one of a kind."

"Now you're two of a kind," she said, showing him the page she'd flipped to.

Kiel's eyes opened to find Dr. Verity bending over him. "AAH!" he screamed in surprise, and tried to push himself backward but found he was strapped down.

"Wow," Kiel said, cringing. "Things don't look like they've gone too well."

"I know," Bethany said quietly. "You need to get back in there and take his place."

Kiel glanced over the page. "He's getting his heart taken out? That doesn't sound healthy." He sighed. "I knew it had to end. That's what the historical documents from the future told us, back when we found the Second Key. I knew I wouldn't live through this. Though having my heart removed does explain a few things."

"We need to get him out of there!" She started to reach into the book, but Kiel grabbed her hand.

"Find a place where he's not being watched, or you're just

going to turn up in the book," he said quietly, all the arrogance of a moment before gone. "I'll switch with him then, and no one will know."

Bethany nodded, and flipped forward a few pages. "Here. He's been knocked out by the Science Robots to have his heart taken out."

Kiel nodded and prepared himself. "I'm ready."

Bethany started to take his hand, then stopped as something occurred to her. "You don't know any magic."

"Doesn't seem so, no."

"But you're going to just switch places with him? You'll be trapped without any spells!"

"I knew it was coming," he told her. "It's been nice having this little break from things, out here with you. But now it's time to get back to the real world." He shrugged. "Or my version of it."

Bethany closed the book. "I'm not going to just let you die."

"It's how things are meant to go, Bethany. You can't change a life story."

She glared at him, hearing her own voice telling Owen the same thing. And then she heard herself snort. "Don't be stupid. We just need Jonathan Porterhouse. He wrote it, he'll change it."

"The book is *written*." Kiel grabbed the copy from her hand and showed her the words. "See? It's all there! Look. Look at the end—"

She knocked the book out of his hand. "Don't look at the end! I'm going to find Mr. Porterhouse, and he's going to fix this. I don't care how."

"You don't even know where he is!" Kiel said. "Just bring me back, Bethany. Owen doesn't belong there. *I* do."

Bethany glanced around the library. "You're right, I don't know where he is. But I can find him."

And she could. She had the magic, after all.

"How? Didn't you say the Magister hid him in one of these books? It'd take years to check them all."

"Not if I use a spell," she said, letting out a deep breath. The location spell she'd learned would find him, of course. After all this time, she knew that magic did what it was supposed to do. The only problem was, this was it. Spells were only good once. Which meant she'd be no closer to finding her father, and nothing good would have come of *any* of this. For a moment she couldn't do it, any more than she could cast the spell the day before in the library.

Bethany glanced up at Kiel, ready to admit she just couldn't. Kiel stared at her with concern, looking like he was ready to catch her if she fell.

Well, okay, maybe *one* good thing had come out of this.

She raised her hands the same way she'd seen Kiel do, then felt the location spell she'd learned to find her father run through her mind. She took a deep breath, then recited the words, and her whole body began to glow with the same warm feeling like hot chocolate on a cold day. And then she released the glow, saying Jonathan Porterhouse's name.

A tiny ball of light appeared in front of her face, then slowly floated off into the shelves of books.

"Follow it!" she yelled, then took off after the light.

The glow passed over and through books, zigging and zagging until finally settling on one in particular. Bethany picked it up quickly, then dropped it in horror.

"It's a Stephen King book," she whispered.

"What's that?" Kiel asked.

"Nowhere you want to go. Ever."

"Eh, I'm not worried," he told her, grabbing her hand. "I have a half-fictional girl to protect me. Now let's go find my creator so we can pull your friend out of my story and get me back to losing my heart, shall we?"

She couldn't help it. She grinned at Kiel, then jumped them both in.

CHAPTER 42

Owen's eyes opened to find Dr. Verity bending over him. "AAH!" he screamed in surprise, and tried to push himself backward but found he was strapped down.

"Finally," Dr. Verity said. "I didn't think you'd ever wake up. Looks like I set the stun setting up just a *bit* too high. Didn't want you using any magic, though."

"AAH!" Owen screamed again.

"Let's move past that, shall we?" Dr. Verity said, beginning to pace. Owen quickly looked around and realized that he wasn't in the audience chamber anymore. Instead, this looked like some sort of dark hallway, lit by the smallest of nuclear explosions on either side. And in front of him was . . .

"The vault," Dr. Verity said. "Notice anything unusual about it?"

Owen frantically looked over the door, but didn't know what to say, so just shook his head.

"It's not OPEN!" Dr. Verity shouted. "Do you not see the problem here, boy? I count one-two-three-four-five-*six* keys here! What kind of hero are you, showing up without all the keys you'd need to find the only weapon that can defeat me?!"

Owen stayed quiet, thinking as quickly as he could. There was no way he could give the mad scientist the last key he needed. No matter what it cost him, he couldn't let Dr. Verity use a bomb to wipe out everyone who'd ever used magic! Not only would that be the entire population of Magisteria, but also Kiel, the Magister, Owen himself, maybe even Bethany!

But how could he keep the Seventh Key from the doctor? If all it took was a selfless heart—

Wait a second.

Dr. Verity peered down at him impatiently. "Well?"

"Well what?" Owen asked, stalling as he walked his way through the plan.

"WHERE IS THE LAST KEY?"

Owen took a deep breath, crossing his fingers, toes, and

everything else. "I know where it is. And I'll give it to you, under one condition."

Dr. Verity grinned. "Look who wants to deal!" He took two steps closer until he hung over Owen like a gargoyle. Slowly, he raised a ray gun right at Owen's face. "You don't really seem to be in the greatest position to be negotiating, though, all things considered."

Owen swallowed hard. "Go ahead. Shoot me—"

"As you command!" The ray gun began to power up, and the doctor grinned wider.

"But if I die, you'll never get the key!" Owen finished quickly.

"If you die, you won't have any say in what happens to the key," Dr. Verity said. "That's starting to look like my preferred option at this point, honestly. At least I never have to look at you again."

"THE KEY IS IN MY HEART," Owen shouted, turning his head away from the ray gun. "If you shoot me and my heart stops, the key will never work!"

Dr. Verity stood back and gave Owen a careful look. "You aren't lying," he said, tapping the still-powered-up ray gun against his glasses. "I can tell, no increase in heart rate. And if you're not lying, that presents a very annoying problem. You can't live, you see. You've caused me far too many problems. But I *want* the Source, Kiel. I don't like loose ends, and this wipes up pretty much every single one. Including you, by the way. So what do I do?"

"Let me live!" Owen said. "There's got to be a way to make sure the bomb doesn't kill me too. Then you'll have your weapon, and I'll go away. You'll never see me again!"

"Pardon me for suggesting this, but if I take a key out of your heart, wouldn't that stop your heart from working? And wouldn't that therefore negate my end of this bargain?"

Owen nodded and took another deep breath. "But you can save me," he said, going all in. "Charm gave me a robot heart, just like hers. Put it in, do whatever you need to do to keep me alive, and the Seventh Key is yours."

Dr. Verity's eyes went wide, and he held up the robotic heart Charm had given Owen back in the Magister's tower. "Well, that explains why you had *this* on you." He began to laugh, harder and harder until Owen wondered if he was going to have a heart attack himself. "You . . . want me to save you . . . with science?" the doctor finally gasped. "YOU, Kiel Gnomenfoot, will become a creature of technology? I don't even *need* a reason. I'd happily do that, just to make everything you've fought for completely worthless!"

"You have to promise I'll be okay," Owen said. "Otherwise there's no deal."

"*Or* I could just take the key out of your heart myself while it still beats," the doctor said, raising an eyebrow.

"That won't work. According to the zombie of the First Magician, the only way to form the Seventh Key is if I give my heart up freely." And selflessly.

Dr. Verity started to swear. "I really, *really* hate magic." He sighed. "I really did want to kill you too. This is turning out to be a very disappointing day, all things considered."

"Trust me, things aren't going the way I hoped either."

Dr. Verity snorted at that, then shrugged. "Okay, one robotic heart for one heart key. Deal. Shake." He held out a hand, and Owen went to shake it, only to remember he was still tied down. The doctor grinned. "Gotcha!"

Owen sighed. "Just . . . just do it already."

"Soldiers!" Dr. Verity snapped his fingers, and two Science Soldiers stepped up next to Owen. "We're going to need a little surgery. Take the boy's robot heart, and switch it with the one in his chest, will you?"

One of the Science Soldiers held Owen down while the

other's fingers folded in to be replaced by knives. "Wait, *they're* going to do it?" Owen shouted. "I want a real doctor!"

"They contain all the knowledge in our medical libraries," Dr. Verity said absently, then gave him an evil look. "Or, if you prefer, *I* could do it."

Owen shivered and shook his head.

"Your loss. Let's move, soldiers! Give our boy a new heart!"

The Science Soldier holding the robotic heart touched his arm, pricking it with some kind of needle, and suddenly the room began to get all wavy and foggy. Owen fought to stay awake, but whatever it was that the robot had injected him with was way too powerful.

"Don't forget, you promised to keep me alive," he said as clearly as he could.

"We'll see!" Dr. Verity said.

"Bethany," Owen said as everything turned to black. "I'm . . . I'm sorry. . . ."

And as Owen fell unconscious, Dr. Verity turned to the Science Soldiers. "Who's Bethany?" he asked.

CHAPTER 43

Owen sat at the front desk at the library, checking in books. Lots of Kiel Gnomenfoot books, for some reason. He flipped through one, and the fact that all the pages were empty seemed odd, but not odd enough to worry about.

Someone laid a book down on the desk to check out, and he looked up. It was Bethany, made out of chocolate.

"I can't believe you did all this," she told him, for once not sounding like she was yelling at him. Actually, she sounded almost impressed. "You played out Kiel's story through the entire book, Owen. All the way to the end."

It was a bit hard to talk for some reason, like his head was foggy in a non-truth-spell kind of way. "I'm *so* sorry, Bethany," Owen told her. "I never should have done any of this. It's all my fault. I don't blame you for leaving me here to die. I deserve it."

Bethany, who was now made of words instead of chocolate, almost laughed. "Leave you here to die? What are you talking about?"

"Kiel Gnomenfoot dies at the end of the book," Owen told her sadly. "And right now, I'm Kiel Gnomenfoot. If I didn't go through with it, all kinds of other people in the book would have suffered for it. I couldn't do that to them. Because it was my fault Kiel wasn't there. All my fault. Fiction is too dangerous. I'm going to leave it to you from now on." He frowned. "Except I can't, because I'm going to die. *Aww.*"

"Owen, where do you think you are?" Bethany started to say, then was interrupted by a boy wearing a sign that said KIEL GNOMENFOOT.

And he was wearing that sign because he *was* Kiel Gnomenfoot! Sometimes dreams were the best.

"I'm really proud of you," dream Kiel said to Owen. "I don't know you that well, Bowmen—"

"Owen," Bethany said.

"But look at you. You're a bigger hero than I am!"

"Keep it modest," Bethany whispered to him.

"Never," he whispered back with a wink.

She sighed, and turned from words into an almost normal-looking Bethany again. "Owen, it's all over. Kiel and I beat the Magister. Everything's okay out here."

Owen looked at her blankly. "Why would you beat the Magister? At what, a game?"

Bethany looked at Kiel, who nodded. "That's right, Owen," the boy magician said. "We beat him at a game. That's all it was. Maybe you should just go back to sleep."

"Sleep?" Owen asked, looking around him at the library, which was now his bedroom. "Oooh, sleep would be nice. But when I wake up, I'm going to have a robot heart and then Dr. Verity is going to kill me, because my heart won't work as a key." He leaned forward conspiratorially. "I tricked him, Kiel. I had to give up my heart selflessly if it was going to open the vault. But I didn't. I made him promise to save me with a new heart and then let me go. That was a selfish deal, since it saved me, so the heart key won't work!" He frowned. "Which means he's going to kill me when it doesn't work. But at least I saved everyone from blowing up."

Kiel grinned. "Sounds complicated, but I like it. Almost as good as one of my plans."

Bethany put her hand on Owen's chest. "Maybe we should have gotten him out *before* the whole robot heart thing?"

"I also got an input for computer chips, too," Owen said, showing her the back of his neck.

Bethany's eyes widened, and she dropped her head into her hands. Kiel smiled wider and patted her on the back. "It'll be fine," he told her. "We can cover that up with magic or something."

"You don't *know* any magic!"

"I bet *he* does," Kiel said, pointing to Owen, who giggled happily at being pointed at by Kiel Gnomenfoot. Even if he did have to go back to playing Kiel and therefore dying.

"Sleep time?" Owen asked.

"Just about," Kiel said. "Tell me one thing. What happened to Charm? She wasn't in the hallway with you when we snuck you out."

Owen's smile faded. "She got hurt. She saved me when the *Scientific Method* exploded. She thought I was you, though. I like her lots." He sniffed loudly. "I hope she's okay after all of this."

Kiel's face clouded over. "Hurt? Where is she now?"

"Dr. Verity has her," Owen said sadly. "Maybe if I don't die right away, I can try to magic her away or something? I don't know that spell, but I'll still try."

"You do that," Kiel said. "Sleep now, Owen. I'll take things from here."

"Sleep now," Owen said, and leaned back into his bed, a relaxed smile on his face.

As he started to close his eyes, Owen saw Kiel Gnomenfoot, Bethany, and some other random guy step away from his bed, which was now much bigger than it'd ever been, surrounded by curtains and marble and all kinds of rich things.

"Well, it's time," Kiel said from a short distance away now. "Take me back."

"You can't go back to just . . . *die*," Bethany said, before turning to the random guy. "*You*. I rescued you from a truly insane horror book, which we will never speak of again, so you owe me. Do something about this!"

"I can't!" the random guy said. "I set all of this up back in book two. Kiel was always meant to . . . um . . ."

"I know," Kiel said. "I knew it was coming. Take me back, Bethany. It's the only way to save everyone."

Bethany paused, then nodded. She took Kiel's hand, gave him a look, then threw her arms around him and hugged him close. Aww! Why did she get Kiel hugs? Then the two of them disappeared into a book.

A moment later, just as Owen started to fall asleep, Bethany came shooting out of the book and turned to the older man.

"I don't care what you've set up," Bethany said to him. "This is *not* happening. I'm not letting anything happen to him. To either of them!"

"You can't change the story!" the older man said. "The books have already been published!"

"Doesn't matter," Bethany said. "Get ready to rewrite it."

Wait . . . *Bethany* said that? Even in his dreamlike state, Owen couldn't believe that.

"You and me," Bethany said to the older man. "We're going to fix this. You're going to find a plot hole, and I'm going to use it."

"But my book doesn't *have* . . . Okay, there are a bunch, but—"

"Where's the closest one to the end here?"

"Well, probably . . . this one." He pointed to a page.

"Good. Watch over Owen. I'll be right back. Oh, and just a real quick note for later—there's a full-size version of the Magister's tower on your lawn, so I'd just tell everyone they're making a Kiel Gnomenfoot movie. Seems like the best excuse."

"Wait, what?" the older man yelled.

But Bethany disappeared into a book, and Owen fell asleep. And thankfully, all he had were amazing dreams of Hogwarts letters telling him he'd just been named High King of Narnia, without a robot heart in sight.

CHAPTER 44

Kiel's eyes opened to Science Soldiers standing on all sides of him, powerful robotic arms holding him down. "What . . . what happened?" he said, struggling against the robots.

"You're awake!" said a voice, and Dr. Verity leaped forward, his face stopping just inches from Kiel's. "Finally! I wanted to wait to actually open the vault until you'd be here to see it too."

"Don't do this, Verity," Kiel said, staring at the doctor with fury in his eyes. "You can't. Billions will die!"

"Say it, Kiel," Dr. Verity said, turning his back to the boy magician. "SAY IT!"

"Say . . . what?"

"Tell me to HAVE A HEART!" Dr. Verity shouted, then broke into maniacal laughter.

"Yikes," Owen said to Bethany as they read the final Kiel Gnomenfoot book together. "That was awful. I wish you'd said something to Mr. Porterhouse about his puns."

"Shh, I'm reading," Bethany told him.

"Listen to me," Kiel said. "They're innocent people who did nothing to you. I can't let you do this!"

"Actually, you can," Dr. Verity said. "The bomb's prepared, and just needs a power source. Now, where did I put my Source again?" He grinned. "Ah, right. Behind this door!" He gestured behind him, as if pulling aside a curtain. *"Ta-da!* See? I can do magic too!"

Behind the doctor lay a door with seven locks, each a different size and connected to large glowing energy bands that spread over the entire door. It was almost impossible to tell from looking at them if they were made from electricity or magic, but either way, the energy looked deadly.

"Want to do the honors?" Dr. Verity asked. "Or are you all tied up?"

"Did he always make these crazy-person kinds of jokes?" Bethany asked Owen.

"He's a mad scientist," Owen said with a shrug. "This is the mad part."

Kiel just gritted his teeth, struggling against his bonds, so the doctor shrugged and stuck the First Key into the lock. "Ah, fresh from a dragon's hoard," he said, sniffing the key. "Mmm . . . you can really smell the fact that this dragon's not going to exist in about two minutes!"

"I know forbidden magic, Verity," Kiel said. "I'll use it if I have to."

"Ah ah ah," Dr. Verity said, holding up what looked like a tiny box with a large red button on it. "Remember, you're the one with a robot heart. Shouldn't make a deal with the devil if you can't pay the price, boy." He laughed. "I added a little part of my own during surgery. If I even hear a word of magic, just *one* word, I'll push this button, and your new little heart goes BOOM."

"Wait, *what*?" Owen said. "The robot heart is in *my* chest, not in the actual real Kiel's! If he pushes it, will my heart explode out here?"

"Of course not," Bethany said. "Maybe he won't push it?"

"Oh, he's gonna push it," Owen said, then shouted into the pages. "Kiel, stop him!"

"You know he can't hear you, right?"

"I'm the one whose heart might explode, so he'd *better* hear me."

"You wouldn't dare," Kiel said to Dr. Verity as the scientist turned the Second Key. "We had a *deal*."

"This key was hidden in the future, wasn't it?" Dr. Verity said, ignoring Kiel. "I hear there are interesting news reports there. Something about how you died of a broken heart?"

Kiel screamed in frustration. "I won't let this happen!"

The Third Key clicked in the lock. "Oh, but you already did. You've done this *all* for me. Finding the keys, playing the role of dangerous criminal to convince the Quanterians that Magisteria was on

the verge of revolt. Everything I needed, you did!"
He glanced between the the Third and Fourth Keys.
"Now which one was melted, then hidden in the ice
in the lair of the Ice Giants? I can never remember."

Kiel closed his eyes and began to cast a spell.

"NO!" Owen shouted, then grabbed his heart protectively.

"What did I say?" Dr. Verity screamed, then
pushed his button over and over. "Die, Kiel Gnomenfoot! DIE!"

But nothing happened.

Bethany grinned and patted the now breathing Owen on
his shoulder.

Kiel laughed, and his bindings burned in a
green fire, releasing him. "Oh, are things not going
as planned?"

Dr. Verity raised an eyebrow, then pushed the
button several more times. "What's wrong with this
thing?" he said, banging it against a nearby robot.

Kiel mumbled the rest of his spell, and the Science Soldiers fell apart at their joints.

"How did you do that?" Dr. Verity said, his eyes wide. "You've never been able to use magic against science that easily before!"

"Oh, I can do a *lot* of things I've never done before," Kiel said, his eyes burning a cold green. He held out his hands, and the robotic parts of the Science Soldiers slowly pulled back together. Soon, the robots rose, zombielike, and turned toward Dr. Verity.

"Oh, come on," the scientist said, and made a cutting motion with his hand. Instantly, the zombified robots crumbled to the ground. "Not that old trick. I haven't seen that for a thousand years, but I've got these things programmed to stop at a signal. You'll have to do better than that."

Kiel mumbled another spell, and green energy shot straight for Dr. Verity. The scientist just snorted, and the spell splayed off an invisible bubble surrounding him. "Really? Magic? On me? Don't you get it, Kiel? I came from Magisteria too!

I have all the protection I could ever need! Charm spells, protection spells, everything a growing boy could want, all to keep idiots like you from coming anywhere close to me."

"What about idiots like me?" said a voice from behind Dr. Verity.

A metal Science Soldier arm slammed into Dr. Verity, knocking him to the ground. The doctor looked up with a dazed expression to find a second Kiel Gnomenfoot standing behind him with a big grin on his face, and just one energy band left on the vault door. "The Seventh Key," this new Kiel said, holding up a large red key. "It had to come from a heart given selflessly, which mine wasn't. You remember that deal we made, the one where I gave up the key to save my life? That's pretty much the definition of selfish, isn't it? Your key never would have worked." He glanced at the key in his hand. "This one, though, comes from a friend of mine who wasn't using his heart for much longer, after it'd just started beating again today. He offered—selflessly, I might add—and I figured, why not?"

"BUT . . . ," Dr. Verity said, then glanced behind him, only to find that the first Kiel now resembled a half-fleshed skeleton wearing a lab coat.

"Nice to meet you," the First Magician said.

"The First Magician?" Owen said, his eyes wide. "But . . . that was me in there! Then you took me out, and put Kiel in. When did—"

"It was a plot hole," Bethany told him. "Jonathan Porterhouse told me about it. You get the First Magician's heart beating and then don't use it, before he falls apart anyway? It just seemed wasteful. So I went back, grabbed the First Magician, and brought him forward, after a quick disguise spell."

Owen just stared at her. "So just so I'm clear on this: You let me get a *robotic* heart . . . when I could have just asked the First Magician to give up his heart instead?"

"Seems to be working okay," Bethany said, tapping his chest. "Besides, it's like a thousand times stronger, I bet. You'll live for way longer with that thing!"

Owen just stared at her openmouthed.

She winked.

"Kiel, this fun has taken far too much out of me," the First Magician said wearily. "I wish you all the best, but I've done all I can. It was nice meeting you, the robotic girl, and that other girl, the one who—"

"Right!" Kiel interrupted quickly. "Me and the robotic girl. We enjoyed meeting you, too. Thank you for your service, my friend." Kiel saluted him, and the First Magician smiled back, then crumpled to the ground, disappearing into dust.

"So much for you not getting mentioned in the books," Owen pointed out.

"Don't think I missed you saying my name already," Bethany said.

Owen sighed. "Saw that, did you?"

"NO!" screamed Dr. Verity. "You can't do this! There's something you don't know about the Magister! If you give him the Source of Magic, he'll use it to—"

"Destroy Quanterium?" Kiel said, tossing the

Seventh Key from hand to hand. "I know. I figured that out *months* ago. Who didn't see *that* coming?"

Dr. Verity blinked. "... What? You *knew*?"

"I know *everything*," Kiel said. "Just like I know you tried to kill him, but failed."

"You can't know that!" Dr. Verity screamed. "You weren't there!"

"Part of knowing everything," Kiel said, tapping his head. "Don't worry. He's fine. And I've got it on good authority that he won't be hurting anyone, no more than you will. Now, let's see what we've got here." He inserted the Seventh Key and clicked the final lock. The ground began to rumble as the enormous vault door began to slowly pull away from the wall, opening to reveal the Source of Magic, the origin of all unnatural power in the entire universe. . . .

Which apparently looked just like a small pile of books.

"NO!" Dr. Verity screamed from the floor. "Where is my power source? It *has* to be there!"

Kiel stepped forward, picking up the pile of books and carefully carrying them out of the vault. "Books?" he said, his eyes full of wonder and curiosity. "Honestly? Books? That's what was in there this whole time? After all of this, there are *books* in the Vault of Containment?" He began to laugh, harder and harder. "That's amazing. I can't wait until she reads this!"

"I wonder who he's talking about there?" Owen said with a wide grin. "Sounds like you two are pretty close friends."

"Shh, we're almost done," Bethany told him, her face turning red like a strawberry.

"That can't be it!" Dr. Verity shouted, and pushed himself to his feet, then past Kiel into the vault. He frantically felt around the empty metal room, searching and scratching the walls for any sign of power. "It has to be here somewhere! The histories all promised a power greater than any other! I *need* it!"

Kiel watched the doctor bang his fists against the wall in frustration, then held out a hand. "It's over, Dr. Verity," he said. "End this. Call off your Science Soldiers. Bring them home. There's still time to stop the war."

Dr. Verity looked up as if noticing Kiel was there for the first time. "Oh, no, there isn't," he said. He pulled open his coat and took out a small cylindrical green device as he stepped out of the vault. "I might not have the Source of Magic, but I can still have Magisteria destroyed. That infinite army has to be good for something, right? And now, as an added bonus, I can kill you, too!"

"What is that thing?" Kiel asked, backing away a step.

"Just a portable nuclear light," Verity said, then twisted off the cap. "Kind of like the ones on the walls all over the palace, only this one's been rigged to blow us up in the next ten seconds." He grinned. "Yes, yes, I'll die too. But *my* mind is backed up on computer and will transfer to a new clone the moment this body sends a signal that it perished. What's *your* backup plan, Kiel Gnomenfoot?"

Kiel paused, then returned Dr. Verity's smile. "I don't know. I guess I've always kept *my* important things locked away in a vault."

And with that, he pushed Dr. Verity and the bomb into the Vault of Containment and slammed the door shut.

"NO—" Verity screamed before the closing door cut off all sound. Kiel quickly turned the first key in the lock, then stepped back and waited.

The Vault of Containment had held the Source of Magic all these years, completely cut off from any outside forces. Either it was strong enough to contain a nuclear explosion, and Kiel (not to mention the entire capital city of Quanterium) would live, or he'd have some complaints to make when he next ran into the First Magician.

Ten seconds passed, and not even a sound escaped the vault.

For a moment Kiel wondered if Verity had been telling the truth about another clone. The doctor *had* survived for thousands of years, after all, and had no magic like the Magister's to keep him alive. Still, if a signal had to be sent out to have a new clone download the doctor's memories, and the vault contained all signals, maybe this really would be the end of Dr. Verity.

That thought sent Kiel falling back against the vault, almost trembling with exhaustion. It was over. Magisteria was safe, finally. No more Dr. Verity. No more Science Soldiers attacking—

Whoops. Dr. Verity hadn't called them off, had he?

Kiel groaned, pushing back to his feet. He had to stop the attacking robots, but how? He had no spell book, and Magisteria was an entire space-travel trip away. If only there really had been a power source in the vault, maybe—

He glanced at the books he'd taken out of the vault, then grabbed the top one. Why hide these if they weren't actually a Source of Magic? And if they were, somehow, then they had to contain *some* power, right? After all, books were the truest form of magic that existed, in a lot of ways. If he'd learned nothing else in the last day or so, it'd been that.

"Oh, come *on*," Owen said, rolling his eyes.

Kiel quickly paged through each book one by one, a disbelieving look gradually spreading over his face. The books *did* contain power, one that Kiel never would have dreamed existed. Could they be true? Had magic actually begun this way? And if it had, did that mean he could—

Kiel carefully set the current book down and picked up the nearest Science Soldier robot head. As he read aloud from the page he'd left open, he focused the magic out from the book and into the robot, lighting both up with a different form of magic than he'd ever felt. The robot's eyes flickered, then slowly powered up, glowing a bright red.

Kiel grinned in spite of himself. "RETURN TO QUANTERIUM," he said, planting the order in this Science Soldier's head. "ALL SCIENCE SOLDIERS

OF EVERY MAKE AND MODEL, THIS IS AN ORDER. RETURN TO QUANTERIUM, THEN POWER DOWN!"

This new form of magic filled the robot's head until it practically burst at the seams, then separated into a million rays of light, each firing off in a different direction. Since the Science Soldiers could communicate between one another, the magic just followed the same paths, delivering Kiel's magical command to Dr. Verity's infinite armies. Even the soldiers on the floor in front of him powered up briefly with the red magical energy, took in the command, then powered right back down again.

Kiel dropped the again-silent Science Soldier head, not believing what he'd just done. Using magic to manipulate science? Who would have believed it?

Apparently, the first magic-users had, the ones who'd begun as scientists themselves. There was more to read in these books, much more. These scientists had experimented with the very foundation of science, and discovered magic entirely by mistake. Even just that idea opened so many doors. And the books contained so much more!

But this wasn't the time to read them. There was something far more important for Kiel still to do. He quickly left the hidden vault behind, making his way out into the Presidential Palace. The fact that he found multiple Science Soldier robots lying depowered throughout the hallways seemed to confirm that his science-spell had worked.

As he reached the Audience Chamber, he slowed and carefully peeked out the doorway, but saw the same troop transport of soldiers that he'd come in with now lying on the floor of the chamber, unmoving. And there in front of the soldiers was Charm, floating on a stretcher.

He ran to her, completely unsure what to do. What *could* he do? He had no magic, no spell book. How could he fix her? Maybe the Source had ideas, but she didn't have time. He needed a doctor, medicine, something!

But what doctor would help a criminal like Charm, or even listen to Kiel's request in the first place? They were the most wanted felons in all of Quanterium.

There was just one thing to do.

Kiel pushed the stretcher out of the Audience Chamber and into the palace proper, stopping only when he found himself surrounded by shocked holograms of Quanterians.

"HELP!" he shouted. "This is Charm Mentum, the daughter of your former president. She needs medical attention now! She's no criminal. She's been a Quanterian spy since the day I met her, and actually just betrayed me, Kiel Gnomenfoot, to save your world. Please, call a doctor!" And with that, he dropped to his knees and held out his hands, waiting to be taken away by the Science Police as the holographic citizens of Quanterium gathered all around him.

CHAPTER 45

"Wait, what?" Owen said. "That can't be the ending! He gave himself up to get Charm a doctor?"

"They thought she was a criminal," Bethany said quietly, touching the page. "I guess he thought they wouldn't save her otherwise."

"There has to be more," Owen said, pulling the book out of her hand. "There has to be! What happened to Charm? Is she okay?" He seemed about as worried about Charm as Bethany felt about Kiel, honestly.

"There's an epilogue," Bethany said, turning the page while he held it. "Five years later." She paused. "But I don't think we should read it. I mean, after everything, it wouldn't be right to just finish the book that way, you know? That's no way to say good-bye."

"Not *read* it?" Owen said, his voice rising as he stared at her indignantly. "But I have to find out—" And then he noticed her hand in midair, waiting to take his.

He swallowed hard, gave her a thankful, relieved smile, then silently took her hand.

Together, they disappeared into the pages.

Five years later

"As you know, the tyrant Dr. Verity caused an accident six years ago that killed my parents and sisters," Charm told the crowd before her. "That accident took my eye, arm, and leg. Science saved me, giving me robotic parts to take the place of flesh and bone. But it took magic to truly make me whole."

She pointed at her now-human eye and held up both nonrobotic arms. "This is what magic and science accomplished together. But it won't stop there. Together, Quanterian and Magisterian will become one and whole, like science and magic healed me. We shall move forward together as one planet once more, with one people of both science *and* magic!" Charm said. The assembled Magisterians and Quanterians below her broke into cheers. She grinned, and waved as she started to step offstage.

For just a moment someone in the crowd caught her eye. While most of the assembled people were cheering or clapping, one boy just stood silently, an almost sad smile on his face. She gave him a curious look, and he waved awkwardly, almost in embarrassment.

Did she know him? There was something about him that seemed almost... familiar. Something she hadn't seen in a long time. Years, even.

And for some reason, seeing the boy now, she realized how much she missed that ... something.

Before Charm could do more than raise her hand to wave back, the boy disappeared into the crowd. She stepped forward, ready to say something, then sighed and let it go, turning back to step offstage.

"I'll never get used to that," she told her assistant, a Magisterian boy just a couple of years younger than her. "I hate talking."

"To crowds?" her assistant asked.

"Or anyone else," she said.

"But you faced down Dr. Verity!" her assistant said. "Visited alternate dimensions! Fought off zombie magicians and deadly computer viruses!"

"None of those were scary," she told him. "I had ... company."

She began to walk back toward the Presidential Audience Chamber, sighing at her list of upcoming meetings. It wasn't easy, bringing the entire population of Magisteria back to Quanterium where they belonged, then convincing two planets full of people that hated one another that they needed each other, that one side had grown complacent and unimaginative, while the other was nothing but imagination. Two sides of a whole, and neither complete without the other.

And yet it had happened, despite the hiccups. Still, there were always more meetings.

"Company?" her assistant said. "You mean Kiel Gnomenfoot?"

She stopped, then turned to face him. "I might," she said.

"What do you think ever happened to him?

After you proved him innocent of crimes against Quanterium right before his execution?" her assistant asked.

She raised an eyebrow. "Why do you ask?"

"It's been five years, and no one's seen him since the trial," her assistant said. "If anyone would know where he is, I'd think it'd be you, right?"

She sighed. "The Ice Giants claim to have captured him and are holding him for a million frozen fires as ransom. I've also heard that he's King of the Infinite Nothingness, beyond the universe that exists. Some even say he took the books he found in the vault and used them to open a school to teach people about the true Source of Magic."

"But those books were just details of scientific lab experiments," her assistant said. "Right? About how scientists actually developed the first magic spells, which were really just quantum connections used on a larger, practical level? That's how he was able to use magic to communicate with every Science Soldier at once, because science at its core is magic, and magic is science?"

"So it stands to reason that a school teaching both magic *and* science might have some use for them," she said.

"But what do *you* think?" her assistant asked. "Where do *you* think he went?"

Charm sighed. "I like to think that somewhere, somewhen, Kiel Gnomenfoot is annoying someone else, with his stupid magic and his stupid arrogance, just like he did me all those years."

Or maybe saying good-bye in the middle of a crowd, the least Kiel Gnomenfoot thing he could ever do.

She smiled, then shook her head and straightened herself, ready to continue bringing together science and magic into one, whole world.

With that, Bethany and Owen slowly pulled themselves out of the book. Bethany closed the cover and looked at Owen. "Well?"

"She's okay," Owen said to himself with a goofy grin, then noticed Bethany smiling at him. "Uh, I mean, I'm glad it ended happily. You know, for, uh, everyone. Charm. And the rest.

Like, everyone else. Kiel. You know." He stopped, realizing something. "So where *is* Kiel? Isn't it a little strange that after seven of these books we don't even get a concrete answer as to what happened to him? I mean, maybe Charm thought that I was him. . . ." He couldn't stop himself from grinning wider. "But that was me, not him. Shouldn't the real Kiel have turned up somewhere?"

"I guess," Bethany said, smiling with him. "Listen. Owen. I've been thinking about things."

Owen nodded, his grin fading. "Me too. You go first."

"Okay," she said, then paused, taking a deep breath. "I've been thinking. I might try looking for my father in some Sherlock Holmes books next, since I used up my magic spell on finding Jonathan Porterhouse. It's been a while since I tried anything from the early twentieth century, so maybe he ended up there somehow." She looked up at him almost shyly. "And I was also thinking, maybe, um, that it might be nice to, I don't know, have some company. Might be more, you know, *fun* that way."

Owen's eyes widened. "You want me to go with you?"

She shrugged. "Maybe. I don't know. If you want. I'm just saying."

He smiled, then shook his head sadly. "I really appreciate the offer, Bethany. You have no idea. But I . . . I think I'm done with all of this."

She raised an eyebrow. "You are? But why?"

"The idea of an adventure just seemed so exciting from this side of the book," he told her, looking at the ground. "But people get hurt. It's *dangerous* in there. And everything you do can put other people in danger too. I almost . . . Charm almost . . . It was too much. I think I'm ready for some regular, boring, quiet life right now. To just read books the normal way, you know?"

She nodded, then reached out and hugged him. He hugged her back, a little surprised, then got up to leave.

"You saved them," Bethany told him as he reached the door. "You know that, right? You saved both Kiel and the Magister. Jonathan Porterhouse told me that originally the Magister did get killed by Dr. Verity, and Kiel died in the end, giving up his heart. Charm never even thought about giving him a robot heart, since he never let on that sacrificing himself even bothered him. All that arrogance, you know."

Owen just looked at her. "It wasn't right, how I did it. Even if it ended well."

"I just wanted you to know that," she said, smiling slightly. "You and I changed the story, together, and saved Kiel's life. No matter what else, don't forget that."

He paused, then nodded, returning her smile. Then, turning to go, Owen said good-bye, leaving Bethany with her books. He was ready for a real, boring, completely safe life again.

CHAPTER 46

Multiplying fractions is one thing," Mr. Barberry said. "But dividing fractions is where life just gets *crazy!*"

It'd been a week since *Kiel Gnomenfoot and the Source of Magic* had come out, and the library's two copies hadn't been in stock once. Owen's mother had surprised him with a copy she'd bought, and Owen had smiled and thanked her, keeping secret the fact that Jonathan Porterhouse had signed a copy to him a few days earlier. Owen had brought the signed copy to school, planning on showing everyone, but for some reason hadn't ever taken it out of his locker.

Just like he hadn't mentioned anything about Nobody to Bethany. How did Nobody know about her? Could he actually be her father? If he wasn't, and Owen told Bethany about him, what would that do to her? Was that just cruel? Maybe Owen could just keep an eye out for Nobody in books, and see what he found. The last thing he wanted to do was get Bethany's hopes up, after everything that'd happened.

"It's really not that different from multiplying, honestly," Mr. Barberry said, turning to the board. "Just the opposite, in fact!"

On Owen's right, Mari sighed, dropping her head into her arms. Owen smiled slightly at this, remembering the feeling. Still, right now, boring just wasn't that bad.

On his left, something hit his arm. He looked down to find a folded note on the floor. He reached down slowly to pick it up as Mr. Barberry continued.

Okay, no Holmes. How about Narnia?
—B

Owen grinned and threw a glance back at Bethany, who was pretending to pay attention to the lesson. It meant a lot that she asked, and really did want him to come. She'd changed so much since he'd caught her in the library, popping out of Willy Wonka. So had he, if he was being honest. But right now, there was no way he could go into another book. It was just too much. Not with how things had ended, with Charm almost dying, with him almost dying, with a robotic heart in his chest now. All just too much!

Still. NARNIA.

He tossed the note back.

> I'm in.
> –O

You couldn't just say no to *Narnia*.

A few minutes later, something else tapped his arm.

> We might have another friend coming too.
> –B

Huh? Another friend? Who was she talking about?

"Mr. Barberry?" said the principal, Mr. Wilcox, from the door. Mr. Barberry looked up from the board. "Class?" Mr. Wilcox continued. "I want to introduce you to a new student. He's going to be joining your class today. Everyone say hello to Kyle!"

Mr. Wilcox stepped aside, and Kiel Gnomenfoot walked into the classroom, a half smile on his face.

"Hey," Kiel said, and waved.

Owen's mouth dropped open, and he slowly turned to look back over his shoulder.

Bethany looked at him for a second, then winked.

Mr. Wilcox started to leave, then turned to give Owen a look. Owen might have imagined it, but just for the briefest of moments, it almost looked like the principal's face melted into nothing, like a mannequin's face, or the face of Nobody.

Owen blinked, and Mr. Wilcox stared back at him, a hint of a grin on his face. The principal's eyes shifted to Bethany quickly, then back to Owen, and the man slowly shook his head. *Not just yet,* the look seemed to say. Then Mr. Wilcox held up an old-looking math book and tapped it twice. *Study hard,* probably.

With that, the principal left the classroom, and Owen turned back to welcome Kiel Gnomenfoot to reality with the rest of the class. Even after everything, he couldn't help but smile as "Kyle" gave him a wink.

Sure, this was the fictional former hero of a series of children's books, now joining the class of a real school in the non-fictional world. But it's not like that *automatically* meant things were going to get all crazy.

After all, how much damage could one boy do?

ACKNOWLEDGMENTS

I never know who to thank, James thought, then paused. *Or why I narrate my own life like this.* He sighed, tapping his pen against his cheek as he thought.

Obviously, he needed to thank Liesa Abrams Mignogna, who from the beginning had asked, "Why can't this James character be an author?" Then, "And can he be wearing a Batman shirt?"

And of course James couldn't thank Michael Bourret enough, given that Michael was his agent, and maybe, dare he say . . . friend?

No, he daren't. So just "agent" it was.

Then there was everyone else at Aladdin: Annie, Mara, Fiona, Carolyn, Katherine, Adam, Laura, Mary, Christina, and everyone who shepherded the book from its start as just a tiny sheep baby (*Lamb?* James wondered) to its current incarnation as full-grown, curly-haired *Mr.* Sheep. James furrowed his brow. A shepherd analogy? Shouldn't there be something with genies, since the imprint is called Aladdin? He shrugged. No one reads these things anyway, so why worry about consistent creative choices?

Not that he *ever* really worried about consistent creative choices.

Then there were those who personally supported James. Your Thaphnes, your Dan and Saras, your Shannons, your Brandons, your Everyone Elses. "Maybe it's not as bad as you think," they'd say, and James would shrug. *Anything* was possible, he supposed. They definitely needed to be acknowledged for that.

But what about all the *fans*? Out of everyone, they were the most important people to say "Thank you!" to! But how to do it? There was no possible way to thank all of them, even with the time machine James's future self had just gifted him. Oh, horrible irony! Was it irony? James frowned, not sure. Twitter would know . . . but that way lay madness.

And then there were the teachers, the librarians, and the booksellers. The magical, selfless geniuses who changed children's lives on a daily basis, and who every so often would push James's books into the hands of a reader who wasn't quite done with fairy tales just yet. Thanking all those people would take months, or *years* if James were lazy about it! Even if he just started with, say, Kim and Katie Laird—

OOOH, NEW CAT VIDEO ON THE INTERNETS!

. . . Ha! Classic, that cat. Now, where was he? Something about thanking people. Right!

Except that thanking people made James wonder what would happen if he left someone's name off by mistake. Would people get offended? Doubt their contribution? Not thank him in *their* books?! That would be horrible! Sure, his family would know he loved them, since James was always incredibly thankful for their support, but everyone else? And even worse, what about those who *didn't* contribute anything, but just assumed James was referring to them when thanking "everyone else"? It made him shudder with horror.

Nope. There was just no good way to do this. James crumpled up the paper he'd been doodling on instead of writing down names like he was supposed to have been doing. And if there was no good way to do something, that meant he shouldn't do it. After all, not everyone had acknowledgments pages, right?

All people really had to know was how honored James was by

anyone reading his work, and how much he hoped they enjoyed it. And what better way to show that . . . than by SENDING EVERY READER A THOUSAND DOLLARS IN CASH! That was a *much* better idea than some clichéd acknowledgments page! If readers finished the book, all they'd have to do was [You're not putting this in. No. —Liesa] and James would send them a thousand dollars in cash!

Perfect. This would be the best acknowledgments page *ever*.